Mouflon

Brigade

Cyberworld Publishing

www.cyberworldpublishing.com

This book is copyright © Gina Drew 2010
First published by Cyberworld Publishing in 2010.
Cover design by S Bush © 2010
Cover Photo - Mouflon Sheep © Tigrajr | Dreamstime.com
All rights reserved.
E Book ISBN 978-0-9808490-1-1
Print ISBN 978-0-9808490-2-8

Cyberworld Publishing
Jindalee St, Toronto, Australia

Koniotis Mysteries Series

Each book in this series stands alone, but they are also all connected in various ways and form the different parts of one story.

Mouflon Brigade

Koniotis Mysteries - Book Three

by Gina Drew

Caitlyn's maps of sites visited in this book

Cyprus

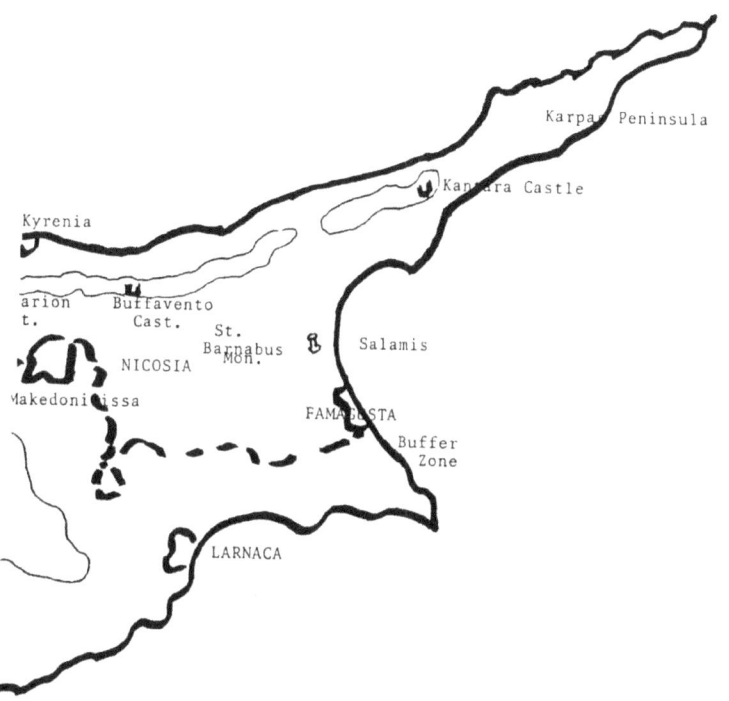

Kyrenia

Karpas Peninsula

Kantara Castle

arion
t.
Buffavento
Cast.
St.
Barnabus
Mon.

NICOSIA

Salamis

Makedonitissa

FAMAGUSTA
Buffer
Zone

LARNACA

Nicosia

A. OLD NICOSIA
B. TURKISH ZONE
C. MAKEDONITISSA VALLEY
D. ACROPOLIS
E. MAIN UN BASE
F. STROVOLOS

1. Border Checkpoint
2. Ledra Palace Hotel
3. Apollo Nights Club
4. Cyprus Museum
5. Stuart's Averof St. House
6. Canadian High Commission
7. Cypriot Police Headquarters
8. Ziya's Office
9. Ziya Flat
10. Koniotis House
11. Hamilton Flat
12. American Embassy
13. Russian Embassy
14. UN Coordinator's House
15. Piccard House
16. Makedonitissa Monastery
17. International Fair Grounds
18. Makarios Stadium
19. Presidential Palace

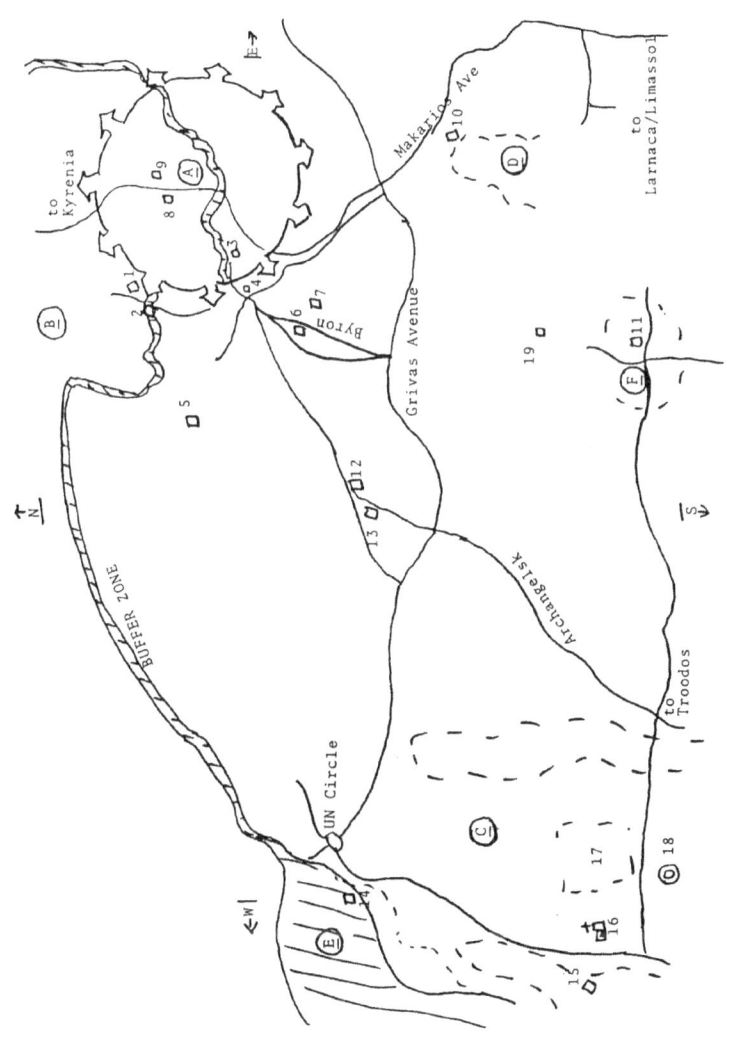

to Kyrenia

BUFFER ZONE

N

W

E

S

(A)

(B)

(C)

(D)

(E)

(F)

Makarios Ave

Byron

Grivas Avenue

Archangelisk

UN Circle

to Larnaca/Limassol

to Troodos

1
2
3
4
5
6
7
8
9
10
11
12
13
15
16
17
18
19

9

PRIMARY CHARACTERS

Androulla—An assistant to Takis Koniotis

Ayman Abu Hani—Lebanese ambassador to Cyprus

Suzanne Abu Hani—Wife of the Lebanese ambassador to Cyprus

Phylaktis Baroutis—A Greek Cypriot lawyer

Ingrid Bittmann—The UN coordinator for Cyprus

Paul Conte—American embassy political officer

Colonel Julio Alberto Funes—Commander of the argentine UN peacekeeping contingent

Widad al-Ghabra—The Asp's second in command

Ginger Nives-Smyth Baldwin Remington Hamilton—Wife of Willie

Willie Hamilton—retired British infantry major; now senior political and crime reporter for the *Cyprus Mail*

Ioannis Herodotou—Greek Cypriot interior minister

Ibrahim—Hizballah band chief

Eric Isaksen—Former Danish foreign minister, former chairman of the United Nations Development Program, and current special emissary of the UN secretary general to the Middle East

Anwar Jabril/Mehmet Tosun/Nabil Jallud—A Beirut copperware merchant

Ahmad Jallud—Anwar Jabril's nephew

Caitlyn Spencer Koniotis—American archaeologist in Cyprus; wife of Takis Koniotis

Takis Koniotis—Chief of Cypriot police department International Investigations Unit

Ellen Larkin—Canadian high commission political officer

Irina Lukenov—wife of Mikhail Lukenov

Mikhail Lukenov—Russian embassy intelligence chief

Pavel Lukenov—Son of Mikhail Lukenov

Uri Lukenov—Son of Mikhail Lukenov

Manuel—Serving man cum spying asset

Demetris Mattas—"Under the Grapevine" columnist for the Greek-language newspaper *Simerini*

Munir Nahlawi—Syrian ambassador to Cyprus

John Paterson—An agronomist working on a grant, at the Middle Eastern University in Famagusta

Sami—An assistant of Turkish Cypriot police official Safa Ziya

Maria Solonos—Greek Cypriot police investigator deputy to Takis Koniotis

Alex Stuart—British high commission political officer

Faris Sukkar—Terrorist hit man

Zenon Tenekides—Greek Cypriot police department chief

The Asp/Abdul Abed-Rabbo—Head of the Mouflon Brigade

Andriko Visiliou—Cyprus Museum director and Caitlyn Koniotis's boss

Safa Ziya—Turkish Cypriot police senior investigator

11

Chapter One

"If ever one sought validation of the second oldest profession," mused Mikhail Lukenov with a secret smile, as he looked northeast over Morphou Bay on the wild, desolate western Cyprus coast, "one need only come to this spot."

The tall, large-boned and well-fleshed, but still distinguished-looking spy chief for the Russian embassy to the divided Mediterranean island republic of Cyprus was standing at the northern edge of the many-roomed cliff-top Vouni palace and staring down on the seaside slopes below at the ruins of the ancient Greco-Roman city kingdom of Soli. As he did so, he was calculating the strategic importance of the wide, slowly curving sandy beach area of the bay below much as the Phoenicians had done some 2,500 years earlier. They constructed this mountaintop aerie to watch over the activities of the pro-Greek city of Soli in pursuit of that second oldest profession—spying.

This area of Cyprus, where the seaside cliffs of the southwest quadrant of the island met the central Cypriot alluvial plain—known as the Mesaoria—which ran the width of the island between the Troodos Mountain Range to the south and the Kyrenia Mountain Range to the north, was now isolated and deserted. In ancient times, however, it had been a major mining and trading region. It was from here that the copper that gave the island its Greek-derived name and that was extracted for centuries from the Troodos Mountains, rising immediately to the southeast, had been shipped throughout the Mediterranean basin. A long, crumbling pier, which was easily discerned from the Vouni vantage point, jutting out to the sea very near and below the Soli ruins, attested to the importance of this industry throughout and beyond the British colonial period, which had ended with the island's independence in 1960.

It was the Turkish invasion of 1974, however, that had divided the island into two ethnic zones—Cypriot Greeks in the lower two-thirds and Turkish Cypriots and Turkish mainland troops in the upper third, buffered by a UN Peacekeeping Forces-supervised neutral zone. This event had largely isolated the Vouni and Soli ruins. Both sites were now in the Turkish-controlled zone. But just barely, as the buffer zone met the sea at the island's western coast a mere five miles to the west of Vouni.

It was just this remoteness, however, that had prompted Mikhail Lukenov to bring his family to Vouni and Soli on this warm late April morning. At this thought, Lukenov turned and, with yearning eyes, gathered his family into his field of vision.

His wife, Irina, and his seven-year-old son, Pavel, were some distance off, returning to where he stood at the northern entrance to the palace from the remains of the temple Athena. This temple once dominated the southern edge of the high plateau and more recently had been refashioned into a Turkish outpost looking out toward the Greek-controlled Troodos Mountains. Irina was walking slowly and deliberately, drinking in the white honeysuckle, the pink and white oleander, and the blue dwarf chicory that sprouted from fissures in the ancient stone blocks underfoot and at hand.

Seemingly like any seven year old, Pavel was scampering away on short independent adventures only to return each time to his mother and to cling to her skirts for attention to what he had seen and found. Lukenov's other son, Uri, was also seemingly the picture of a typical eleven year old, standing in the core area of the original palace, located in the northwest quadrant of the site, and staring directly and intently out to sea.

But all was not as it appeared at a distance, which Lukenov well knew and which became more readily apparent as Irina and Pavel approached and as Uri turned to gaze at the rest of his family. It was this tenseness and vulnerability of his wife and sons that was the basis of Lukenov's choice of this lovely, yet remote, spot for the family's first outing since they had joined him in Nicosia during the previous month.

As Irina and Pavel grew closer, the hollow-eyed strain on Irina's face was ever more evident and fearful looks that accompanied little Pavel's retreats to his mother's skirts could be clearly discerned. For his part, as Uri worked his way around the edge of the site to where his father stood, what could originally have been taken as a dreamy independent speculation on the world around him and of his future was revealed as a boiling anger that was barely held in check by a large dose of surliness. This demeanor led him to shrink from the gaze and touch of his parents while, at the same time, positioning himself so that both were in view at all times.

14

"When will they recover and when can we be the close, happy family we once were?" Lukenov lamented inwardly, as he managed a broad, welcoming smile and prattled on to his gathering kin about Vouni, Soli, and Cyprus history and geography in general.

He could not—and did not—blame his wife and sons for their mournful, tense attitude. He knew that they had every right to mourn. No, he could only—and constantly did—blame himself for not having insisted that they accompany him directly when he first traveled to his Cyprus posting nearly a year ago. However, Irina had been too taken up with the new-found freedoms of the post-Communist era Moscow, and Lukenov, who had quite selfishly never taken his family on a foreign posting before, had not been able to convince his sheltered bride that life was even more free and abundant in worlds beyond the new Russia. For their part, his sons had not been at all anxious to leave their friends. It therefore had been too easy once again for Lukenov to leave his family behind and to take yet another plum posting with the expectation of full freedom to dabble in the local sexual delights as and when he wished.

But then remorse had gotten to him and he had insisted that his family join him in Cyprus—an almost ideal posting, where the people were highly educated and friendly, the economy was healthy, the air was clear, and the weather was nearly always delightful. And his family had acceded to his summons. But first, en route, Irina had wanted to visit her family and to let them see her growing sons for the first time.

Lukenov would never forgive himself for agreeing to this visit. He had known it wouldn't be safe, but he had only known this from the privileged information that came to him in his position as a senior intelligence agent, and he couldn't bring himself to warn his wife off. His devotion to duty—or what he had taken to be his devotion to duty at the time—had prevented him from telling his wife of the building trouble in her home city, because he knew that her father was one of the dissident leaders and he didn't want a warning of danger to reach the old man's ears. And he knew that his superiors were scrutinizing his actions for any sign of favoring his wife's family. Lukenov was sure, in fact, that this assignment to Cyprus had been engineered to get him out of the nerve center, in Moscow—a better solution Lukenov admitted, than would have been initiated by previous regimes in Russia.

So Irina and the boys had innocently set off from Moscow to Grozny, near the Caspian Sea and in the shadow of the Caucasus Mountains, in the late fall for what was intended to be a short stopover with her family while traveling farther south to Cyprus. They were already on the last leg of their journey by train when the people of the Grozny region irrevocably voiced their intent to form the new, independent state of Chechnya and the Russian leaders in the Kremlin just as irrevocably decided that an example must be made of these rebels to prevent the further breakup of the Russian nation.

As the train bearing Lukenov's family rolled into Grozny, the shelling by Russian troops had already been going on for nearly a week. Irina had heard of the fighting soon after leaving Moscow, but she felt she had nowhere else to go; she was desperately homesick to see her family once more before going out into a strange, new, and— to her—terrifying world beyond the lowered Iron Curtain; and she had assumed the reports of the fighting were worse than reality. Besides, her family was one of the leading families of Grozny. Surely they had made provisions for their own safety.

Whatever provisions Irina's family had made, however, had quickly come to naught. She was indeed able to see her family—but only after their large, old house had been leveled by Russian shells and they had all been dead for three days. It was she and her sons—all in shock—who had dug through the ruins of her childhood home and who had found her mother, father, and maiden aunt. The shelling had been so intense and the destruction had been so widespread that no one else had had the time, energy, or inclination to recover her parents' bodies and to give them a decent burial.

What had followed for Irina and her boys over the next two months, set adrift in the dying city of Grozny, was so numbing, terrifying, and foreign to their previously relatively privileged life in Moscow that their internal defense mechanisms had blocked most of the events from their memories.

But, in the end, it had been their privileged positions as the family of a senior Russian intelligence operative that had been their salvation. After having seen in internal reports the name of Irina's father among those of other prominent Chechen dissidents as a probable "kill" and not having heard from his family in weeks, Lukenov mustered all the insider's influence at his disposal and managed to have his family located and extracted from Grozny and sent on to him in Cyprus.

But the three near zombies who were assisted off the plane at Larnaca International Airport a month previous to this first sightseeing trip to the seaside were hardly identifiable as his family.

Initially Irina shrank from Lukenov's embrace and leveled a damning stare at him that marked him as one of the Russian government murderers who had taken her family from her. And little did she know, Lukenov kept berating himself, just how accurate her unvoiced accusation of his complicity was. But when he got her home to the Russian compound, which contained both the embassy proper and the residences for the Russian diplomats, and when Irina had at last been freed of sole responsibility for her sons and was able once again to think primarily of herself, she broke down and cried—sometimes in anger and sometimes mournfully—for hours. At the end of her tears, she fell into her husband's arms and only very slowly subsequently began to creep out from her husband's shadow to relate to the new world around her.

Little Pavel similarly clung to his mother in panic, and, sometimes, to her great frustration cried uncontrollably as well. He had nearly driven Lukenov to distraction during Irina's day-long breakdown and still remained glued to her to the exclusion of all others, even to his father, whom he barely seemed to recognize.

In some respects, Uri's behavior was the most distressing. He still seemed to be in shock and would not look his father straight in the eye or respond civilly to the most simple of questions and guidance. This was in stark contrast to his former ties with his father, a man whom Uri had idolized and followed in every action and mannerism when Lukenov had been with the family. At the same time he was always there, in the fringe of Lukenov's vision, almost as if waiting for his father to instantly erase the eternity of the pain, fear, and grief he, his mother, and his brother had absorbed in two short months in Grozny.

It was with an extremely heavy heart he was valiantly trying to cover with an air of good humor and ease that Lukenov ushered his family back to the embassy Volvo and started down the Vouni Cliffside to visit the Soli ruins below.

* * * *

It was soon after the Lukenovs reached the Soli ruins that the miracle began to happen. In hindsight, for what it mattered, which, in the end, wasn't much, Lukenov could see that the warming of the ice around his loved ones' hearts had started to occur at Vouni. Uri's stare became less truculent than before, and he moved closer to his father than at any previous time since he had arrived in Cyprus. Lukenov had similarly already marked the little flights of adventure Pavel took from his mother's skirts and the notice Irina took of the wildflowers bravely pushing their way out of the stones of Vouni.

Almost immediately, during the tour of the excavated mosaic-floored early Christian basilica at the lower end of the Soli complex, all three appeared to be less tense and more prone to actually see what they were looking at and even, in Irina's case, to flash a tentative, but very real, smile at the little delights that accosted her—an unusual flower or the sudden realization of what a mosaic was depicting.

And, thus, when Lukenov pointed up a staired pathway and told the boys that one of the best-preserved Roman theaters was carved into the hillside above, it was with great pleasure that he saw the boys start off together and up the hill—just the two of them, moving beyond the protection of their parents—and, eventually, Uri challenging a race to the top in the way that brothers the world round do.

"Yes, I was right to have brought them out into the fresh air and to one of the fascinating sites of Cyprus," Lukenov thought happily to himself, a happiness that was magnified a thousand times when Irina placed her arm through his with a contented sigh and quickened her own ascent up the pathway.

The exploration of the theater—which quite evidently was still being used for concerts or open-air plays—out of the way, the family laid out the blanket they had brought on the hillside and settled down to enjoy the light refreshments Lukenov had carefully assembled that morning, not with any real hope at the time that the family would actually be able to achieve the level of happiness and contentment that had marked such outings in years past in and around Moscow. As Lukenov unpacked the bag he had brought along and distributed the drinks and hunks of village bread to his suddenly animated sons, he looked over at Irina. She appeared almost angelic and fully relaxed as she gazed out over the slope down toward the sea.

What was barren ground much of the year was now covered with a short, but very green, carpet of grass, that was interlaced with a profusion of violet-colored flowers Lukenov gently identified to his wife as bearing the fascinating name of Venus's Looking Glass, and taller plants, with delicate yellow flowerets, that Lukenov said he thought were called Mullein. Irina's eyes glowed with a pleasure that Lukenov had not seen for more than a year. He knew how fond she was of wildflowers and also knew that it was fortunate that their outing had coincided with the period in which Cyprus' countryside was most colorful.

Irina sighed and picked up the tour book Lukenov had brought along. She read about both the Vouni and Soli sites, occasionally aloud to the boys, who, to Lukenov's delight, were showing signs of awareness and appreciation for the rich history on exhibit around them.

"Oh," Irina said at length, "It says here that there's another large temple complex at the top of the hill over there. That's where they say they found the Aphrodite of Soli. The book says this is the most famous statue found of Cyprus' patron goddess and is now in the Cyprus Museum in Nicosia. We'll have to go to the museum and see it, Mikhail."

"Yes, we must," responded Lukenov shortly, trying to hold back the tears of relief that were building up in his eyes and trying to still the quaver in his voice that he was sure his wife and children could hear.

Irina looked up toward the top of the hill for some moments and then stood, wavering for an instant. Then she tentatively took a step or two toward the path that could barely be seen rising up the slope. Pavel instinctively moved toward his mother. Irina cast a pleading look at Lukenov, who instantly understood that Irina wanted to discover the temple alone and called Pavel back to look at an interesting picture in the tour book.

As Irina climbed the hill toward the beckoning temple ruins, Lukenov pulled both of his sons toward him and started leafing through the guide book, telling them about all of the interesting sites they would visit in Cyprus over the coming months.

Such was the glow for all three at this intimate time together that they completely lost track of time. It was the rising, cooler breeze accompanying the dipping of the afternoon sun that jolted Lukenov out of his mood and made him realize that Irina had been gone an unusually long time. He was suddenly alarmed, but the last thing he wanted to do was convey this alarm to his children and send them back into the shock that he had fought so hard to negate. He rose, as if to stretch, and glanced up the hill. he thought he could see something glinting in the sun momentarily from the brow of the hill, but then it was gone. He tried to take a step, but Pavel clung to his leg.

Bringing all the calm he could to his voice, he casually said, "It's about time to go. Let's go up the hill and find your mother."

But that wasn't going to be possible. When they reached the top of the hill, they found the temple ruins right where they were said to be, but there was no sign of Irina. There were no buildings or other sign of human habitation in the hills beyond the temple. From this shallow meadow, the hills undulated up toward the lofty Troodos peaks toward the southeast. And, although the vegetation on the rising slopes grew thick, it did not grow tall, so Irina should have easily been seen if she were anywhere around.

Pavel began to cry, and Uri moved slowly and deliberately around the temple ruins, as if he was examining the very cracks between the ancient stones for evidence of his mother. In guarded panic, Lukenov turned back toward the slope leading down to the sea. There was no other sensible place for her to have gone. Perhaps she had gone back to the Volvo for something. But he could see the automobile near the basilica several hundred yards below, and the familiar figure of his wife in her sky-blue skirt and blouse was not there.

There was a piercing, heart-chilling call of "Father" behind him. By now Pavel had returned to the only available refuge, his father, and was clinging to his trouser legs so tightly that Lukenov could only move toward Uri at a slow, crab-like pace.

Taking the young boy up in his arms, the Russian diplomat reached Uri's side and followed his intent gaze. There, upon what may once have been an altar stone, was a piece of sky-blue material. He lurched at the stone and took up the material. it was a blouse—Irina's blouse—and it had been lodged under a large stone. As Lukenov lifted the blouse, a piece of paper also flew off the altar and floated to the ground. Silently Uri picked up the paper and turned it over and over in his hands, although he was not looking at it. Pavel began to wail for his mother and to twist and turn in Lukenov's arms. Tightening his grip on his son, Lukenov snatched the paper out of Uri's hands.

He felt he must be hallucinating. The paper did not make any sense. It was just a brochure for Cyprus Airlines. What was a Cyprus Airlines brochure doing out here in the countryside? And, in particular, what was a brochure for the airlines of Greek Cyprus doing in the Turkish zone?

"And just why, damn it," Lukenov thought in frustration and anger, "do I give a shit about a Cyprus Airlines brochure? My wife is missing. Where is my wife?"

He started to toss the folder away, but then he noticed that it had something written on it. The letters MB had been scrawled with a thick black marker across the front of the brochure. Even in his confused and agitated state of mind and even as his elder son crumpled to the ground in a faint and his younger son resumed his squirming and yelling, Lukenov had the presence of mind to slip the folder into his pocket, to take one last scan around in the hope of finding a rational and benign explanation for his wife's whereabouts, and to race for the Volvo and its high-powered mobile telephone.

Chapter Two

Alec Stuart rolled out of bed, pulled his briefs up his wiry legs, grabbed a pack of cigarettes and a book of matches from the nightstand drawer, and maneuvered his gangling frame to the glass door overlooking his small, walled bedroom garden. The once-barren nook was now a miniature forest hideaway, with shaded ferns and spring pink and white cyclamens and white and red anemones, peeking out of and around artfully and deceptively arranged broken pieces of Greek and Roman columns and cornices.

Stuart tried to move as quietly as possible as he reached the door, lit a cigarette, and stared out into the garden in an attempt to martial his thoughts. He knew that Suzanne must have also been awakened by the ringing of the telephone. In truth she could not have had much time to have drifted off to sleep after their lovemaking, and, this being late afternoon, she probably had not even intended to sleep—only to rest a bit before a third passionate coupling preceding, for them both, an early evening return to their separate lives. Stuart smiled to himself in spite of the concern that was introduced by the telephone call. He had never encountered anyone like Suzanne before. She was both incredible and insatiable. And what did such a sophisticated, raven-haired beauty see in an unpolished, common, mid-level British government bureaucrat such as he was depicting himself to the world, anyway? Could it be that she could look through to the real him? Or did she know more than he had thought she did?

Whether or not she was asleep, he wanted her to have the impression that he thought she was asleep so that she might leave him to his thoughts for a few moments. He took two quick puffs on his cigarette and gazed intently into the garden, purposefully avoiding looking back at the bed at Suzanne in repose. He must focus his attention on the problem at hand; if he dared look at Suzanne and she was awake, he knew he'd be back in her silken arms in a flash. She had woven a charm around him that he could not—and almost did not want to—break.

The inviting, small, stoned-floored garden, with its single wooden bench and its array of earthen jars, many containing exotic succulents, revealed an aspect of the tall, red-haired, and florid-complexioned Britisher's personality that few who knew him casually would have imagined.

In fact, the very house in which Alec and Suzanne were not liaising would have surprised most of Stuart's business and social acquaintances. Stuart's house was a lovely old British colonial-period Cypriot mansion that had been lovingly and painstakingly restored under the guidance of Stuart himself over a five-year period. Few would have believed that the long-serving, boisterous British high commission political officer, who looked most comfortable with his foot planted firmly on a bar foot rail and his hand wrapped tightly around a pint and sharing coarse jokes with working-class comrades, could have either the tastes or the means to restore an old Cypriot villa.

The house was one of those deceptive old buildings that looked like it was a one-story bungalow but that actually was two stories and contained ten large rooms. The living level sat on top of a three-quarters above-ground basement level, which was, in fact, at ground level at the back of the lot, overlooking a beautiful garden area. The residence was covered in renewed, off-white stucco, and its corners were dressed with ochre-colored sandstone blocking, which anchored the building visually in its lush garden.

As with many of the Cypriot mansions of that era, the large entry hall, with double wooden entry doors framed at each side and above by windows covered in delicately winding ironwork and its massive crystal chandelier, was inset in a balcony located at one corner of the building and reached by a sweeping and curved stone staircase at the front of the house. All of the shutters and woodwork were freshly painted in a traditional glossy dark green. The house looked its best in the current, early spring season, as it was framed by mature orange and lemon trees, which were now in full fruit.

The interior of the residence had been as tastefully, lovingly, and expensively decorated as the building itself and had been restored with British and Cypriot antiques, Persian rugs, and the myriad complementary Oriental treasures Stuart had acquired during an earlier posting in Singapore.

But very few of his friends and acquaintances had seen this residence on Nicosia's old Averof Street or this side of Stuart's personality. When asked where he lived, Stuart truthfully noted that he resided in the old, but now unfashionable neighborhood that was called Ayios Pavlos. Coveted during the British colonial era for its proximity to the administrative center of the new city and to the Ledra Palace Hotel, the focus of the then-social, political, and business world of Cyprus, Ayios Pavlos was now known mainly for its rotting, unheated, and largely derelict houses; for being the district in which the central prisons were located; and for being much too close to the "Green Line" buffer zone, which slashed through the center of the capital city like an ugly scar. Most diplomats and people of any note now lived out in the newer, southwestern suburbs of the "new" city of Nicosia.

The "old" Nicosia, dating from the twelfth century, was located within a circle of dry-moated stone walls that had been raised by the Venetians in the sixteenth century in an unsuccessful bid to hold back the invading Ottoman Turk armies. The "new" city—or at least that which now rose above the ground in the areas surrounding the old Venetian walls—dated largely from the nineteenth-century period, during which the British displaced the Ottoman Turks. The use of the word "new" was somewhat of a misnomer, however, as many of the buildings outside the present city walls rose from Greek, Roman, or even older civilizations, some areas of the city having been dated back to the Neolithic period of 5500 BC.

The now-desirable suburbs of Nicosia were those of Strovolos and Engomi, which had swallowed up old once-independent villages, and the Makedonitissa Valley, which ran alongside the city's western buffer zone adjacent to the main United Nations Forces base and the Nicosia International Airport, which had been locked in the buffer zone and which had not been in operation since the 1974 Turkish invasion of the island.

When asked why he lived in Ayios Pavlos when nearly all other diplomats lived in more fashionable areas, Stuart was able to maintain his chosen character by answering that his residence in the area suited him fine, being halfway between his office, the British high commission—which had stubbornly held to its long-occupied location in the northwest corner of Ayios Pavlos and almost surrounded by the buffer zone—and his favorite pub, the Navarino Wine Lodge, traditional haunt of the foreign press corps and champion European tipplers of all backgrounds.

And when pressed for an address, or when required for business purposes, Stuart even had a seedy flat in a rundown building on Rupel Street, just one block over from his own elegant mansion, where he could live the character that he had established for himself and that had a telephone that rang in the Averof Avenue residence as well.

For Alec Stuart was not all that he seemed. He was not a working-class, low-level high commission flunky. He was, in fact, the son of an earl with impeccable pedigree, connections, and education, and he also was the long-serving chief of British intelligence in Cyprus, a country that had never lost its strategic importance for British interests in the Mediterranean and Middle Eastern regions.

The telephone call he had just received had brought him quickly and coldly back from his erotic reverie with the luscious Suzanne and into the world of reality.

"The report said that five of the embassy vehicles, all with several men inside, rushed across the Ledra Palace border checkpoint from the Greek side to the Turkish side." He mulled this over in his mind as he stared into his garden without actually seeing anything there. "Now, what would be so important that it would draw that many Russians over into the Turkish zone? Lukenov. I'll have to try to find out where Lukenov is and how the Russian spy chief may fit into all of this."

Stuart started to turn toward the bedroom and his clothes and telephone, but he was suddenly transported back to the other world of enchantment. Suzanne had stolen up behind him and had wrapped her shapely, diminutive, olive-colored body around his. Her tongue went into his ear and her heavy breathing vibrated through his body. Her arms were wrapped around his chest. The fingers of both of her hands expertly traced sensuous circular designs around his smooth, hard pectoral muscles and then circled down lower until they disappeared between his briefs and his heating, expanding flesh, and centered there, still in motion.

"Come back to bed, Alec," Suzanne whispered huskily. "I'm bored."

"Sorry, love," Stuart managed through clenched teeth. "No more for this afternoon, I'm afraid. I have something to contend with."

"Yes, I could almost hear the voice on the other end of the line." She had not stopped her teasing motions. "Something about Russians on the move?"

Stuart flushed and was jolted into action. As he turned and placed Suzanne at arms' length, he said, in a very serious tone, "It is nothing. Just something about business. About a Russian firm trying to enter a formerly British-dominated business area here in Cyprus."

And, moving toward the rumpled clothes that he had laid neatly over a chair, he went on in a softer tone, "Besides, it's getting late, and I have to go to the UN coordinator's house tonight to wine and dine some visiting UN big shot. There isn't time for any more today."

But Suzanne was too quick for him. She reached the chair before he did, turned full face toward him, sank to her knees, and reached out for him just as he arrived.

In the event, they made time.

* * * *

The peace and quiet that normally reigned in the central square of the village of Strovolos except during the brief rush-hour traffic that saw motorists short-cutting through the narrow town streets in an effort to get from somewhere to somewhere else was shattered by the only other challenge to the villagers' sanity.

The Hamiltons were in residence.

For the better part of the early afternoon, (British Infantry) major William (Willie) Hamilton (retired), a florid bantam rooster of a man in his mid sixties and current senior political and crime reporter for the island's only country-wide English-language daily, the *Cyprus Mail*, had ranted and raved. Every anguished word echoed from one thinly walled room to another in the couple's five-room city flat in an old, but well-preserved ochre-colored stone block of flats that had been located opposite the village's Orthodox church on the town square since the 1920s.

The topic had been a familiar one to the neighborhood and no longer was of scintillating interest to any of the local citizens who managed to keep up with Hamilton's heavy, Anglais brandy-slurred Welsh accent—if indeed the topic had ever been scintillating to those who had seen the second Mrs. Hamilton at close quarters.

As usual, Ginger—Mrs. Geneva Nives-Smyth Baldwin Remington Hamilton—a blonde, pencil-thin, former model type of fifty-six, who had lost the battle with age some time ago but who hadn't accepted that she had even seen combat yet—had been a naughty girl. The previous evening Willie had driven his ancient Morris Mini the over one-hour distance to the southern port city of Limassol, Cyprus' second-largest city and its industrial and commercial center, to pursue what had turned out to be a false story in a possible Customs Department scandal. He had quickly decided there was nothing in the story and had thus returned to Nicosia earlier than expected.

He didn't know what—other than intuition when he found his flat deserted—led him to the Camelot Pub in the Makedonitissa Valley near the main UN base, but when he arrived at the nightspot strip just off 28 October Street, his wife's baby-blue BMW convertible stuck out like a neon light. He found her sitting on the bar and fondling whatever she could reach of several drunken—and quite possibly either very myopic or avid car buff—UN soldiers. Willie presumed both, the last because, while Ginger was discussing the varied uses of private human parts at the top of her lungs—but barely over the blare of the CD player—the soldiers seemed busy trying to find out where she kept her car keys.

"In the ignition of her car," Willie had thought bitterly, as he waded into the UN lines. The soldiers must have recognized an officer when they saw one—and/or must have been shocked out of their drunkenness enough when he lit into them with a fierce bellow that they had gotten a sober glimpse of Ginger and had decided to bail out of the Camelot.

32

Thus, Hamilton had spent a good part of the following afternoon adding chapter and verse to his favorite novel, *The Sins of Ginger*, which even the heroine of the tale could tell him was largely fiction and was certainly longer on wordage than on action.

For her part, Mrs. Hamilton had spent the entire afternoon at her dressing table—first developing a game plan for her disguise for the UN coordinator's dinner they had inexplicably but delightedly been invited to that evening, then in resolving that she would not continue to keep her auto keys in the BMW's ignition (she didn't block out everything her husband said) but that she *would* plant fake keys on and about her body and return to Camelot to see if she could revive the magic of the place—at least what the soldiers had said they were willing to do to find her keys had sounded interesting—and, finally, in the painstakingly and seemingly unending execution of her cosmetic plan for the evening.

As the light began to dim everywhere in the flat except for the vicinity of Ginger's dressing table, which was graced with a larger ring of light bulbs than a star's dressing room at the theater, Willie stopped in mid tirade and looked at his wristwatch. If any of the local citizenry were paying a bit of attention to the unwelcome caterwauling coming from the Hilton's flat, they would have discerned that the major had changed tactics at this point. Now he was trying to hurry Ginger up with her toilet. First, while he himself was changing, he cajoled her to get a move on and suggested that she had applied several layers too much powder already. And then, when this had no effect, he turned to screaming and threatening her for endangering his chance at a really juicy column from what he could glean from the pre-dinner cocktails, which most certainly must have already gotten under way at the coordinator's residence.

At length, he stormed out of the flat and down to his Morris Mini, where he sat, threatening the health of everyone within miles with his carbon monoxide emissions, honking his horn while screaming insults up at the balcony of his flat, and revving the vehicle's engine. The Mini answered every goosing of its gas by dying completely with a very ungentlemanly burp of its muffler.

Mrs. Geneva Nives-Smyth Baldwin Remington Hamilton tooled away, steady hand carefully redrawing eyebrows a good inch above those she had just plucked out.

At length, the lights in the flat slowly went out, one by one; Ginger made her grand exit from the building's front door; stopped briefly in front of the Morris Mini; raised one perfectly arched, obviously fake eyebrow; walked to—and past—the passenger door; folded herself into the BMW parked a bit farther down the street; and glided through the square and westward toward the Makedonitissa Valley.

Willie hit his steering wheel with both hands and with enough frustrated strength to bend yet another attachment of the Mini slightly askew; revved the engine, which immediately flooded with gasoline and died; restarted the engine; and roared off in pursuit.

The sound of the engine completely obliterated the anxious ringing of the telephone in the flat above, that, had Willie been home, would have apprised him of a much more interesting event on the island than the dinner party he was off to.

The citizens of the Strovolos town square let out a collective sigh of relief. The Hamiltons were no longer in residence.

Chapter Three

Caitlyn Spenser Koniotis finished what she had thought would be an interrupted playing of Chopin's waltz in C-sharp minor, rose from the piano with a sigh, and absentmindedly ran long and delicate, yet strong fingers through her shoulder-length honey-blonde hair.

"What could be keeping Takis?" she wondered, smoothing out the stylish emerald-green taffeta cocktail dress that elegantly set off her tall, thin, but pleasingly proportioned figure. "He was just finishing dressing by tying his tie when he threw me out of the bedroom with the flustered comment that he couldn't get it tied while I was watching. Well, he apparently can't get it tied any better when he's alone. His office is entirely too informal if its dress code has allowed him to forget how to dress for a dinner party."

She became aware that she was tugging slightly at her dress again to smooth out an extra pucker. "One too many mezes this month," she thought, both damning and celebrating the Cypriot national dinner menu, which translated as "tidbits" and which was manifested by a succession of some thirty separate, small dishes of Mediterranean delicacies served in a steady stream over the course of a three- or four-hour meal. "Well, hopefully the UN coordinator won't be serving Cypriot style tonight—although Austrian cuisine won't look any better on my figure."

She sighed again and appreciatively rubbed her hand along the burnished mahogany of the Petrof baby grand. This had been the most pleasant surprise she had encountered in the Koniotis house when Takis had first brought her to her future home. She had had no idea that Takis would have such a nice home; when they had married. She had prepared herself for a messy bachelor's flat.

Caitlyn and Takis had first met a couple of years previously. She was a promising young American archaeologist, who had won a short-term Fulbright grant to participate in a Neolithic Era dig in the foothills of the Troodos Mountains. Takis had been the inspiration behind and first chief of a specially formed Cypriot police division charged with focusing specifically on crimes committed by and against foreigners in Cyprus. The formation of such a unit had been considered—and was subsequently proved—to be advantageous, because, although the strongly family-oriented Cypriot society itself was traditionally nearly crime free, the island was sp strategically located on a major crossroad between Europe and the Middle East and the Occident and Orient that it had become a favorite base and meeting ground for those who wished to pursue international crimes elsewhere.

It had been just such an assortment of crime schemes—a case of murder, drugs and arms trafficking, and logistical support for an international terrorist organization—that had brought Caitlyn and Takis together. Caitlyn had unwittingly and innocently become swept up in the events of the case, and Takis had been in charge of the investigation that had finally unraveled the intricate network of crimes and foreign villains.

Neither Caitlyn nor Takis were particularly aware of each other at the time or knowingly looking for a commitment. They had been married three months later, though. Takis had brought Caitlyn to this, his parents', house in a once-outlying and now quite central suburb of "new" Nicosia that had sprung up in the 1960s. This area of the city, which was very close to where the major north-south road, Markarios Avenue, intersected with the main east-west artery, Grivas Dhigeni Avenue, was formally called Acropolis—because this had once been the high ground upon which the Greek-era city had been centered. The neighborhood was now known, however, as the Hilton area, in honor of the city's only five-star hotel, located a half mile south and up the hill from the Koniotis house.

The Koniotis residence, which had been left to Takis intact, furniture and all, when his mother and father had been killed in a motoring accident more than a decade earlier while being posted to the Cypriot embassy in Germany, was located immediately adjacent to the base of the central acropolis hill—more a mound, where centuries of dirt and dust had buried the ruins of the Greek public buildings under layers of soil under which the remains of even older civilizations were buried.

In fact, the house's usually secluded, pine tree–bordered garden and the cemented open breezeway under the bedroom wing of the unusually designed split-level building, was even now littered with excavation gear and tagged artifacts. This was because, highly talented archaeologist that she was, Caitlyn, who now worked for the Cyprus Museum as its chief carbon dater, had struck a major historical find almost literally in her own backyard when a lot just across the road and backing into the acropolis cliff side was being prepared for construction of a house.

Caitlyn had seen signs of an ancient tomb where the bulldozers were biting into the hillside and had subsequently found a royal grave site, which dated from the Early Bronze Age. In recent months, she had brought a whole new definition to bringing one's work home, as she had been working out of her own house and garden as the team leader for the dig.

But now her thoughts returned to her husband, nervously struggling to dress to perfection for what she knew—and appreciated—was a very important dinner for him.

Of course Takis personified perfection whether dressed or undressed, Caitlyn mused naughtily. She had found Cypriot men—at least in visage (their attitudes in general toward the role of women, she thought, often left much to be desired)—to be the very definition of the Greek gods that many women dreamed of upon considering a Mediterranean holiday. And Takis, in his prime at thirty-two, with his classic, chiseled beauty and his trim figure, had a full share of a lineage descending directly from Adonis. Fortunately, Caitlyn had found beyond the handsome exterior a man who also was extremely intelligent and, if a little too stubborn, highly principled and with a humor and gentle nature that belied his no-nonsense policeman's image.

If he had not been educated in the United States, having taken a master's degree in criminology at the University of Texas at Austin, he probably would never have been prepared for or been able to adjust to the very independent and outgoing Caitlyn, however. As it was, the two were perfectly matched. They were both highly motivated and ambitious in their separate, chosen professions. But they also were mutually supportive and—usually—highly sensitive to according each other with the space needed to solve their separate challenges. Both, in their own way, had chosen investigative professions that called forth the greatest of problem-solving techniques and talents.

Sighing for the third time, Caitlyn gently lowered the cover over the keys on the Petrof and headed for the half set of stairs to the bedroom level. As expected, she found Takis red faced and staring into the mirror, his tie still awry. Moving between her husband and the dresser, Caitlyn reached up and expertly began to knot the tie.

"It will be fine, honey. You know your worth and you know how well your unit has done. And so do many others. I'm sure that's why the UN official has stopped here; there couldn't be any other reason we've been invited to this dinner. And you know what's coming yourself, or you wouldn't be this nervous. Just relax and enjoy yourself."

"Relax and enjoy myself, you say?" asked Takis, turning on that sensuous, boyish smile that made Caitlyn melt in her shoes and slowly wrapping his arms around her waist. "In that case, who needs dinner?"

"Not a chance, tiger," Caitlyn retorted in mock anger as she broke away and headed for the bedroom door. "I have *no* intention of missing a free dinner. And I have *no* intention of getting this dress more mussed than it already is. This is the second gown I've put on this evening. The one I really wanted to wear doesn't fit at all, and even this one is too tight. I'm not in the mood to face the shock tonight of discovering how many of my favorite dresses I no longer can get into."

"Come along," she continued as she trailed down the hall. "You have two choices: We can either go to dinner or go dress shopping, and both require getting into the car."

"Are you remotely aware, my love," Takis called after her as he followed her out onto the front veranda and down the broad, marble steps to the garage below, "of the cause and effect of going to dinner and not fitting into your dress? Would you like to wait for me to call a crane to help you into the auto?"

"Beast!" Caitlyn yelled over her shoulder as she maneuvered around a small wooden table in the garden upon which an array of tagged pottery shards had been neatly arranged, slipped into the passenger side of Takis's old Jaguar saloon, and slammed the door.

The old-world widow who lived next door looked up from her weeding, startled. "Their first fight," she thought, with satisfaction. "Good. Maybe now he will get that American siren under control."

The Jaguar pointed its nose toward Grivas Avenue, which led to and ended at the main UN buffer zone encampment at the western end of the city. The elegant vehicle purred around the corner from Z. Papantoniou Street to Goryiou, the playful, animated bantering of its occupants looking for all the world like angry fodder for an evening of gleeful neighborhood gossiping.

* * * *

Only a couple of miles but a cultural and political ocean away, Takis Koniotis's Turkish Cypriot counterpart, Safa Ziya, had also been standing and fiddling in front of a broken mirror in a sparsely and poorly furnished flat in a nondescript building in the Turkish-controlled sector of Nicosia. She also was nervously preparing for the dinner at the UN coordinator's residence, which, since it was located in the buffer zone and on the main UN base, was one of the few venues on the island—the Ledra Palace Hotel being the most notable other location—where Greek Cypriots and Turkish Cypriots could be brought together.

Her position as the chief Turkish Cypriot police investigator of foreign-related crimes was not the only thing she had in common with Takis Koniotis. She too was a brilliant and highly successful and tenacious investigator; she also had studied criminology in America at the University of Texas at Austin—and, in fact, she held a doctorate from and had taught at that institution, and she too had lost her family in tragic circumstances, most of her kin having gone missing in the internecine warfare between Greeks and Turks that had led up to the 1974 Turkish invasion. The two also shared an unusually high regard and deep respect for each other that had recently resulted in an unprecedented but highly productive round of regularly scheduled bicommunal—Greek Cypriot and Turkish Cypriot—meetings on cross-buffer zone criminal activities. These meetings had been established by the mutual request of Koniotis and Ziya at the Ledra Palace Hotel under the sponsorship of Alec Stuart of the British high commission.

There were many things as well that the two did not share. Whereas Koniotis had command of a large staff and could marshal considerable national and international resources to help solve his cases, Ziya only had a single assistant, who only recently had been assigned to the investigator full time, and partial claim on two other detectives. And, since the Turkish Cypriot regime was only recognized

41

as a legal entity by Turkey, Ziya could develop information from outside of the economically blockaded Turkish Cypriot zone only with great difficulty and via communication links through the Turkish mainland.

Also, whereas Koniotis's success had led to a comfortable lifestyle, Ziya—the better educated of the two by far—lived in nearly abject poverty, which did not, however, distinguish her in any way from most of her fellow Turkish Cypriots. The elaborate villas being constructed all over the scenic northern zone, with its castle-crowned Kyrenia Range peaks and the breathtaking views from its coastal mountain slopes and picturesque rocky coves, belied the lot of most Turkish Cypriots and bespoke, rather, of the exploitation of rich foreign industrialists providing for their annual month in the sun.

But the most frustrating difference to Safa Ziya at the moment was that, whereas Takis Koniotis was gifted with beauty and grace—and a fairytale bride—his Turkish Cypriot counterpart was much older (she had just turned forty-four), painfully plain, quite overweight, and slightly lame—and she had always come home to an empty flat.

She had just run her face under the tap in disgust to erase an hour's wasted effort at powdering and painting in preparation for the special dinner, and she could only stand there, surveying the damage, in mounting depression. The UN vehicle that would take her across into the UN base at the highly restricted unofficial crossing point would be there at any minute and she still looked a drudge.

"Ugh," she said accusingly to herself in the mirror. "No matter what you do, you are a drudge. And, yuck, just look at this dress. Even my bulges have bulges. Doesn't anything fit anymore? Too much donner kebab."

"Well, you are what you are," she declared at length with resignation, as she squared her shoulders and tried to force a strand of gray hair back under her headband. "Get a grip on yourself, Safa. It wasn't your pretty face or curvaceous body that got you invited to this dinner for a former Danish foreign minister. And how many pretty Turkish girls can say they had been invited to such a dinner?"

She started to reapply her lipstick but was interrupted by sudden darkness. The electricity in this sector had failed again.

"Damn. Shit," she exclaimed as she felt the lipstick jag onto her cheek. But, as she grabbed a tissue and headed for a window to catch the retreating evening light, she heard the sound of an automobile horn. A white vehicle flying a blue and white flag was wedged into the narrow street below and was already attracting a large crowd of curiosity seekers.

Safa's spirits lifted a bit. "That's my transportation. I may not be able to exit as a beauty queen, but my neighbors won't soon forget this evening."

Such was her distraction at the scene in the street below as she left the flat that she didn't hear the telephone begin to ring insistently behind her. She descended to the street level in a better mood than she had held for the entire day and thus was smiling broadly when she entered the rear seat of the vehicle—only to be caught up short by the presence of a pudgy, bearded, and bespectacled face grinning back at her from inside the car.

"Are *you* Safa Ziya, Safa Ziya the famous criminologist?" the pudgy face asked in a distinctly British accent and with an edge of awe.

Safa was too taken aback to more than nod, although the manner in which the question was posed helped her to retain her smile and lifted her mood.

"I am *so* happy to meet you," her surprised companion gushed as the vehicle gingerly started out, picking its way between pedestrians and street stalls. Above their heads, in the now-dark and empty flat, the telephone maintained its plaintive ringing.

"My name is John Patterson," the other passenger continued. "I'm an agronomist working on a grant at the Middle Eastern University in Famagusta. I've heard so much about you and your work, and I had no idea until this afternoon that you'd be going to this dinner as well. I'm just fascinated by that murder you solved of that art collector in Othello's tower. And that Italian woman who was washed up on shore in a belly dancer's costume . . ."

"And what is a pudgy little agronomist at a remote university in the eastern coastal old city of Famagusta doing as a guest at the UN coordinator's dinner?" Safa was thinking as the UN vehicle cleared the congested city inside the walls and picked up speed. "And, boy, can he talk."

But she found she was still smiling and her unusual happy glow was, if anything, increasing. And, for the life of her, she did not know why she was suddenly in such a good mood. She took her compact out of her purse and, in the fleeting glare of the headlights of passing cars, attempted to check the damage. But here, in the soft light of the advancing evening, she thought she didn't look nearly as bad as she had in the unforgiving blaze of her bathroom light. She had no idea that her now-radiant smile made all the difference in the world.

Chapter Four

"Why won't that telephone stop ringing? It's not my responsibility to answer that phone. Ibrahim explicitly said that it would ring only at predetermined times and that he or one of his men would always be here to answer it. It wasn't going to be in my way. All they needed was a bit of space and privacy. For that they would keep my return from the notice of the police. Pah! How do I get myself into these messes?"

The merchant left his tiny office behind his copperware and antiquities shop and dragged his bulky frame through the bulging showroom and over to the entry door, hoping to put enough distance between himself and the storeroom behind his office to deaden the sound of the telephone. But the instrument just continued its ringing, stopping intermittently in parallel with the pattern of the regular cuts in the Lebanese telephone lines, and then starting up again, demanding attention.

"Ah, telephone service continues to be bad here in Beirut," Anwar Jabril mused as he loudly blew his nose on his flowing burnoose—his cloak—sleeve. The material was so dirty it was stiff, and he scowled at the chaffing against his tender skin, a scowl that was unusual on his perpetually, albeit, insincerely, smiling visage.

"However," he continued the thought, "services have not been nearly so bad since I returned. When I left, the shelling was terrible. The pearl of the Middle East was being completely ruined by this senseless warring between the Christians and Arabs and the Palestinians and the Israelis. But even then I would not have left—just as most Lebanese didn't leave, hunkering down in the flats during the shelling and gunfire of the day and coming out in the evening in their finery to party the night away in whatever nightclub had survived the day's carnage. No, I would not have left even then if the police had not been hot on my trail. And if I had not come back to my old neighborhood, where too many people knew me, I would not have been swept right back up into this mess."

Jabril sighed and cocked an ear to the storeroom. "Good, the ringing has stopped. When Ibrahim comes in, I'll say I'd been out to see what had come in at the docks today, so he will not be angry if he hears the call was important and no one answered.

"Oh, Ahmad. My nephew, Ahmad. What did I get you into? We could not stay in Cyprus, and then I discovered I could not stay in Turkey, and so I dragged you back here to Beirut. And now they have taken you away and are forcing you to become a terrorist. You could have stayed in Turkey. Why did I insist that you come here with me? But if you had not come, you might never have seen Beirut. And for a son of Lebanon never to be able to see Beirut . . ."

Jabril turned back to the doorway and surveyed the busy street outside. There at the end of the street, on the cornice with the blue Mediterranean as a backdrop, was the Holiday Inn Hotel, being restored now as a symbol of Beirut's readiness to bid to regain its reputation as the Paris of the Mideast.

Jabril had returned to a Beirut taken up in a construction frenzy, to a city anxious to try to erase the craziness and destructiveness of the previous two decades. The incessant door-to-door fighting that had seemed to perpetuate itself forever and often for no particular reason had run its course and had appeared to move, like a capricious plague, to Eastern Europe and the former Soviet Union.

Anwar Jabril, aka Mehmet Tosun, aka Nabil Jallud, had hoped to slip back into Lebanon under the cover of this busy activity and to take up the strands of his former life—his simpler life that had been interrupted by years of merchanting, thieving, and spying in Europe, Turkey, and Cyprus. But this was not to be—because of the likes of Ibrahim and the Iranian-backed Hizballah terrorists who still held out in the otherwise regenerating city.

"Yes," Jabril thought with an anger dampened by fear and desperation, "the Ibrahims of the Middle East will never leave either Beirut or me at peace."

And as if the very thought of the name drew his attention, Jabril looked across the street to the open-air café to find Ibrahim's eyes locked on him. The gaze was both penetrating and malevolent, and his smile was one of the puppeteer as he made the strings dance.

The telephone began to ring once more. The half-wit shop assistant moved toward the office at the back to answer it, but Jabril stopped her, irritated because she never could seem to discern the ring of that telephone from the business phone.

"Damn," Jabril exclaimed inwardly. "He knows I am here now. If the caller complains that the telephone wasn't answered, who knows what he will do? And it might be just as bad if I answer the telephone myself."

What else could he have done? The balloon-figured tradesman performed an exaggerated double take, as if he had just heard a far-off telephone unexpectedly start to ring, turned dramatically and pirouetted into the shop, came up short as if realizing that it was the "special" telephone that was ringing, turned back to the doorway in a show of great concern, and started to gesture wildly to the street, bringing his hand up to his ear as if he was holding a receiver.

Ibrahim got the message. Everyone within two city blocks got the message. Ibrahim scowled, his eyes dancing with fire. He slowly, and as unobtrusively as possible—which was not at all possible, since now everyone in the café connected his movement and direction to Jabril's theatrics—rose and sauntered over to the copper shop. And although everyone in the vicinity knew what had transpired between Jabril and Ibrahim, they all turned their eyes away and would conveniently forget that there was any connection. Because this was Beirut and they were all survivors.

Ibrahim stiff-armed Jabril to the side and very musically into a string of pots suspended from the ceiling as he passed the merchant when entering the open-fronted shop.

"Kind sir," Jabril mouthed obsequiously from within the jangle of copperware. "The telephone. Your telephone. It is ringing, and I did not want you to miss your call."

Ibrahim did no more than grunt menacingly as he disappeared into the back of the shop, pushing a lolling shop assistant aside who wasn't showing any intention of moving out of the way on her own.

Obviously, calling the Hizballah band chieftain to the special telephone so publicly hadn't been the right answer either.

* * * *

Mikhail Lukenov tried to adjust his position in the backseat of the Volvo without awakening little Pavel. The boy had screamed and whimpered himself into a state of exhaustion. He had finally gone to sleep in the Volvo, his head on his father's thigh and his arm wrapped around Lukenov's waist as if from fear that his father would suddenly disappear just as his mother had disappeared hours earlier.

Lukenov felt trapped and frustrated as he sat pinned down in the Volvo, watching developments through the vehicle's open door. The beams of light from flashlights that were wavering around on the hillside above Soli looked like so many fireflies in some sort of frenetic dance. The Dance of Death. No, he couldn't think such thoughts, he demanded of himself. He should be out there, helping—commanding.

The five Russian embassy vehicles had roared into the Soli excavation parking lot just over an hour after he had gotten through on the mobile telephone. This was record time for a journey through Greek Cypriot Nicosia—called Lefkosia by the Greeks—across the buffer zone at the Ledra Palace checkpoint, out of Turkish Cypriot Nicosia—called Lefkosha by the Turks. Clearing the capital, they had raced across the central Mesaoria plain on rough roads, and, finally, through the Turkish-held town of Morphou before hitting Morphou Bay and turning west to Soli, just short of the buffer zone once more.

Just as he had directed, the Russians had answered his call immediately and without having raised the alarm among the Cypriots. This had to be handled discreetly. He still couldn't believe that Irina had just completely disappeared or had come to any harm. But why had she not returned by now? To be honest, he couldn't believe she had just vanished into thin air. But, with the onset of night and the advance of time, he had to accept that she must have wandered off farther than she had intended to and had come to some sort of incapacitating harm. She could, certainly, have fallen into a fissure or, possibly, have been bitten by a snake. There were species of poisonous vipers on Cyprus, but he would have thought it was too early in the season for them to be out. And reports of snake bites were rare; even the vipers were not aggressive on Cyprus.

"Or have you been approached by a snake of a different caliber? A human snake, perhaps, who has come upon you by happenstance and taken advantage of coincidence?"

"I'm rambling!" Lukenov exhorted himself in disgust. "Be professional," he commanded, as he moved his leg and pinched and rubbed his calf with his hand in an attempt to improve the circulation in his limbs. Pavel moaned and turned slightly but tightened his grip around his father's waist. Lukenov laid his arm across his son's body and patted his leg until the youngster had settled down.

Despair began to set in. "Why was she suddenly so euphoric just before she wandered off? Had she made some sort of decision? Has she tried to leave me out here in the wilds? Is she trying to make some sort of statement about what I let happen to her family—and what I let her and the boys walk into in Grozny? Where are you, Irina?

And are you alive, or have you done something to yourself for spite and revenge? If so, you know just how to crush me."

Lukenov beat on his temple with his free hand. "Focus, Mikhail! Focus. You are the chief of Russian intelligence here. She must be found, and this must be contained before it becomes public."

But it was already too late for that.

Lukenov looked up toward the hillside once more. The dancing beams of light had increased significantly in number. But there were two distinct sets of lights now. The nearer ones, fanned out on the hillside immediately above and beyond Soli, were his Russian searchers. But beyond those and separated by nearly half a mile were other lights. And then a flare went up from among these lights and out over the hillside where the Russians were searching. And then another flare. It was as if daylight had returned, if only fleetingly.

Now that his attention was torn away from his thoughts, Lukenov realized that he could hear a loud humming noise as well, although that sound didn't seem to be coming from the direction of the hills.

One thing was obvious. The Russians were no longer alone.

It was then that Lukenov noticed that Uri had not returned. He had said he was just going off into the bushes to relieve himself. He had already bid on joining the Russian crew in the search of the hillside soon after they had arrived, and Lukenov had firmly denied the request. He could not bear the thought of another of his family members out there in the dark, alone. But, if truth be known, he was far more concerned that it might be Uri who did find his mother and that she might not be alive. Lukenov could bear the thought of that even less. Uri had been extremely angry but had complied and had stayed near the automobile with his father. But he had asked for, and received, one of the water canteens the search party had brought along.

Lukenov looked around the Volvo as best he could. The canteen seemed to be missing as well. He broke out into a cold sweat, faced now with the two new concerns of who was in the hills above and beyond his search party and where Uri had gone.

But without notice, there was a third, even more compelling concern.

Blinding lights riveted the Volvo into the ground from three different directions, as several hulking battle tanks roared into the parking lot and trapped the Volvo in their sights. Pavel woke with a convulsive jerk and screamed and screamed and screamed.

"Well, so much for anonymity, and the mystery of the humming noise is solved," thought Lukenov, as he wearily rose up out of the Volvo and raised his arms above his head.

* * * *

Ahmad had never been so scared in his life, and he had seen more than his share of fear in his young life. He had been brought along on this operation because he had lived most of his life here in the Turkish-controlled zone of Cyprus. But he had never been in the area around Vouni and Soli before today. His uncle's antiquities shop had been in the Turkish sector of Nicosia, very near the Ledra Palace checkpoint, and the rest of his movements in the north had been either in the northern coastal harbor castle town of Kyrenia or in the walled eastern coast port of Famagusta.

But Ahmad hadn't had the courage to tell The Asp that he couldn't guide the band across the buffer zone to Vouni and back.

Ahmad sensed that his life would have been at an end if he had admitted this. As it was, the unwilling youth had not gained the respect of the terrorist band that would have ensured his place in their ranks. He did not want their respect or to be in their ranks, but he had not been asked what he wanted. What he wanted was to live. And to live, he had to continue to pretend he was committed to this band and to prove himself as useful to them during his stint in Cyprus.

The band was here to train in mountain maneuvers and to toughen themselves for service elsewhere. But The Asp was ambitious. He didn't think *he* needed any training or toughing, and he planned to prove his worth to his superiors quickly and in different ways than they anticipated.

From these simple thoughts had arisen the plan. And the plan had gone even more smoothly than The Asp had imagined it would—with, possibly, one small glitch. Having received word of the Russian political officer's plans for an outing at Vouni, The Asp had quickly laid down an operational scheme. His purpose had been twofold: to make an international splash that would make even his superiors take notice—in this case, to deliver a senior diplomat of one of the major powers—and to test the new, shaky recruit from Beirut.

The Asp had serious doubts about Ahmad Jallud. He had instantaneously gotten the feeling that the youth didn't belong and wouldn't fit in. And, like the viper from which he had taken his battle name, he usually acted on his feelings immediately. If he had not been told that Jallud had lived most of his life in the Turkish Cypriot zone and thus could prove useful to the band in some small way—The Asp planned to spend most of his time in the Greek zone, which was beyond Jallud's experience—Jallud would have been eliminated on the first day he came to them.

But now that they were safe at the base camp in the old monastery just outside the remote Greek Cypriot Troodos Mountain village of Vroisha, The Asp had to admit that the youth had served them well. He also found the young Ahmad to be handsome and attractive, and The Asp had special uses for such men. Thus Ahmad could live for another day at least. At first Jallud had seemed so panicked and disoriented that The Asp almost shot him just outside the monastery gates. But then the boy had taken hold and had led the band across the buffer zone without any signs of Greek, UN, or Turkish troops.

The Russian family and their Volvo had been in the area when the band had arrived. They were up on the heights at Vouni, however, and The Asp had not seen any way they could be reached without attracting attention. He had taken the chance that they had not stopped at the other ruins, Soli, yet and that they would do so after they left Vouni. He positioned his band just above the ancient amphitheater and awaited the chance to snatch the diplomat.

He didn't want the whole family, and he didn't want to just run in and take the diplomat from within the embrace of his family, which, in this isolated spot, he knew that he easily could have done. No, the rules of this game were subtlety and the establishment of fear—the fear that terrorists could surgically remove whoever they wanted from wherever they were and that no one who defied their masters was to be safe.

However, the diplomat himself never separated from the family, and while they were at Soli, the sons seemed to be plastered to him as if they could hardly believe he was flesh and blood and that he was there with them. However, the woman did wander away, coming up the hillside and very near to where the band lay in waiting.

And then The Asp had his inspiration. The wife. That would almost be better than the diplomat himself for this first exercise in surgical extraction. Who would care, really, if a Russian diplomat was taken? This one couldn't be too important. He was merely listed as a political officer, and Cyprus was not a major posting. And being a target was part of his job. No, the biggest splash for the initial operation would be someone who would evoke instant sympathy. Who better than an innocent woman, a simple housewife and mother?

The snatch itself was anticlimactic and did not give The Asp that orgasmic surge that had made this work so thrilling for him. There had been no resistance, and, beyond the initial brief exclamation of unexpectedly encountering glowering people in full commando gear, the woman had made no sound. It was as if a thick protective veil quickly fell over her face at the realization that she was trapped and in grave danger. She had not struggled against the gag; she had hardly flinched when Widad had reached over and ripped the blue blouse away from her body, and she did not fight the bindings they wound tightly around her wrists.

When Widad, The Asp's chosen deputy, started jerking the woman cruelly toward the rising slope, The Asp noticed the subtle way in which Ahmad insinuated himself between the two women and more gently led the Russian up through the fragrant hillside of sage. Widad's attention was easily distracted, and she had not seemed to notice the displacement at all. But The Asp had seen and recorded the event.

"No, not the right material for our band," he had registered. "It will help us move faster as long as she remains compliant, but you have not done this to help us move faster, Ahmad. No, there is a softness about you that is not acceptable and cannot be trained away. I can see that I was right, and you are not long for this band—or this world. But, if this helps us get our prize through the buffer zone and back to base quicker and more safely, I will do nothing for now. Besides, I believe I have another use for you."

As the others were silently and swiftly fanning out onto the hillside above the temple of Aphrodite of Soli, The Asp placed the torn blouse on what appeared to have once been a stone altar and stooped to pick up a large rock to anchor the material.

"The Russian diplomat must know that this was no accident. He must have time to fully know fear, confusion, and uncertainty before we drop the big surprise on him."

The Asp started to leave and then remembered the other marker that he had devised to leave here. He unbuttoned and reached into one of the long pockets on the leg of his fatigues and pulled out an airline brochure covered in black markings.

"You won't know what this means now," he chuckled to himself, "but you will come to know what it means. And you will see it again and again and again."

He paused and peeked over the brow of the hill and down toward the meadow below through his binoculars. The Russian diplomat was just looking up the hillside, a mild look of concern on his face, and was trying to stand. The youngest son, however, was holding his father closely and hampering the man's movements.

The Asp quickly pulled back from his vantage point and slithered off through the sage and up the hillside.

* * * *

He stood, fully exposed like a surprised deer, in the glare of the first flare. But by the time the second flare was arching its way over the hillside below, Uri had dropped to his knees between a carob tree and an oleander bush. And it was a good thing for him he had reacted so quickly, because as he disappeared into the foliage, two figures passed by just a few feet from where he had been standing.

"Can you see them?" one was whispering to the other. "Where is the line? We can't go beyond the line."

"Christ almighty," answered the second voice, a bit louder. "What the shit is going on down there anyway? A hell of a way for Turks to invade—with a few scattered flashlights. What are we doing out here anyway? This was supposed to be the Argentine's sector. Why haven't they deployed yet?"

The voices faded out over toward the coast. The two hadn't moved any farther down the slope. They must have thought they were close to the Turkish line at the buffer zone. Uri realized that he must have reached and entered the UN-controlled buffer zone. His stomach started to churn and he clutched the canteen closely to his chest. The thought that the trail had moved into the buffer zone somehow steeled his resolve.

This wasn't just his mother escaping the family and the horrors she had experienced. He had realized that almost immediately upon inspecting the temple area. He had been the best of his elite section of Young Pioneers, the ones who had been trained in mountain survival and tracking. And he had known right off that there had been others where his mother was last seen and that she had left the same way they had. He had tried to tell his father, but Pavel would not stop screaming, and his father had—surprisingly to Uri, who had always thought he father was the world's expert in such matters—been too confused and disoriented to pay any attention to Uri. Even when Uri had wanted to join the hunt, his father had gotten that panicked expression, and Uri's explanation had hardened in his throat.

But Uri had seen evidence of where his mother and the others had gone. He was shocked that none of the other Russians could see the trail. They were useless. All of them. Including his father. No, that had been unfair. His father had been hampered by the screaming Pavel. And, knowing what Pavel had been through, Uri was not about to take from him what little stability he could cling to in the face of his mother's disappearance.

Uri had managed to maneuver his way through the ranks of the Russians without attracting notice and had followed the trail farther up the hillside by the time the second set of lights appeared above him. At first he thought these were the people who had taken his mother, and he climbed as quickly as possible. But now he knew that these must be UN troops within the buffer zone who had been attracted by the unusual night-time activity of the hunt by the men from the Russian embassy in the normally deserted coastal hills above the isolated Soli site.

During his initial climb, Uri had not taken the time to even think about what could have happened to his mother. He just knew that the trail included a soft-soled shoe print along with those of sturdier boots, and he grasped at this as evidence that his mother was alive and moving with an unknown group of people. He had originally thought he could quickly locate where his mother had been taken and call in his father and the rest of the Russians for help. Now that he knew the trail moved into the buffer zone, he realized that this would not be a simple or quickly concluded search. The Russians could not follow here.

After the UN soldiers had moved off, Uri climbed a bit more until he had reached a better vantage point from which to watch the activity below and above. He picked a spot that also offered concealment nearby to which he could retreat as needed. The activity seemed to be intensifying below. There appeared to be some sort of military convoy forming in the parking lot at Soli, around the family's Volvo as well as the five sedans from the embassy. The lights from the flashlights of the Russian searchers seemed to be coalescing and moving back down the hillside toward the parking lot.

Uri knew that he would have to hole up here until everything got sorted out below and above. He seriously doubted, however, whether his mother and those with her would get sorted out as well in the process. There was something deeper going on here. He took comfort in the evidence that his mother had apparently come at least this far on her own feet. If she was to be killed, it seemed this would have already happened, probably at the temple ruins below. Uri had just been through hell in Chechnya. He was prepared for the worst. However, now that he had come this far he was not prepared to timidly return to the embassy and to let others sort this out without his help. He wanted to know where his mother was, why she had been taken, whether she had gone willingly, happy to abandon her family. He was the only one of the lot who had been able to track her this far. He was no longer a boy, despite his age. He was a trained mountaineer. He had lived through the siege of Grozny, and he was now a man. He would follow this trail and solve this mystery. He was his father's son—stronger now even than his father.

* * * *

Later, in the early light of the new day, when the terrorist band had returned to the isolated monastery, when the Russian woman had been locked in the storeroom under the watchful eye of Faris Sukkar, and when the bar on the heavy wooden outer door of the monastery compound had been shot home, The Asp and Widad retired to the abbot's room and made wild, noisy, and purposefully audible sex.

It was thus for The Asp after every operation, whether it was a simple, straightforward killing or a full-scale planned program such as the previous day's cross-border kidnapping. Danger and the excitement of the hunt brought out the juices in The Asp. To his excitement, it seemed to have the same effect on his recently assigned deputy, Widad. Before Widad, The Asp had always had to have sex after an operation, but, before Widad, there had not always been such a strong woman at hand—nor, as a matter of fact, had there always been *any* woman at hand. But that had never stopped The Asp from this ritual.

When he and the woman had exhausted their lust and she was leaving him, he said, "Make the call and report the snatch. You'll need to make delivery arrangements as well."

"But, Abdul," Widad quickly responded, "It's not time. We were told always to report at the designated time."

"This is not routine. This is a new game, and we will now make our share of the rules. Make the call now."

"Yes, of course." She left quickly. No one else could question The Asp even as far as she had done. And no one else in the unit could use his real name and survive.

To mark this special operation, he had originally planned to call for the Russian woman after he had done with Widad. But, when it came time for him to send for her, he was caught short by the recollection of the strange look of defeat and calm acceptance in her eyes at the point of her first realization that she was trapped. That haunted, yet resigned, look disturbed the terrorist as nothing else had in all his years of cruelty. He knew that he could not enjoy the act under those circumstances. In fact, he doubted whether he could even perform under those circumstances—certainly not with a woman.

But, at the same time, the recognition of his impotence in the face of the Russian woman's martyred response to her situation challenged his pride. So, instead of sending for her, he sent for Ahmad.

"It's time he learned the full meaning of discipline within this unit."

Chapter Five

The last lingering light of the setting sun—providing precise definition to the term "evening glow"—was brushing against the red tile-roofed white and beige houses that climbed the two sides of the Makedonitissa Valley as Caitlyn and Takis Koniotis drove out Grivas Avenue, across the mouth of the valley, around UN Circle, and up the old international airport road to the entrance to the main UN forces base at the western end of the city.

This was Caitlyn's favorite time of the day in Cyprus. Takis, who had lived here all of his life, seemed oblivious to the magic that was created by the glow of the setting sun reflecting off red roofs, white and ochre walls, sandy earth, and lush greenery. But Caitlyn was smitten by the Cypriot twilight—and especially in this wealthy western suburb of the capital. When she had first come to Cyprus, her friend and benefactor in her archaeological project, now recently and tragically dead—murdered in one of Caitlyn's husband's more celebrated police cases—lived in a house on top of a mesa on the western ridge of the valley, just above the old Makedonitissa monastery, tucked away in its pine grove ringed with giant palm trees. Caitlyn visited the house often and had told her friend, Eleni Piccard, that she had fallen in love with the place. She had found the view from this house—especially at this time of the evening—to be breathtaking. From the rear garden of the residence she could see the entire Makedonitissa Valley unfolding below her, while the rest of Nicosia peeked just over the rise of the eastern ridge. And riding above this scene was the full east-to-west stretch of the nearby sharp, rugged Kyrenia Range, invariably purple in the sinking sun, with the dancing lights of mountain villages flickering on and growing stronger in the waning natural light.

The view from the front of her friend's house had been almost as impressive. The UN base, with its mature stand of trees—an unusual sight on Cyprus' central plain—hovered on top of the next ridge to the west, the last ridge between Nicosia and the central Mesaoria plain as it marched down to Morphou Bay on the western coast. The base, which now delineated the widest band of buffer zone between the Greek and Turkish sectors and which now included, just to the south, the buildings and runways of the island's former international airport, had been a military encampment as far back in time as anyone could imagine. Before housing the headquarters of the UN peacekeeping forces, which arrived in 1964 to try to stem the intercommunal troubles that had only increased in the wake of the withdrawal of colonial Britain and the formation of the Cypriot Republic four years previously, this had been the main British forces base. Its buildings still were wholly reminiscent of British colonial architecture. And before that, as it commanded the western approach to the city, it had been a Turkish encampment, and before that Venetian, and, even earlier, Roman and Greek . . . and back into the earliest eras of settlement on the ancient, richly historic island.

Eleni's house was one of a handful that occupied the top of a mesa that was riddled with crumbling fortification walls and a zigzag of personnel trenching around the periphery.

This was another aspect of Cyprus and its history that Caitlyn could feel—that was palpably alive to her in ways that weren't felt by most visitors to the island but that were felt by the Cypriots themselves—the continuum of history on the island. But even though Takis felt this, for some mysterious reason he didn't feel as steeped in it as Caitlyn did. It was part of her gift that made her a good archaeologist and had given her the reputation of a "locator of archeological finds." Caitlyn could stand on the soil of Cyprus in almost any location and feel—palpably experience—the layers of history and the people who had been here. This was particularly so on the mesa where Eleni's house stood—a strongpoint that had guarded the approaches to Nicosia for centuries and that pulled at Caitlyn with the whisperings of valiant defenses and treachery and grief from earlier civilizations. And when Eleni had been alive and they had stood here together, Caitlyn—because of her close affinity to Eleni, as much in past lives as in the current life—had been more in touch with the history of place than at any other time and place. This despite the recent massive construction in and habitation of the small valley.

In the valley between the two ridges, luxury villas were beginning to rise—as a sign that now, twenty years after the Turkish invasion of the island that had only been stemmed at this point by the presence of the UN base, the Greek Cypriots were beginning to feel safe enough to build this close to the buffer zone. And, just as the Kyrenia Range dominated the view to the rear of the house, the view from the front of the house, from north to south, swept from the western end of the Kyrenia Range, across the plain leading down to Morphou Bay—red- and indigo-hued in the setting sun—and to the far off, often snow-capped Troodos Mountain Range in the south, which was cast in various shades of blue in the evening light.

Caitlyn sighed, as the Jaguar cleared the UN checkpoint and turned into the drive to the residence that had been assigned to the UN coordinator for Cyprus, a walled compound that looked more like a fortified outpost from the outside than a residence. The main building inside the compound was a squarish, columned villa that was suspended on the eastern slope of the Makedonitissa Valley near its northern mouth and that could be reached either through the UN base or, via a valley, from the Greek sector.

As much as she liked the Koniotis home in the shadow of the old acropolis and immediately adjacent to the busy commercial center and the main avenue leading to the nearby old walled city, Caitlyn was mesmerized by the vistas that could be seen from the slopes of the Makedonitissa Valley, and she wished that she could muster the courage to ask Takis if they could move to this or some other area where she could see the mountains—and where people down through the ages whispered to her in the quiet moments. Of course, she rationalized to herself, it probably would be so much worse if she spent very much time on the island's coast. Nicosia was in the center of the island and thus did not benefit from the added glory of having the sea as part of the equation. She could readily understand why so many Europeans were choosing to retire to villas on the hillsides around Paphos and Limassol, which sloped from the Troodos Mountains down to the crystal-blue Mediterranean.

The sight of the UN coordinator's front gate, blazingly lit up by a combination of the lights over the entrance and of several back-lit television camera crews, brought Caitlyn out of her reverie, as Takis nosed the large, old Jaguar into the side curb and, in the process, barely avoided contact with a blue BMW convertible, which had skidded up to the entrance from the other direction, braked hard, and shimmied slightly toward the left into Takis's lane.

Caitlyn knew that this potentially was a very important night for her husband, and she was determined to be supportive. At the same time, she was a bit concerned. She had heard that the guest of honor, Eric Isaksen, could be irascible and that he distained archaeologists, Americans, and women. So she was starting off the evening at a great disadvantage. Well, perhaps the UN coordinator, who she was quite fond of, would be an ally in time of trouble.

* * * *

Willie Hamilton had a great deal of trouble trying to keep up with Ginger as she sped westward out of the village of Strovolos on the road that dissected the Makedonitissa Valley between the International Fair Grounds and the national sports complex. As he crested the eastern ridge at the Apollonion private hospital and dipped down toward the village floor, he was hit with sudden dismay.

A soccer match in the Makarios Stadium was just breaking up, and the road ahead was congested with people and automobiles, an obvious potential for disaster in a country that reveled in good-natured and macho chaos. Ginger's approach to the problem had quite evidently been to press down on the accelerator and weave her way through the congestion as quickly and maliciously as possible to reach the other side of the valley. Actually, the Greek Cypriots were

66

accustomed to this manner of driving, so she was probably in better stead than if she had tried to maneuver the road more carefully.

With a curse, Willie decided to exercise good sense. Pulling over to the side of the road long enough to anxiously observe his spouse's miraculously successful journey across the valley floor and disappearance beyond the old monastery before the departing stadium traffic had a chance to encumber her high-speed flight, Willie maneuvered the beat-up Mini across one of the ubiquitous dirt connecting roads that the Cypriot public had created across empty plots of ground to circumvent official designs to cut down cross traffic in residential areas. Once back on pavement, he wove his way along the eastern ridge and across the valley until he could reach the downslope approach to the UN coordinator's mansion.

He arrived just in time to see Ginger pull past—and almost through—a television crew and a large Jaguar saloon car and neatly cut off a UN vehicle that had started to park in a space that was now occupied by Ginger's convertible.

To his dismay, Willie saw that the senior police inspector, Takis Koniotis, and his American wife were the occupants of the Jaguar. Willie began to sweat. He couldn't afford to cross the inspector; both he and Ginger had barely missed out on going to prison the last time they had dealings with Koniotis.

As the couple exited their vehicle, Willie pulled to the side of the Jaguar and quickly offered an apology through the window. "I'm so sorry about that, Takis. I'm afraid Ginger and I had a little spat, and she's in somewhat of a tiff."

"No, I don't believe it," Takis returned with a mocking voice and knowing grin. "You and Ginger fighting? I cannot imagine that."

The battles of the Hamiltons were the stuff of legends in the expatriate community.

Caitlyn began to surface a chuckle of her own, which, however, stuck in her throat, as Ginger wafted by and into the mansion's entrance, bestowing a saucy grin at Takis as she did so and throwing a stinging comment over her shoulder toward Caitlyn. "Beautiful dress, Caitlyn, but putting on a little weight, are we?"

Once more Willie started to form an apology, but the effort was rendered unnecessary by the arrival of the occupants of the UN sedan that Ginger had cut off.

"Safa!" Caitlyn exclaimed with real and warm pleasure. "How nice to see you here. Takis gets to meet with you every week, but I rarely get to see you."

The face of the Turkish Cypriot senior police investigator lit up. "Caitlyn. Takis. It's so wonderful to be able to socialize with you again." She pumped Takis's hand and hugged Caitlyn closely, after which she pecked the younger woman on both cheeks as was Cypriot style. "Good evening, Mr. Hamilton," she said with a bit more reserve, as the *Cyprus Mail* investigative reporter entered the grouping.

"Oh," she continued, as she pulled a somewhat rotund little bald man forward into the circle, "Let me introduce Mr. John Patterson, who came across from the Turkish side with me in the UN vehicle. I just met him now myself; he's an agronomist at the University of the Middle East in Famagusta. Mr. Patterson, Mr. and Mrs. Koniotis, Mr. Hamilton."

"Oh, yes, I have already met Mr. Patterson," said Caitlyn with a smile.

All eyes—including Patterson's—turned quizzically toward her. But before anyone had time to say anything, the Greek Cypriot television crews had seen Takis and Safa together and had descended on the group.

"Mr. Koniotis; Ms. Ziya," called a male voice from within a blinding circle of light, "What can you tell us about the former Danish foreign minister's mission here? Is it true that the United Nations wants the police departments of Cyprus and the Turkish pseudo state to merge?"

And then the convergence of another pool of light and a female voice. "Have the two of you uncovered yet another crime implicating a UN official? Is that what you are here for?"

"No," answered Takis amiably as Safa Ziya involuntarily shrank from the glaring lights, "We're just here for dinner. And, no, neither Ms. Ziya nor I know of any plans—or external pressure—to extend the cooperation of our two police departments beyond the current regular—and highly beneficial, I might add—review sessions on investigations that affect the entire country."

An insistent follow-up from the first reporter: "Can either—or both—of you tell us about what is happening on the Green Line over on the Morphou coast? Has there been a Turkish incursion of the buffer zone? Perhaps Ms. Ziya would care to comment?"

Three microphones stabbed out toward the Turkish Cypriot police official.

The video cameras caught both Takis and Safa looking startled, a clip that played the airwaves for a couple of days thereafter.

"Border fighting . . . ?" Safa murmured. But before she could say more, John Patterson moved between her and the microphones;

69

Caitlyn Koniotis pulled at her husband's suit sleeve and whispered, "Perhaps we should go in"; and Willie Hamilton started hustling the other four through the entrance court and toward the villa's massive front doors. While the group moved toward the villa, Willie smiled to himself and started formulating plans. If the hunt for news was on, he didn't need all of those television cameras around.

* * * *

Ibrahim slammed down the telephone and stalked out into the main room of the copper shop. He glowered at Jabril without even seeing him; the rotund shopkeeper shrank into a hanging display of small carpets just as if he had been seen. The terrorist was muttering to himself, and Jabril wished he hadn't heard what had been said.

"I'll kill him when I see him, the uppity little turd. I'll tear him limb from limb. Training and practice was all he was supposed to be doing. Training and practice. There were no orders to actually carry out an operation. Ambitious little bastard."

Ibrahim was pacing the room—at least to the extent the narrow passageways between the merchandise tables would permit. He stopped just parallel to Jabril, broke out in a wide grin, and threw both arms out at full extension. This sent brass bells into concert at one extension and flipped the merchant's preposterous red velvet fez sailing across the shop at the other extension.

"What balls!" Ibrahim yelped, changing tact upon a rethought. "He's put us into the game, and there's no way I can lose. If we pull this off, they will credit me. If something goes wrong, he brought it on himself. OK, so be it." He headed for the sunlight outside the shop.

At the frame of the wide opening at the front of the shop, where the wall of the shop met the exterior wall of the building, he remembered Jabril, cowering in his rugs. Ibrahim returned and put his face, menacingly, directly into the face of the shopkeeper.

"I'll be gone for two days. Do not, during that time, answer that telephone. Understand?" And then, when Jabril just continued to gaze at him like a startled deer, he repeated, "UNDERSTAND?"

"Oh, yes sir, I understand perfectly." Jabril came to life, pulled himself up to his full height—such as it was—and slid to the door with the terrorist, patting and brushing at Ibrahim as if he had fallen in a tub of flour.

As they reached the doorway—Jabril brushing and Ibrahim flapping his hands away—the shopkeeper began to prattle.

"Yes, certainly, I understand. All of the plans are working well. The one who telephoned had an operation and is a turd, and you are going away for two days. When the telephone rings, I will tell the turd you won't be back for two days."

"No, you idiot. That's not who I don't want to talk to for two days. I said not to answer the telephone at all!" Pulling Jabril off of him as if he were a leech, Ibrahim gave the fat little man a withering look and marched back to the storage room. With a jerk, he pulled the telephone cord from the wall and walked back to the door, instrument in hand.

"Here, little man. Your telephone is broken. Get it fixed on Tuesday. Not on Monday and not on Wednesday. Tuesday. Can you understand and remember that?"

"Certainly, sir. Thank you, sir," Jabril gushed as Ibrahim strode out of the shop and toward the sea.

As the terrorist turned the corner down near the Holiday Inn, Mehmet Tosun/Ahmad Jallud/Anwar Jabril straightened his back and narrowed his eyes.

"Now, what was all *that* about?" he wondered to himself. "Obviously his operations are *not* going quite to plan and he doesn't want to be in contact with the Iranians before he can figure out his next move. Two days? Why not two weeks or two years—or two lifetimes? How did Ahmad and I get into this mess? And, more important, how are we going to get out of it?"

A couple of European tourists were approaching the shop. Jabril's eyes darted to a mirror, wherein he adjusted his face to one of his silliest and most obsequious grins, and then, after sticking the unattached telephone receiver under a pile of made-in-China silk pillow cushions, he headed for the street. Business was business. He did it all to be able to stay in business.

* * * *

Mikhail Lukenov was physically exhausted and emotionally drained, but the cacophony of anxious chattering about him had cleared his mind and put him back on a professional footing. The commotion of the search by his Russian compatriots on the hillside above Soli had brought out a squad of British-national UN soldiers who had been patrolling this sector of the buffer zone, and the combination of these two activities had produced a whole tank squadron of the Turkish forces stationed in the Morphou area.

The Turks had permitted the captain in charge of the UN patrol to come down to the Soli parking apron to discuss the situation, and the mukhtar of the nearby Turkish Cypriot village had also arrived. Lukenov had the presence of mind to consider that the combined animated conversation among his Russians, the British, the mainland Turks, and the Turkish village official, all being observed by a large gathering of local residents who would likely remember this day longer than any other, more festive occasion, would have been very amusing to him under other circumstances.

Thorough professional that he was, he also had the presence of mind to mark that there had, as yet, been no sign of a Greek Cypriot force of any kind at the Green Line in this sector. He tucked this indication of a low threshold of readiness in the back of his mind as the subject of a cable to Moscow. This cable, however, would be greatly misleading. There had been eyes aplenty viewing this spectacle from the Greek Cypriot line. Unfortunately, these watchers had not gathered quickly enough to have seen either Irina Lukenov and her captors or her son pass into Greek territory and beyond. But they had reached the area as quickly as the Turkish tanks had, and they were lying in wait for developments.

Surprisingly enough, the disappearance of his older son, Uri, had a calming effect on Lukenov rather than heightening his anxiety in the wake of his wife's disappearance. He somehow recognized that Uri must have seen something and was following it up. It gave him hope that the boy apparently was off pursuing a clue. That meant to him that there must be a more complex and still hopeful explanation for Irina's disappearance beyond a fatal accident. If either Irina or Uri had suffered a deadly or disabling accident, surely the searchers would have found them—or one or more of them would have suffered the same fate and also now be missing, which wasn't the case. He feared for Uri as much as for Irina in this situation, certainly, but he could feel in his soul that his son was well and was in pursuit of the mother. In this, Mikhail took both comfort and pride. Today his son was a man.

Mercifully, Lukenov's other, younger son, Pavel, had finally drifted into deep sleep, oblivious to all of the ineffectual fussing going on about him.

"Yes, ineffectual activity," Lukenov admitted to himself. "There's nothing more we can do here tonight. The mukhtar can arrange his own search in the morning's light. If he then finds the answer to this riddle, it is not likely that my presence will be needed— or known by my wife and son. There are other ways to approach this problem. I can feel it in my bones that the action has shifted to the Greek Cypriot side. I'm beginning to think that this is a more insidious, purposeful event than it has first appeared to be. I have assets on the Greek side. I must get to them—and quickly. I must let the search dogs loose."

He rose from the backseat of the Volvo and grimly turned to the chattering circle of men representing so many and so varied a collection of authorities and began to take charge, to shut the activity down for the night.

* * * *

Eric Isaksen, former Danish foreign minister, former chairman of the United Nations Development Program, and current special emissary of the UN secretary general to the Middle East, stood at the mirror in the UN coordinator to Cyprus' guest room and tried to straighten his tie with shaky fingers. He didn't have palsy, nor did he suffer from old age—although he was old, older and more shriveled and more sour of disposition than he had ever thought would be possible. He blamed this on all of the treachery and misery he had seen

74

in his life. But, no, it was not illness or age that made him tremble; it was raw fear. And it was a fear that he could not show—not now, and most certainly not after he had moved on to complete his mission.

For the hundredth time that day he missed his wife, Anna. She had always given him strength. No one had ever known that it was she, not he, who had mustered the courage to see him through his long, distinguished, and very dangerous career. When that terrorist's bullet had missed him five years ago and taken Anna instead, the world had rejoiced—at least publicly—that he had not been the victim. They had not purposefully denigrated Anna's life, of course, or purposefully been insensitive to her tragic death, but the world of the peacemakers considered Isaksen as indispensable in negotiating amity in a world of hate and had declared in editorials read around the world that mankind was saved when he had escaped assassination.

Little did they know. Anna had been their salvation. He had only been the façade. Anna had been the steel in his back—and the conscience that wouldn't let him just give the fight up. And now Anna was gone—by the will of a terrorist's bullet—and Isaksen had drawn the task of walking into the lion's den in Beirut and negotiating the departure from that city of the Hizballah. He trembled at the thought. Yes, he was so afraid of this mission that he could not tie a simple knot and appear on time for the dinner party that had already started downstairs. But it was not personal fear. It was fear that the bitterness he had kept locked inside this past five years would erupt in much more than just the sharpness of tongue and the hardness toward women that had become his reputation—a persona that had been brought on by the incongruity of his anger at Anna for leaving him and at himself for having put her in the line of fire. It was fear that he would let his true feelings toward the Hizballah and all such terrorists out and thus doom the people of Beirut and Lebanon to further decades of hell.

But he couldn't let the fear and bitterness overtake him. He dug his fingernails into the palms of his hands, and the pain calmed his nerves. He could not dwell on the task ahead in Beirut, even though the whole world was watching. The Hizballah had publicly announced they were prepared to negotiate a withdrawal from Beirut and even from Lebanon and offered safe conduct to Isaksen—and only Isaksen—to initiate the dialogue.

Isaksen could not turn down this call. It may never come again. But he was much more interested in the project that he had been called away from—the establishment of an anti-international crime organization, which would include terrorism, within the United Nations Secretariat, and he had purposefully stopped over here in Cyprus on his way to Lebanon because he had heard that the Cypriots had gained some experience in this area. He straightened his tie as best he could and moved toward the door. Both terrorism and fear would have to wait for another day. There was something more important to him to pursue here in Cyprus over the next couple of days.

As he descended the stairs to the familiar sound of clinking glasses and happy babble from below, he put on his studied, frosty smile meant to tell the world that "I am polite and distinguished, but don't come near me." A sudden pain made him look quickly toward the staircase wall. The hundredth and first thought of Anna had breached the defenses of the day. When he looked back, however, there was his studied smile again. And there, at the bottom of the stairs, was the smiling UN coordinator for Cyprus, ready to take him

76

to his appointed reception spot for the latest in a never-ending chain of "vitally important" diplomatic dinners

Chapter Six

Eric Isaksen, frozen smile in place, reached the bottom of the curved staircase in the two-story entrance foyer at the same time that the escaping Koniotises, Safa Ziya, William Hamilton, and John Patterson swept into the front door. The lights from the television cameras and the microphones from various extended arms intruded beyond the threshold, but the Cypriot media were too well trained and polite to encroach any farther. There, midst mutual glances of relief, the newly arrived guests came upon Ingrid Bittmann, who flashed them welcoming smiles and then turned to the staircase.

"Here, Eric, let me introduce you to our most recent arrivals. Several others are already in the main lounge, and you can meet them over cocktails."

Ingrid Bittmann had only been the UN coordinator for Cyprus for a couple of months, although she had been deputy coordinator before that for several months following the death of her predecessor at the ancient Greco-Roman-period Curium archaeological site on one of the huge British sovereign base areas on the southern coast to the west of Limassol. Although this death had been attributed to a fall off the Curium cliff at the time for public consumption, it had been part of one of Takis Koniotis's first major international crime investigations following the formation of his special police unit—and the UN coordinator had been up to his eyeballs in schemes to trade drugs for arms.

Ingrid Bittmann's association with Cyprus had gone back even further than that, however. In fact, anyone with a long-time connection with the United Nations was likely to have had contact with Cyprus, as the thirty-year peacekeeping effort on the island constituted the UN's longest continuous support operation. When last in Cyprus, during the mid 1970s, Bittmann had been the coordinator of the UNHCR, the international organization's refugee office. Her offices during this period had been in a couple of old corrugated tin barracks buildings not more than a couple of hundred yards from her current plush residence. In the wake of the 1974 invasion, with its massive exchange of Greek and Turkish populations across the Green Line, Bittmann had been a very busy lady during this previous tour and had distinguished herself in ways that had moved her career with the UN into the higher profile political arenas.

She was a well-dressed, statuesque, large-boned, still very attractive Austrian national in her late fifties, who always bore the healthy, rosy glow of someone who had just departed the ski slope in victory. And this indeed was her persona, as she had been a European downhill ski champion in her younger years. Although the Mediterranean island of Cyprus, with its mild climate and inviting beaches, seemed a far cry from the ideal posting of a skiing champion, the Troodos Mountains, in fact, had enough snow on them during the winter months for Bittmann to get sufficient exercise when she could not get away for weekends in her native Austria.

Isaksen's eyes took on interest when he was introduced to Takis Koniotis and Safa Ziya, and he murmured something about wanting to talk with both of them privately at some point during the evening. But his expression became frozen with a slight hint of pain when Caitlyn Koniotis was introduced to him as an American archaeologist. After a polite acknowledgment, he immediately moved on to Willie Hamilton, whereupon his eyes became more guarded when Hamilton was introduced as the columnist with the *Cyprus Mail* who was to interview him later in the week. When he reached John Patterson, however, the former Danish foreign minister's eyes lit up and he enveloped the little professor in a giant bear hug.

"Ah, yes, it's so good to see you again, my friend." Holding him out at arm's length, Isaksen declared proudly, "Yes, it's hard to believe, but here stands one of the world's truly great investigators."

Everyone but Caitlyn looked bemused; she only looked amused.

"You know, John and I worked together in Asia for many years. We were both with the UN Development Program. And John was a wizard. A regular Sherlock Holmes. In fact, he could tell almost precisely where someone had been anywhere in the region just by examining the soil and plant residue on their shoes. He was working for us as a master agronomist, but he was often brought in by the authorities to help trace the movements of murder victims. He was phenomenal."

Sweeping Patterson up with his arm, the UN official turned and moved toward the lounge. "Well, Ingrid, I guess it is time to meet the rest of your guests. I do appreciate so much your thoughtfulness in having included my old friend."

Trailing along behind him, Safa Ziya whispered to Takis Koniotis, "I guess that explains why *he* was invited."

"Yes," Koniotis whispered back as he pulled his wife within earshot, "but not necessarily why Caitlyn had met him before."

"He really is famous, you know, for his ability to extrapolate useful information from fragments of the environment," Caitlyn answered. "His work has had archaeological application, and I met him at a seminar in New York. Although he seems not to have recognized me. Did you see, by the way, the ugly expression Isaksen gave me when we were introduced? Maybe I should just cut out and go home before he fully realizes we are together."

"Screw him," Takis whispered back. "He takes us together or not at all."

Caitlyn started to answer, knowing how much the planned discussion with Isaksen could mean for her husband's career, but they had been talking sotto voce as they walked and the procession had reached the lounge, where the bright lights, bubbling conversation, and clinking glasses indicated that the party had gotten off to a good start and that they were expected to be mingling.

* * * *

Several small centers of conversation could be seen in various areas of the lounge and in various degrees of animation as the official guest entered the commodious room. Ingrid Bittmann separated off Isaksen to take him, British agronomist still in tow, over toward the southeast corner of the room, where the twinkling lights of the Makedonitissa Valley could be seen through tall French windows and where the commander of the Argentine UN peacekeeping contingent, Colonel Julio Alberto Funes, and his wife were in polite—and probably very diplomatically stuffy—conversation with Lebanese ambassador Ayman Abu Hani, the wife of the Syrian ambassador, and the newly arrived Canadian high commission political officer, Ellen Larkin.

The rest of those who had met Isaksen in the foyer turned in the other direction, toward the now-closed double doors that led into the dining room and behind which could be heard the clinking of silverware and china and muffled expletives in a mixture of Greek, Tamil, and Tagolic. Several servers, carrying trays of savories and drinks, were wandering among the guests in the lounge. Their obvious wide differences in origins helped explain the equally wide variety of languages drifting through the woodwork from the dining room.

The Koniotises and Safa Ziya almost naturally moved into a conversation group that included Takis's young, beautiful, and brilliant deputy, Maria Solonos, and a handsome, if a bit chunky, young, and serious-looking Cypriot male. Maria was very popular among the younger, yet well-placed professional crowd in the capital, and this young man must be her latest conquest. Although the couple was having a somewhat private conversation as the Greek and Turkish Cypriot senior investigators approached, they were actually attached to a conversation circle that also included Paul Conte, a political officer at the American embassy and a close friend of Caitlyn's, and the Cypriot interior minister—and Takis's ultimate boss—Ioannis Herodotou and his wife.

Willie Hamilton, ever on the make for a good story, surveyed the room in well-concealed panic to determine where he could make the best use of the golden opportunity. The diplomats at the southeastern corner of the room did not seem to be discussing anything of importance—and he would be getting his private shot at Eric Isaksen in a couple of days in any event. If the discussion heated up between Isaksen and the Lebanese and Syrian ambassadors, however, that would make good background for his planned article. He would have to keep an ear on that conversation. Ginger and the British high commission "political officer" Alec Stuart—Willie, of course, knew who he really was—were making very small and perfunctory talk at the fireplace. Ginger was pouting. Willie started to move in their direction but decided discussion with Ginger would just have to wait, and he doubted that Alec would stay with her any longer than politeness dictated.

As he turned away from the fireplace and toward the northeast corner of the lounge, Willie saw the Syrian ambassador, Munir Nahlawi, and the young, sensuous wife of the aged Lebanese ambassador in very close conversation in the shadows.

"I wonder what *that* is about?" Willie thought. "I'd like to hear that conversation, but they don't look at all in the mood for being joined by a third."

And with that thought, he turned back to the group the Koniotises and Safa Ziya had approached. Perhaps he should start by trying to find out what the television crews outside were trying to pry out of the two investigators. He also decided, as he sidled quietly up to the group, that he should call his office as soon as possible to see what they knew about reports of a disturbance on the Green Line.

Willie Hamilton was not the only person present who was madly setting mental priorities on where to eavesdrop and making unobtrusive approaches to likely interesting conversations. The Filipino servant, Manuel, had also been working the room in an entirely different way than his official employer had intended. Tonight would be a bonanza for him, he gloated, as he passed close enough to the Syrian ambassador and the Lebanese beauty to make him blush at what he heard. This evening alone should earn his wife's passage to join him here in Cyprus.

After happily greeting Takis, Caitlyn, and Safa, Maria took the arm of the young man beside her and proudly introduced him as her new boyfriend, Demetris Mattas. At the mention of the name, both Takis's and Caitlyn's eyebrows lifted in unison. Even Willie Hamilton, who had known who Demetris was the moment he saw him, gave a snort from the periphery that ruined his efforts at invisibility. The Demetris Mattas name had cut quite a striking and controversial swath across the capital's political scene in recent months. Mattas was the writer of a column called "Under the Grapevine" in the powerful and influential Greek-language paper *Simerini* in which he provided very satirical—and telling—jabs at national and international political figures and institutions. He had a writing style that caused his readers to begin to laugh uproariously and then to have their laughter stick in their throats in realization that their most sacred cows and leaders were being cruelly and fairly skewered.

In embarrassment Takis and Caitlyn almost instinctively and in unison moved to open the circle to bring in the conversation that was ensuing between the interior minister and Paul Conte. Herodotou and Conte had been bantering back and forth concerning the helpfulness—or lack thereof—of the United States, and especially of the American embassy in Cyprus, to the Greek Cypriot cause in the intercommunal problems on the island. Herodotou had just been making a good-natured, but stinging, comment on Washington's claimed inability to understand or appreciate national struggle and Conte had countered with the comment, "Oh, but, Mr. Minister, America *does* understand the struggle for independence very well. Just like Cyprus, we threw the British out. The only real difference is that the Americans shouldered responsibility for our own problems ourselves thereafter."

Just at that moment, Takis and the rest of the group turned fully to this side conversation.

"Well, moving right along, Mr. Conte," Herodotou responded with a broad, but forced smile, "Have you met my wife, Olivia? She's British."

Conte took one look at the flashing eyes of the minister's wife and retreated a step in acknowledgment of the broadening of the conversation group. He turned to Caitlyn and said, "There you are, Caitlyn. I haven't seen you in ages. I've been meaning to ask you something."

But before Caitlyn could respond, Alec Stuart had joined the group from one side and the Syrian ambassador and the Lebanese ambassador's wife had been swept in from another angle.

Introductions were repeated around this growing group. At the end of these, the Syrian ambassador turned to Alec Stuart and said, "And last, but not least, this is Alec Stuart of the British high commission. Have you met the Lebanese ambassador's wife?"

"Yes," Alec smiled charmingly, "Suzanne and I know each other well."

"Yes, absolutely," intoned the luscious Suzanne huskily with a lusty laugh.

"Even biblically," the incisive and very well-informed writer of the "Under the Grapevine" column muttered to himself as he turned from the enlarged group. As he did so, he found himself looking directly into the pensive and questioning eyes of Maria Solonos. But what disturbed him was that he was also looking into the much too attentive eyes of one of the serving men.

Startled, Manuel's eyes telescoped to mere slits. As he moved quickly on toward the other group with his tray of savories, both sets of dining room doors were dramatically and simultaneously swung open and a dinner bell began to toll.

As he took Maria's arm and pulled her back so that the diners could enter to the supper room in proper ceremonial order, Mattas scanned the room for the serving man he had been sure was eavesdropping on the conversations. But either he could not pick him out of those present or the listener had vanished from the room.

* * * *

The UN coordinator's mansion boasted what might have been the largest dining room table on the island. But its fame was not as a dining room table—and it *was* famous enough that viewers throughout the island saw it on television at least weekly—but as a negotiating table. This was the only room, and the only table, at which the leaders of the two communities on Cyprus, the Cypriot Republic president and the leader of the Turkish Cypriot pseudo states, came together on the island to trade demands, to voice hurts, and to otherwise inch toward—and just as often, away from—a solution of the division of the island. The lesser players in the continuous dance of one-upmanship between the two communities on Cyprus met in the Treaty Room at the Ledra Palace Hotel in the buffer zone at the single official crossing point across the Green Line. But the chiefs of state themselves met here. They often met in New York, London, or Brussels, to be sure, but this was the only room that heard them being honest with each other—and about each other.

The table easily accommodated the twenty-one people who sat down to the sumptuous French cuisine, graced with more-than-adequate Cypriot wines, on this early spring evening. And this was no simple meeting of random friends, either, Ingrid Bittmann thought proudly as the guests circled the table in search of their name cards. All of these people—well, nearly all, she brought herself up short as she glanced with slight irritation at Ginger Hamilton and Demetris Mattas and with more contemplation than irritation at the Canadian, Ellen Larkin—were here for a purpose that would serve both Eric Isaksen's varied missions in the region and her own professional advancement.

Even the placement at the table had been precisely worked out beforehand. The Lebanese and Syrian ambassadors had been invited because of Isaksen's primary mission in Beirut after he left Cyprus. For diplomatic reasons, Isaksen must be in constant contact with the Lebanese officials. However, because the Lebanese government remained virtually powerless within its own country, he needed also to meet with the officials of Syria, which was one of the most powerful—and at the current time stabilizing—influences in Beirut. If she had really wanted to bow to reality, she would have invited the Iranian ambassador as well, but it was diplomatic taboo to openly point to Tehran's control of the Hizballah—the "Party of God"—terrorists in Lebanon. So, she had the two ambassadors and their wives sitting immediately next to Isaksen at the opposite end of the table from where she was sitting so that they could talk about the main mission.

She had almost not put Suzanne Abu Hani at Eric's left hand, however, she now remembered as she stared at the woman's brazen flirtation with the Syrian ambassador on her left and in the direction of Isaksen on her right. The woman was entirely too distracting, and Ingrid wasn't at all sure she want Isaksen to have Suzanne to compare with herself. Ingrid didn't know how the Lebanese ambassador, sitting across the table from Munir Nahlawi, could tolerate his young wife's lewd behavior—but, upon reflection, perhaps her activities were part of the fabric of his own ability to rise and flourish in the Lebanese foreign service. But, as Ingrid could see with a great deal of satisfaction, Eric was ignoring Suzanne's flaunting of her undeniable charms and was concentrating instead on the comparatively very plain and dull Syrian ambassador's wife seated at his right.

Ingrid had seated the Argentine UN contingent commander, Colonel Alberto, and his wife across from each other just a bit farther up the table. Isaksen would be taking a UN Green Line tour under the protection of the Argentine colonel on Tuesday, two days hence. She had originally been scheduled for this tour as well, but unexpected pressing business was taking her to Geneva the next afternoon.

Eric and the colonel had started discussing the arrangements for this tour shortly after the appetizer had been served. He called down to Takis Koniotis and the interior minister, who were sitting at his left between the colonel's wife and Caitlyn with the hope that they would join the expedition, which was scheduled to start out at the village of Astromeritis near the buffer zone to the west of Nicosia and the south of Morphou in mid morning on Tuesday and both answered in the affirmative.

Manuel, eyes averted, approached from Isaksen's right and placed his fish course while clearing the appetizer plate and fork.

Ingrid looked down the left side of the table to Ellen Larkin, who had been placed at the last minute between the Argentine colonel and the Lebanese ambassador. She looked so young and fresh. It was hard to believe that she had replaced John Dunsford at the Canadian high commission. She was certainly old enough—and intelligent enough, as Bittmann had already discovered for herself—to be a Canadian political officer. But Dunsford had also been the Canadian intelligence chief on the island. Bittmann wondered whether Larkin had taken over that role as well. It certainly seemed unlikely, but it could also be a brilliant example of someone not being quite what she seemed.

Larkin hadn't been invited to this dinner in her own right, but Bittmann did not begrudge her presence. Both the American, Conte, and the Brit, Stuart, had been invited as the usual bow to the American and British diplomatic missions, and they had both been told they could bring an appropriate date. Conte had brought Larkin, which, of course, was appropriate. Stuart had not brought anyone, which was a relief to Ingrid. She considered him such a lower-class type that she had half expected him to bring a pub waitress. How *he* had risen to be chief of British intelligence on the island was much beyond her.

Moving her attention closer to her down the left side the table, Ingrid could see that the decision to seat John Patterson and Safa Ziya together had been a good one. She had always both admired and pitied Safa Ziya. She admired her because she was much respected in her profession internationally—and fully because of her ability and intelligence rather than her beauty, which was, unfortunately, nonexistent. Except tonight. Tonight she had a happy glow about her that made her almost attractive.

At the same time, Bittmann pitied the Turkish Cypriot official. Before the 1974 Turkish invasion, Ziya's family had lived in a small enclaved Turkish village near Larnaca on the southern coast. After the difficulties, Ziya had returned from the States, where she had been teaching, with the intent of finding her family among the refugees Bittmann had been in charge of resettling at the time. Ziya had come to Bittmann for help in locating her family, but they had all vanished from the face of the earth. None of them had been among the ethnic Turkish refugees who had streamed into the northern Turkish zone. The only real explanation for this was that they had perished in the pogroms. Hers was just one of many such tragic stories on both sides of the line, and Ingrid had never been able to steel herself against such meaningless atrocities.

Bittmann had known that both Ziya and Patterson would be very shy and uncomfortable at a dinner such as this—she had only invited Patterson because she wanted to impress his great friend, Isaksen. But the two had obviously found each other and were happily enjoying each other's company.

This end of the table was another matter. Ingrid instinctively liked Takis Koniotis's wife, Caitlyn, who sat at her right between Stuart and the interior minister, but she knew that the American archaeologist would upset Isaksen. But how could she have told Koniotis that he was wanted but his wife was not because she resembled Isaksen's dead wife, who had also been an American and an archaeologist?

As she was thinking of Caitlyn, she heard Paul Conte, who was sitting across from the American woman, arranging a sightseeing trip to the Turkish sector. Stuart had asked Caitlyn if she, as an archaeologist, had ever seen the most famous Greco-Roman excavation on the island, the city state of Salamis, which was on the east coast just north of the port of Famagusta and which had been involved in the sack of Troy and had been the entry port for St. Paul's third journey across the Mediterranean.

Caitlyn responded that she had, at which point Paul Conte, in his booming voice, said, "That's what I wanted to talk to you about. I remember I had promised to take you to Salamis, but we never got there. Ellen Larkin and I are going to Kantara Castle, the Lusignan crusader castle in the Kyrenia Range above Salamis, next Thursday." He turned then to Ellen and asked, "You still can go, can't you?" Ellen Larkin beamed back an assent. "And so I wondered if you might like to go along as well," he said as he turned back to Caitlyn.

"Certainly, if neither Takis nor the interior minister mind," Caitlyn answered with a smile and turned to her husband. Greek nationals—or even people whose names sounded Greek to the Turkish border guards—were not permitted across the Ledra Palace checkpoint and into the Turkish zone, even on a day pass, Caitlyn was sensitive about the propriety of her going across even though she still had a valid passport in her maiden name of Spencer.

Takis, in turn, looked quizzically at the interior minister, who answered, kindly, "As we don't recognize the legality of the Turkish border anyway and as it appears you will be in the hands of capable diplomats, I see no reason why you should not go."

"Takis?" Caitlyn whispered hopefully to her husband.

"I never could keep you away from a ruin," He answered. "I won't let my bitterness at not being able to go to the Kyrenia Mountains prevent you from doing so. But, we really should ask Safa if she has any objections. We cannot pretend you are just an American tourist."

"Oh, I have never approved of boundaries between our people," Ziya quickly responded. "We would be honored to have an archaeologist of Caitlyn's fame visiting the ancient sites. I'll ensure she is safe."

"I'm not really worried about her safety from your people," Takis said with a twinkle in his eye. "I think Paul once had designs on Caitlyn. I'm not sure I would let them wander in the romantic Kyrenia Mountains alone. But, if Ms. Larkin will be along . . ."

Both Caitlyn and Paul looked down at their plates in embarrassment—as Caitlyn's fish course was whisked away by Manuel and replaced with her meat course. They had, indeed, had a single night together before Caitlyn had any notion she would ever be part of Takis's life.

As this conversation died down, it was replaced with a question Isaksen directed down the table at the interior minister. "What is this I hear about the training of terrorist squads in the two mountain ranges of Cyprus, Mr. Herodotou?"

"There's nothing to it. Absolute rubbish," the minister shot back.

"And is that your answer as well, Mr. Koniotis?" the UN official asked pointedly.

Takis looked uncomfortable. He knew this was some sort of test. He looked at Caitlyn and then at Safa Ziya, both of whom gave him encouraging smiles.

"Well, sir," he said as he cleared his throat and marshaled his response, "there have been reports of suspicious shooting and the appearance of armed bands in the mountain areas. And there have been press reports claiming that the PKK—the Kurdish Workers Party—is being permitted to conduct anti-Turkish guerrilla training in the Troodos Mountains. And alternately there have also been claims that Turkish infiltration bands are being trained in and are operating out of the Kyrenia Range. There have been reports as well that Cyprus is being used by Middle Eastern interests for terrorist training and support—"

"Sheer speculation; not a shred of evidence," the Syrian ambassador exclaimed.

"On the contrary, Mr. Ambassador," Safa Ziya quietly interjected. "Not long ago Mr. Koniotis's special unit uncovered both a plot to exchange arms for drugs from out of a Middle Eastern country . . ." the Lebanese ambassador turned ashen at this point, ". . . and an arrangement by which a major terrorist organization's travel was set up and its money was laundered through Cyprus. I think most of us around the table are aware of this case, even though it did not become fully revealed to the public. And even an international organization official was implicated in this scheme." It was Ingrid Bittmann's turn to look embarrassed, as she contemplated the real reason behind the death at Curium of her predecessor as deputy UN coordinator.

"As I was saying," Takis spoke with growing strength into the void that had been caused by Ziya's pointed comments, "we also occasionally uncover a cache of arms in various places in the mountains and at the seaside."

"All caches left over from the struggle against the British," Herodotou broke in with a huff.

"Modern hand-held rocket launchers?" Demetris Mattas spoke up sweetly.

"We do run across many such reports," Takis continued. "Many seem pretty farfetched. But we check all of the reports out, and we are continually working with the Turkish side, through Safa Ziya, and are keeping a database of all of the reports and of our findings. We are not discounting the possibility that there may be some truth to these reports."

Most of the high officials at the table looked quite unhappy. But Eric Isaksen said, "Thank you, Mr. Koniotis. Ms. Ziya. You have been very frank and helpful." And then he turned back to the ambassadors at either side, bringing in pleasantries and compliments that quickly smoothed ruffled feathers.

Manuel stooped to the side of the Syrian ambassador and whispered something in his ear. Then he took away the diplomat's meat plate and fork and replaced it with the salad course.

As individual conversations revived, Ingrid's thoughts returned to her guest list. She had purposefully seated the journalists at her end of the table, Hamilton on her right, and Mattas on her left. The inviting of Hamilton had been unavoidable. Isaksen wanted to give a major exclusive press interview on his activities to a Cypriot English-language paper, and there simply was no other reporter than Willie Hamilton who could have quoted him accurately let alone spelled his name correctly. Hamilton had insisted he could—and would—only do the interview if he had enough prior access to Isaksen to get a "feel" for the man behind the legend. Well, she would give him this "feel," but it would be from this end of the table. And why he brought his slut of a wife, Bittmann could not fathom. But it had been her own fault, she sighed, for not having seen to it that the invitation pointedly specified that only Hamilton was invited.

"Look at the old bag," Ingrid thought with disgust, as she gazed down the left side of the table, where Ginger, seated between Demetris Mattas and Paul Conte, was bestowing unwanted attention on both.

"Serves Mattas right, though," the UN coordinator mused with a stifled giggle. "I don't know how he crashed this party. I invited Koniotis's assistant, Maria Solonos, because Isaksen wants to discuss the Cypriots' special police international investigations department with more than just the interior minister and the chief of the unit, but could I have known she would bring the most dangerous political gossip columnist in the city with her? I don't even want to think how this dinner party will be written up in his column this week."

At that moment, Manuel rushed into the room and over to Safa Ziya and whispered in her ear. Mattas's head snapped up in recognition, and he half rose from his chair as Ziya followed the Filipino servant out of the room. She was back quickly, whispering to Ingrid that she had been called back on police business and giving her apologies around the room. When she got to Patterson, she realized

95

that he had shared the UN vehicle that had brought her across the buffer zone, and she was stopped short in consternation.

"Please, don't even think of the inconvenience, Ms. Ziya. I will go back with you now, as well." And he trotted off to give his good-byes to Eric Isaksen. In the meantime, Safa Ziya went to Alec Stuart and spoke quietly and earnestly to the British diplomat.

Another servant entered the room, and Takis Koniotis was whisked away just as Ziya and Stuart were headed in his direction. Koniotis was back in a flash, whispered something to the interior minister, Ingrid Bittmann, Maria Solonos, and Caitlyn, and all rose from their seats.

Willie Hamilton took that opportunity to ask the UN coordinator if he could use her telephone and he was gone before she could respond.

Suddenly, there was a yelp from Paul Conte, who gave Ginger Hamilton a startled look and lurched out of his chair, which fell over on the floor.

Mattas turned to Ingrid Bittmann and said, "I must talk to you right now."

"Not now," Bittmann hissed. "I'll talk to you after the others have left." And then in her best hostess voice, "It seems that some of our guests have pressing and unexpected engagements. Thus it is on the world scene. Shall the rest of us take our desert and coffee in the lounge?"

As the others moved across the room, Munir Nahlawi and Suzanne Abu Hani seemed to hang back a bit and both circled toward the French windows in a movement that would not have been noticed if no one was closely observing. But someone was. They met and brushed together for the briefest of seconds in the darkness near the windows.

Suzanne inclined her head and murmured, "So, until tomorrow at Pissouri Beach."

"Until tomorrow," the Syrian ambassador intoned, and then both circled back and folded into the ranks of the dinner guests as they headed toward the lounge.

From the shadows of the veranda, Manuel watched the now-depleted, but no-less ceremonial, procession from the dining room back to the lounge. He slipped through the hibiscus hedge and was gone from sight.

Chapter Seven

In Tuesday's early-morning light, the nondescript little fishing boat putted slowly into Pegeia Harbor at the foot of the ancient Agios Georgios—Saint George's—basilica atop its cliff, honeycombed with an extensive network of early Christian-era rock-cut tombs. Although tired and sore from the eighty nautical-mile, nearly direct northwestward churn through rough seas, much of it within sight of the Cypriot coast from Limassol around to Paphos and then north, Ibrahim didn't want to attract any attention. He just wanted to make the pickup as quickly as possible and be gone.

Not attracting any attention would be difficult. This harbor just to the south of the western-most Akamas Peninsula was probably the most quiet and least populated coastal area in all of Cyprus. Luckily, just as and where Abdul had said he would, he had found a boatman who had often used this isolated little man-made harbor— immediately adjacent to one that had first been constructed by the Achaeans in the twelfth century BC. If they moved swiftly and his men kept out of sight, they should manage to tie up long enough to get the job done and then to slip back out of the harbor and back across the Mediterranean.

Ah, there they were. Up near the Grecian ruins. They were coming down the hill on the southern side, away from the main dirt road that descended to the harbor from between the ancient and the merely very old basilicas and away from any prying eyes on the top of the cliff.

Maybe he wouldn't kill Abdul after all. Everything seemed to be working just as Abdul said it would. He signaled the boatman not even to cut the engine. They would lay out to sea during the rest of the long day. They could even do some fishing. Surely no one would be suspicious of that. That's what the boat was supposed to be doing anyway. They'd make the run home after dark.

* * * *

Caitlyn dragged herself down to the kitchen to make herself a cup of tea. She had awakened with nausea again and with a pounding headache that wasn't helped a bit by the noise that had begun outside her window shortly after dawn.

"Well, I've discovered the *real* problem of working at home," she groggily told herself. "It doesn't help to call in sick."

Until she had started feeling ill with this cold or flu—or whatever it was—she had not noticed just how much commotion was being caused in her garden and the open space under the bedroom wing. She almost regretted that she had offered the space as a staging area for the excavation that was being conducted at the base of the acropolis hill across the street.

She suddenly thought about how bothersome this all must be to her neighbors, who most certainly did not share her passion for archaeology and therefore must not share her tolerance for the mess and noise that were inevitably associated with a dig. At the same time, she reasoned, if her find of a royal tomb had not stopped the clearing of the lot across the street and at the base of the acropolis hill, the neighborhood would still have been subjected to bothersome noises for a year or more—and noise that inevitably would also have started at dawn. Her find had stopped the construction of a house. And in Cyprus, the construction of a house was a long, involved process that included construction noise at the most inconvenient times of the day, not to mention the high-pitched voices of various relatives of the family constructing the house as they each had their turn at tinkering with this and that and sidewalk supervision.

There were no professional construction companies to speak of on the island for residential building. No one to come in and quickly and efficiently erect a house during convenient office hours. People tended to design and build their own houses, taking a long time and subcontracting various aspects of the project out—most often to relatives with permanent jobs of their own, who could only work early in the morning, late in the evening, on weekends, or during the formal early-afternoon siesta time.

Siesta had once been a time when people went home for a nap in a cool, dark room during the hottest time of the day, and during these hours it once had been illegal even to let your children play outside, because it was supposed to be a quiet time. Those days were gone for good. The siesta break still existed in Cyprus, but the Greek Cypriots were so industrious and ambitious that they now used this time for a second job or to work piecemeal on building or expanding their homes.

The cup of tea was not settling her stomach today. Caitlyn reached for the phone and called Dr. Lambros, who could not give her an appointment until Friday morning. She would just have to endure. One thing she knew; she would not let this illness cancel her trip to Kantara Castle on Thursday. Luckily, she always felt better in the afternoon, and Paul had called to tell her that they would have to get a late start, as Ellen Larkin could not leave the high commission until just before the noon hour.

* * * *

Uri woke with a start, the morning sun reaching his eyes. He had been so exhausted that he had barely reached the top of the hill that looked down into the small monastery—it was obviously a monastery judging by the large, dominating stone church that took up two sides of the small compound—before he had snuggled up behind a large boulder, drunk the last of the water that had been in his canteen, and promptly slept. When he arrived the night before, there had been lights behind loosely shuttered windows down in the compound and there had been considerable activity in the compound's courtyard. There had also been muffled music and occasional drunken and profane exclamations that challenged the thought that the monastery still housed a religious order. Two small, closed van trucks were parked outside of the compound's shuttered doors. Something intuitively told Uri both that his mother and whoever she was with were down in that compound and that it would be folly to walk directly down to the monastery and pound on the large wooden doors.

Uri sat bolt upright in the early-morning sunlight. Every joint in his body ached from the long, two-day walk through the foothills of the Troodos. Initially the path had led through pine forests with no sign of habitation. During the last evening, as the trail approached a valley speckled with small villages, however, he had to move in a crouching position along stone walls through vineyards, whose regimented knotty vine bases threw out freshly sprouted vines that had not risen more than four feet off the ground as yet.

Something was wrong. Something was wrong other than the fact that he had allowed himself to drift off into a sound and long sleep when he had intended to remain awake. It was too quiet. He peeked over the rim of the boulder and down into the monastery compound below. It was now empty, deserted—or at least it gave every indication of being so. The vehicles were gone, the wooden entrance gates were yawning open, and there was no sign of activity in the compound courtyard.

All the same, Uri spent a good half hour in his approach to the complex. When he reached the flat ground just in front of the compound's entrance, he could see fresh tire marks in the dusty road that led down the hillside. The road stopped here at the monastery's door. There was no established road or pathway going any higher, and there was no evidence of any houses or any other sign of habitation in the vicinity.

If they had left in the vehicles, Uri's hunt was over. He could not follow tire tracks any farther than the closest oiled roadbed. Uri dropped to his haunches in the dirt, cradled his face in his hands, and allowed a forlorn sob to escape his lips.

Had it all been for naught? Had he tracked them for two days over this rugged, mountainous country only to be left alone and motherless in the dust of this isolated monastery?

The boy rose and carefully entered the compound. The monastery didn't look as though it had been abandoned. If this was some sort of hideout, perhaps the gang that had taken his mother would return at some point and he still could pick up her trail by observing them from the hillside. But he needed food. And now, the last of the meticulously rationed water that had been in his canteen was gone as well; he needed water. Perhaps he also could tell something useful from what they had left behind.

However, as he poked through the church and the rooms off the cloister, his spirits began to fail him. They had left practically nothing. Certainly, the monastery was still furnished, and the adornments in the church supported his hope that the compound was not just a derelict, long-abandoned shell. But there was little food—enough for him for a short time, of course, but not enough to support a band of gangsters—or whatever they were—for any length of time.

Perhaps that was where they had gone—down into some village to obtain rations. But why then would everyone have gone—and especially his mother? Surely she hadn't gone with them willingly, although, admittedly, he'd seen no sign of struggle either in the meadow above Soli or along the route.

"Maybe she's still here. She must still be here. She must be locked in somewhere. A prisoner—or worse."

No, he would not allow himself to think the worst. He looked back at the entrance gate, as if in search of deliverance.

There, near the gate. In the dust. As if it had fallen out of someone's backpack in the haste of departure. Some sort of pamphlet. There must be clues somewhere. Everything had to be checked out.

Uri walked deliberately and calmly—he had to remain deliberate and calm, he told himself—over to the gate and bent down to pick up the pamphlet. It was some sort of guide. In English. It seemed to be of this, the Paphos, district, and the front cover was a map. He could see the western portion of Cyprus. In its upper right corner, the map almost ran up to Vouni and Soli, where this horror had all begun. But, no, the horror had begun for Uri and his mother—and for his brother, little Pavel—back in Grozny. This was only the anticlimax. Perhaps, he thought, that was why he was able to be so calm and deliberate in his actions.

He fanned at the paper edges of the pamphlet, and it opened at a page nearly halfway through the booklet. Another brochure fell out of the pamphlet. It was for an airline company—Cyprus' own Cyprus Air, the airline Uri and his mother and brother had flown to the island on. Uri picked up the brochure and stuffed it back in the booklet, which he stuck in his waistband against his spine.

He would examine this better later, but he needed to take another look around the compound. He still could not believe that this monastery had been abandoned. There was a small door he had not noticed before at the right of the entrance gate. It seemed to go into a small room at the front corner of the compound. Probably some sort of storage room or woodshed.

Uri pushed open the door and discovered that the monastery, indeed, had not been abandoned when The Asp's band acquired it as a short-term hideout. The stench sent him reeling back out into the courtyard but not before he had seen the bodies and held the rise in his gorge long enough to make sure his mother wasn't there—and not before that scene had been engraved on his brain—bring imagines of the short time they had spent in Grozny flooding back into his mind.

The boy's recoil carried him back through the entranceway and out of the compound. He collapsed just outside the doorway, vomiting violently into the dry earth.

He broke down into wild sobs. He had now simply seen too much of death and horror. He could go no farther. Rising up out of his despair, though, there were soothing words. Words of comfort. Russian words. But they were not Uri's words. He was not alone. A hand was laid on his shoulder and he turned and hugged the legs of the figure that loomed over him, a figure that whispered words of solace—in Russian.

* * * *

It had taken Alec Stuart far too long to arrange the special meeting between Takis Koniotis and Safa Ziya at the Ledra Palace Hotel. In the few brief moments Safa had to converse with Stuart at the UN coordinator's dinner two days previously, she had quickly told him that she had just been informed that the wife and son of Mikhail Lukenov of the Russian embassy—both Ziya and Stuart well knew what his real position in the embassy was—had disappeared in Soli. The Turkish Cypriot police authorities had been trying to get hold of her ever since five Russian embassy vehicles had rushed through the Ledra Palace checkpoint. They had missed her at her flat and had discovered the reason for the movement of the Russians before they had managed to get patched through to Bittmann's villa via UN communications lines. Before leaving the villa, Ziya had asked Stuart to set up a meeting between Koniotis and her so that they could coordinate the police response to the situation. She had also wanted to inform Takis, but he had been called to the telephone as well and obviously was receiving the same news from his own sources.

This had explained the questions the television crews had shot at them outside the villa's entrance. It might also have explained the presence of so many of the media at the UN coordinator's that evening.

Safa had no idea why it had taken Stuart two days to arrange the meeting in the usual bicommunal meeting place in the Ledra Palace's Treaty Room. It had turned out to have been capriciousness on the part of some rather junior, militant figure in her own foreign ministry. Her government had fallen just a week previously, an occurrence that was happening all too frequently of late in the Turkish zone, resulting no doubt from the continued frustration of the economic blockage of the Turkish Cypriot pseudo state by all nations except Turkey, itself no economic giant. The new occupants had not realized that Ziya's ongoing contact with Koniotis had been cleared at the upper-most leadership level in the Turkish zone—which meant that Ankara approved it, as Turkish Cyprus was still very much under the thumb of mainland Turkey.

As a result, Tuesday morning was the earliest Stuart had been able to arrange a meeting, and Koniotis had thus been forced to cancel his participation in the Green Line trip with the visiting UN official, Eric Isaksen.

"Oh, well," he rationalized as he sat down at the conference table in the historic Treaty Room and opened his briefcase in preparation for merging his own notes with those of his respected Turkish Cypriot counterpart, "Isaksen has been insistent that we will get together to talk about the International Investigations Division concept before he leaves. Tomorrow is another day."

But sometimes tomorrow never comes.

* * * *

The Asp had been watching her the entire day. After they had left the monastery outside Vroisha, the band split and went their separate ways. They would meet up again for the next operation by mid afternoon. When they left the monastery, they acquired two more vehicles so they could all move quickly to the next rendezvous. One of the rules of this game was to always keep your opponents off guard.

After having received the message, The Asp drove down from the hills—alone—to the Colombia Pissouri Beach hotel, an isolated resort on a black sand beach between Paphos and Limassol and in the center of Cyprus' oldest grape-growing region.

Suzanne Abu Hani was there at Pissouri Beach, just as he had been informed she would be. She spent much of the morning on the sand, roasting her luscious body. As the sun approached its zenith, however, it apparently became too hot for her on the beach, and she retreated to the protection of the hotel. The Asp had watched every move she made from the corner of the rocks on the cliff that jutted into the sea and marked the western boundary of Pissouri Beach. He could barely contain his desire.

He knew what room she was in. It was conveniently located on the second story, just above the lobby lounge. Instead of having balconies as the rooms on the floors above had, the suites on Suzanne's floor opened onto a wide, shared veranda. The Asp had no trouble entering a service compound just to the north of the hotel entrance and behind the tourist shop or climbing to the veranda level above.

The glass doors to Suzanne's suite were open. The Asp quickly stripped off his clothes in the shadows of the balcony above and slithered into the room without making a sound. Suzanne had removed her one-piece swim suit, with its deep cleavage and its high-cut side panels, and was languorously pulling on a diaphanous negligee. She was humming an Arabic melody to herself and was facing away from the glass doors and their probing sunlight.

The Asp was on her in a flash, one arm snaking around her throat, a hand clamped tightly over her mouth. He brutally dragged her across the room and pushed her to the floor and onto her back between the bed and the wall, hidden from view from the veranda—straddling her body and increasing the pressure, ripping, lifting, opening, thrusting. The struggle was short and largely uncontested.

* * * *

They certainly should have taken notice and reacted sooner. But it probably would not have made much of a difference. The sound came in on the late afternoon breeze wafting across the central plain, up from Morphou Bay. At first it had just been a soft crackling noise, not even noticeable to the Argentine soldiers arrayed around the UN sector headquarters at Astromeritis, just off the road from Nicosia up to Mt. Olympus through the Solea Valley and between and within sight of both the road and the buffer zone. The men were trying to keep cool, and to do that they had to slow down their metabolism and dull their senses, just as the lizards behind the nearby rocks did. Soon the sun would set, and they would no longer have to curse their fate at being here on the hot, dusty plain instead of on the topless beaches of Ayia Napa on the southeastern coast.

But eventually the sound broke into their collective consciousnesses. Even then, however—and even when they had identified the sound as distant gunfire—they were slow to react. There was a Turkish army firing range at the rifle brigade headquarters not far across the Green Line and to the northeast, in Philia.

"Philia?" the squadron commander exclaimed as he came to life and rose from a recline to the fully erect position in one smooth movement. "The sound is coming from the other direction."

Once mobilized and on the move, the Argentine unit performed magnificently. But they were too late. Of course, it had all happened so quickly that they would most certainly have been too late to prevent the carnage in any event. But they may have been in time to have gotten some inkling of who the attackers had been and where they had gone.

It was little solace that the Argentine contingent commander, Colonel Julio Alberto Funes, would speak no word of rebuke at their failure to rescue those on the special high-level tour of the western sector of the UN buffer zone. The colonel was dead. As was everyone else in the tour group as far as they could tell on initial inspection.

But, wait. They knew all of these victims. Most of them were their own comrades, who had made up the honor guard for the tour. And there was Colonel Alberto. And there was the Greek Cypriot interior minister, Ioannis Herodotou. Both dead. But where was the high-level official who was being given the tour? That UN official. That former Danish foreign minister, what's his name? Eric Isaksen. Where was Eric Isaksen? Not here. Not anywhere around here. It was so desolate here that there had been no place to hide from the attackers. Their only hope would have been if they had time to retreat inside one of the three APCs and closed the hatches. But they obviously had not had time and had been caught completely unaware.

And how could they have guessed? Nothing like this had happened in Cyprus since the rebellion against British rule more than thirty years previously. The Greeks and Turks rarely fired at each other across the line anymore. They certainly never had intentionally fired at UN soldiers. And this was not a simple cross-border firing incident. This had been a full-scale attack.

Having become adjusted to the madness about him, the squadron commander started barking orders, and the news started to flash out toward the capital.

That done, there seemed nothing else to do but to examine the bodies more closely. No particular reason for doing so, of course, but he felt he had to be seen to be doing something constructive while they waited for the world to find them. Maybe he'd find something significant to pass on.

Where were Eric Isaksen and that other Greek Cypriot official, Takis Koniotis? That weighed heavily on his mind. A simple firefight attack on a UN patrol was one thing—that was simple and straightforward, if entirely unknown here before. But an attack on major UN and Cypriot figures and a missing high-level UN official? And where was Koniotis's body. His name had been on the tour list too. Suddenly this all was becoming very complex and especially sinister. What did it mean? Had they taken Isaksen—and was that the whole reason for the attack? If so, what did they want with Isaksen? What would they do with him? And who the hell were they? And—his eyes slitted–how had they known about this tour?

Having approached the body of the Argentine colonel, the officer noted that a wad of paper was sticking out of his uniform shirt. The soldier pulled the paper out. Strange. It seemed to be some sort of

110

glossy pamphlet. An airline brochure, all smeared with blood and also with black markings. "MB." The markings seemed to be two letters, scrawled in heavy black ink. Initials?

Turning to the body of the interior minister, the office saw the same pamphlet crumpled up and sticking out of Herodotou's shirt pocket. A quick check revealed the same annotated brochure—for Cyprus Air—had been left on Herodotou's body—and on each of the other bodies as well.

"Well, I did find something to show them," the officer thought, his mind still numb from the unlikely, but very real, unfolding of events.

A covey of helicopters swooped in from the east—all efficiency, but too late. The world had found them.

But where in the world was Eric Isaksen? And the Greek Cypriot, Takis Koniotis?

Chapter Eight

Takis Koniotis sat down on the stone lip of the well in the courtyard of the small monastery in a fold of the foothills of the Troodos Mountains and just over the rise from the village of Vroisha. It was deceptively peaceful and inviting in this setting. He sat near an almond tree that had almost lost all of its blossoms, sending clouds of small white petals swirling around the flagstone walkways, the shrubbery, and the cloister porches. The rich yellow flowerets of the winter jasmine vine climbing the cloister arch to his left were in full bloom, and the magenta of the bracts of the bougainvillea that encased the entire building opposite him was just beginning to show through.

From here, the father and son who were seated and engaged in close conversation on the steps into the church were the model of a tableau of the passing of wisdom from one generation to the next. But if he could see the two at closer quarters, he knew he could see the concern and grief that passed between the two like an electric current.

Immediately upon having been interrupted during his meeting with Safa Ziya at the Ledra Palace Hotel by the urgent message from Mikhail Lukenov, Koniotis had mobilized all of the forces at his disposal—except for Maria Solonos, who he had left to handle information control at the office—and requisitioned a helicopter. During the flight up the Solea Valley and then across the Kykko monastery, high in the Troodos, and finally down the northwestern side of the range and to the isolated village of Vroisha, Lukenov had said little.

"The man must have nerves of steel," Koniotis thought grimly, as the helicopter swooped down into the foothills above Paphos. "He's also quite lucky that I was here to get his telephone call. I'm supposed to be on a Green Line tour. And that's where I would have been if this emergency hadn't developed."

Lukenov had only told Koniotis enough to mobilize this highly unusual flight. After ascertaining that the Greek Cypriot investigator knew his wife was missing from a family outing to the Soli ruins, the Russian diplomat had energized Koniotis by asserting that he thought the kidnapping was probably politically motivated and that his son had tracked the kidnappers across into the Greek zone and to a mountain monastery, where he had lost them but found several murdered monks. He said that he wanted to get to his son as quickly as possible and would provide more information if Koniotis could arrange a helicopter for a rescue of his son.

Lukenov obviously wasn't in the mood to answer further questions about how he knew about his son's whereabouts or what he would do if Koniotis couldn't offer transportation assistance. The investigator was fully aware that five Russian embassy vehicles full of muscle had been mobilized to scour the Turkish Cypriot countryside two days previously. He did not want the Russian doing the same on the Greek side—if he hadn't already done so—but he knew the spy master's reputation well enough to believe he might do just that if left to his own devices.

When they landed on the flat ground just at the monastery's entrance, they found exactly what Lukenov had said they would find, although Maria had called the Paphos police, and several officers and vehicles had arrived before the helicopter. Lukenov's son, Uri, was hunched up outside of the monastery doors and was being comforted by what looked to be a Greek vineyard worker from the area. The attention of the policeman from the Paphos district was more focused on the bodies of the priests that had been found in a small room just inside the gate than on Uri.

Koniotis went to talk to the policemen after instructing the investigators he had brought with him to fan out and look for signs of the kidnappers. Takis then came into the courtyard to have a smoke and to think—and to permit Lukenov a bit of time alone with his son before Takis started trying to get more complete details out of both of them.

As he looked at the pair over near the church entrance, it occurred to him that he had not seen the Greek farmer in the area since the helicopter had landed. This was strange—and Takis had yet to find out when and how contact was made between son and father in this remote place.

"It's time for some answers," Takis told himself as he stubbed out his cigarette and moved toward the church. He had to get his smokes where he could. Caitlyn had thought he had given them up— or so *he* thought, of course, as he seemed oblivious to the fact that his clothing was permeated with the smell of smoke whenever he couldn't help from lighting up, which occurred most often when he was faced with a big case and had not yet figured it out.

Koniotis never made it to the side of Lukenov and his son, however, for, as he was drawing near, his assistant, Androulla, quickly brushed by the pair and accosted him with a very serious look.

"Maria has called over from Astromeritis and says you must get over there right away," Androulla announced breathlessly.

"Maria's in Nicosia, and there couldn't be anything more important for us to do than there is here right now," Koniotis responded, slightly peeved.

But he was wrong on both counts.

* * * *

"Aha, got you, my deadly beauty." Ellen Larkin swung her shapely legs around in the squeaky wooden swivel chair behind the gigantic desk. The desk had been the legacy her unfortunate and now-deceased predecessor, John Dunsford, had left behind in the Byron Street Canadian high commission office she'd inherited. The ceiling fan made soft, mesmerizing pocketa-pocketa sounds as its blades slowly moved the air in the large corner office that could have come straight out of a Humphrey Bogart film.

The pert little Canadian diplomat, who had been brought in to fill Dunsford's shoes when they discovered he was a double agent who had gone very bad and committed suicide when trapped by Takis Koniotis's police unit, looked like she had come out of films herself. Or perhaps from one of the colder and more athletic entertainments. Perhaps it was her petite, well-formed figure, or her friendly, girl-next-door face, or her smartly flipped hair style that had been made famous by a near-twin ice skating champion of the previous decade. Whatever it was, it certainly didn't finger her as an intelligence agent. This, in itself, quite possibly was why the young lady had so quickly reached success in her profession.

She hadn't been on the job long here, but she sensed that she may already have achieved her first big breakthrough in weaving together some illusive strings of the workings of various terrorist organizations in the Middle East. Following the party at the UN coordinator's villa the other evening, she had run some routine name checks on the diplomats who were in attendance, and, surprise, surprise, one name had set off "watch list" bells.

Having sat close to Suzanne Abu Hani, the wife of the Lebanese ambassador, at the dinner table, Ellen had not really been all that surprised that Suzanne's name had evoked interest. The woman had blatantly put the make on nearly every remotely presentable man at the dinner—her aged husband not really being included in that category—and the interest had been returned—to different degrees, but returned nonetheless—by everyone but, thankfully, Paul Conte, and Eric Isaksen, who appeared to have been invulnerable to the attraction of anyone but himself. The electricity between Suzanne and the Syrian ambassador, Munir Nahlawi, had been particularly strong.

Mrs. Abu Hani had not been highlighted in the search by anything known about what she currently was—or might be—engaged in. But because of both what was known and what was unknown about her past, she was recorded in the system as being of continued interest. Nothing had ever surfaced and been recorded in the intelligence files about her origins. She first appeared on the international scene in Cairo, where she was a flamboyant antiques dealer, and where she was sharing wine, food, and bed with an

American military attaché, an Egyptian police official, a known Russian intelligence official, and a central figure in radical Palestinian Liberation Organization circles—simultaneously.

Ayman Abu Hani had been the number two official in the Lebanese mission to Cairo at the time but had not been linked in the Cairo period to Suzanne. However, suddenly and without prior notice, Suzanne had disappeared from Cairo, leaving antiquities, flat, and lovers in the dust. Until Ellen had filed her queries on the guests from the recent dinner party, this was the last that had been known about the whereabouts or activities of the fair Suzanne. The new information that she now was the wife of Ayman Abu Hani, Lebanese ambassador to Cyprus, was a new, *very* interesting aspect to the story.

"Yes, my dear Suzanne, you bear very close watching." But then Ellen's cheeks turned red, even though she was quite alone and nothing had been said in her office. The very thought of closely watching Suzanne had brought back, for the first time since the other night—the memory of the embarrassing scene she had witnessed at the UN coordinator's house. During the pre-dinner cocktail hour, not long before the call for dinner was anticipated, Caitlyn Koniotis, the interesting American archaeologist wife of that handsome police inspector, had excused herself to "powder her nose." This had set off a general exodus of the women present to the ladies room. While Mrs. Koniotis and Suzanne were sitting before the mirror—and Ellen was waiting behind the pair for her turn—Suzanne had turned to Caitlyn, smiled the same smile she had been throwing to the Syrian ambassador in the corner of the lounge, placed her hand on top of the American's, squeezed, and remarked on the beauty of Mrs. Koniotis's skin. Mrs. Koniotis had mumbled something polite in acknowledgment but had been so taken aback at the unusual movement that she had quickly risen and backed out of the room—followed closely by Ellen herself.

Until this moment, Ellen had not thought to identify what had troubled her or had made her leave the powder room right behind Mrs. Koniotis, but now she knew why. Suzanne had been as openly flirting with the American woman as she had been with any of the men in the lounge that evening. As the two left the ladies room, they heard a full, husky laugh from behind them. It was only now that Ellen understood why she had found that laughter so unnerving.

* * * *

Munir Nahlawi dove into the scrub on the usually completely deserted Troodos mountainside near the village of Chakistra. The Syrian diplomat had almost shot off his rifle by reflex as the helicopter had quite unexpectedly roared overhead just above him and disappeared to the west just as quickly as it had appeared from the east. Luckily he had had the safety catch on. Now that the helicopter was gone, Nahlawi realized that there had been no reason for him to hide at all. The hillsides here were covered in pine trees to a density that would have made him, clothed as he was in his mountain fatigues, functionally invisible on the ground from the air unless he was being specifically sought.

But was he perhaps being sought? Ever since that UN official, Eric Isaksen, had raised the topic at the UN coordinator's mansion the other night of terrorist bands training in the Cypriot mountains, Nahlawi had been on edge. Would he be found out? There was too much reporting and discussion going on about such activity in the mountains. Maybe he should stop.

But it was in the blood. He didn't think he could stop. And it was safe in this area—or at least he had thought it was safe and secluded until that helicopter whooped over him. The easiest way to get to the Chakistra area by land was over the Troodos ridges, to the Kykko monastery, and then farther north on a solitary road that only went to the nearly deserted mountain village. Within a couple of miles farther west of the village area, farther into the Paphos national forest preserve, it should be perfectly safe for his activities. Or at least it had been very safe until now.

But maybe they should discuss the whole operation again. He would have to bring the topic up when he rendezvoused with the others.

Without notice, Nahlawi dove into the bush again as the unmistakable and increasing humming noise of a whole covey of helicopters could be heard approaching from the northwest.

* * * *

Demetris Mattas had written—and torn up—the column three times. He didn't know why he was having such a struggle with this; this was exactly the type of material he included in his political satire column, and there was nothing wrong with what he had written. All three columns were brilliant, biting, and, in his experienced judgment, among the wittiest he had ever written. No, it was not what he wrote; it was whether he should write it up at all.

A young copyboy appeared form out of the chaos of the main *Simerini* reporter's room and slowed down—hopefully—one more time and looked meaningfully at his watch as he passed Mattas's desk. Mattas let out a string of curses that hastened the boy's departure.

It wasn't the copyboy's fault, of course, Mattas acknowledged as he pulled at his hair. The deadline for the "Under the Grapevine" column was long past, and the last-minute submissions were reserved for the news reporters.

He started into the column for a fourth time and jerked it out of his machine for yet a fourth time. There was nothing new in revealing the incongruous affairs—sexual, not political—of the politicians and diplomats. And this affair was easy to jibe, not only because the British were considered stuffy to the point of asexuality, but also because the British and Lebanese did not make good political bedfellows and Alec Stuart was no prize, whereas Suzanne Abu Hani was luscious. No, he had had no trouble making the imagery of Stuart in bed with the Lebanese ambassador's wife amusing.

But what was gripping him was the propriety of writing this up. He wasn't disturbed at the possible political implications and the damage the story could do to Alec Stuart's career. That was what Mattas's column was all about, and the British were considered fair game for lampooning in Cyprus. No, it was because Mattas could not be sure he could separate out his own motives for writing about this affair. For he was quite possibly not a disinterested observer. How could anyone be sure they had reached—or could ever hope to reach—the position of disinterest where Suzanne was concerned?

The conundrum was because Mattas once had been precisely where Stuart was now—in bed with Suzanne. His own affair with Suzanne had not lasted long, and Mattas felt that his current liaison with Maria Solonos had cured him of his feelings toward Suzanne. But how could he be sure? At least, how could he be sure that he wanted to write this story out of the same public domain interest as the rest of

120

his columns and not out of jealousy of Stuart and longing to have Suzanne back? Suzanne had dropped him—not cruelly, to be sure, but by just not being available enough to maintain the heat. Could he honestly tell himself that *he* would ever have broken off with Suzanne?

Mattas reached into his bottom drawer and took out one of the general contingency columns without time sensitivity he kept there for those panic days when he had writer's block. This wasn't writer's block, but it was close enough.

When the copyboy had built up the courage to pass by again some five minutes later, he found a column in Demetris Mattas's out basket, and he found the columnist himself slouched down into his chair, chewing on a pencil and staring into his computer terminal. The expression on his face still was not friendly.

* * * *

The lawyer gave up trying to get through on Caitlyn Koniotis's home telephone number and replaced the receiver. He had already unsuccessfully tried to reach her at the Cyprus Museum where she worked. And he had similarly tried yesterday, as well. These modern women—especially these American women. Why didn't they stay home where they belonged? He couldn't understand why any Cypriot man would marry outside of his country and his religion.

Well, she would just have to wait a few days. He was flying to Athens later today on business and would not be back until late on Thursday. She no doubt would want to hear this news as soon as possible, but the papers had already taken several months to clear to the point where she could be notified. A couple of more days couldn't hurt. The museum had informed him that she had no plans to leave

121

the island in the near future, so there didn't seem to be any danger that it would take him much longer to make contact.

But, then, what do lawyers know?

* * * *

Manuel nervously paced the tiny living area of the flat that he had shared with three of his Filipino compatriots since the evening of the UN coordinator's dinner party. This was not working out as he had anticipated. He had been so sure that he could quickly save the money to bring his wife to Cyprus when he had taken on the second job. He had been reassured that he would not be in any danger. But now maybe he was going to lose his first job—and his work permit— and maybe he would be sent back to the slums of Manila.

He had called and reported the information just as he had been instructed to do. And they had attentively listened to what he provided and had seemed to be pleased. But they had not let him reach anyone in authority who could talk to him about helping to bring his wife to the island. And when he had said that he may have been detected and maybe couldn't provide any more information on the UN coordinator's activities, they had been agitated and had tried to find out where he was calling from.

Some unconscious sense of self-preservation had caused Manuel to avoid telling them where he was—Manuel was not particularly bright—and they had become abusive and had refused to give him his money unless they could hand it to him in person, so he had finally disconnected the line.

Now he realized that he had done all of that work for nothing. But at the same time a plan was starting to form in his mind. They had liked the information and wanted more. Maybe he couldn't get more—he wasn't sure he could go back to the UN coordinator's house, because he had left that night scared because the UN coordinator was asking to speak to him directly herself, and he was told she seemed angry about something. But maybe he could use what he had heard more than once.

That reporter, Hamilton, from the *Cyprus Mail*. He seemed to be all ears at the party, Maybe *he* would pay for the same information. Manuel picked up the telephone directory for Nicosia and started looking up the newspaper's number. As he did so, his thoughts returned to the others and to the money they owed him. Well, he wouldn't tell them where he was or meet them personally, but he could see no reason why he couldn't tell them to deliver the money here to his friends in this flat. There was no reason for them to know that he was staying here as well now. This wasn't his flat. They would think he was staying at his own room, not here. After he called the *Cyprus Mail* reporter, he would call the others back.

He needed the money. He missed his wife.

Chapter Nine

It had never been this chaotic in the Nicosia divisional offices of the International Investigations Division of the Cypriot police. It was not only that the eyes of the world were beaming in on Cyprus because of the unprecedented attack on a UN force on the island, and most important, because of the disappearance of the internationally acclaimed Eric Isaksen. The scene was also in turmoil because, with the death of the interior minister, Ioannis Herodotou, the head of the division's support had been cut off at the worst possible time. The disappearance two days earlier of a Russian diplomat's wife had not helped the situation either, although that was an event that still wasn't widely known.

Both the Greek Cypriot National Guard and the occupying Turkish army had mobilized in mutual suspicion that the other had been involved in the attack at Astromeritis, and many in the Greek Cypriot House of Representatives were calling for a turnover of the investigation to the defense establishment.

In the past Herodotou had been a strong spokesman for the international police unit, but now Herodotou was gone. It remained to be seen how well the police department chief, Zenon Tenekides, could step into Herodotou's shoes in protecting the department's role in the investigation. Koniotis could not even be sure that Tenekides would try. They had always gotten along well enough, but Koniotis and his unit had become such a favorite cause with the interior minister that Koniotis could not be sure Tenekides had not become jealous and put out about all the attention directed to the international unit. With Herodotou now suddenly and irrevocably out of the picture, the unit was about to find out what Tenekides really thought.

While remaining current on other aspects of the investigation and giving direction where needed and possible, Takis Koniotis had tried to keep his mind clear to concentrate on the angle of the disappearance of Mikhail Lukenov's wife. He had the gut feeling that her disappearance and the attack at Astromeritis were related, and he was going to hang on to the Russian diplomat like a bulldog until he was confident he had uncovered all that the Russian knew about what was going on.

As he put the telephone down from yet another unsuccessful attempt to reach Lukenov through the Russian embassy switchboard, Androulla came over to his desk with a file.

"I know this isn't the time to be pursuing this," Androulla apologized beforehand, "but I thought that you would at least want to know that the Larnaca airport transit database we set up is beginning to have results."

"No problem," Takis responded. "I'm at loose ends at the moment anyway. It looks like I'll have to go to Tenekides to try to get some official support to make Lukenov talk to me. What did the computers come up with?"

"It's still slow going, I'm afraid—which is a bit unfortunate in this case—but our cross checks on known terrorists reveal that one of the low-level baddies has just been in Cyprus."

"Oh, who?" Koniotis asked.

"A low-grade triggerman who has been variously associated with the Iranians and the Hizballah arrived in Cyprus through Larnaca three weeks ago. Name's Faris Sukkar, a Lebanese national. Not the name he used to get into the country, of course, but we traced the alias he used through the records we seized last year when we rolled up that travel agency here that had been handling travel for the Abu Nidal Palestinian faction. The only problem is that his name also popped out of the computer as having left again this morning."

"Yes, a pity we didn't catch him while he was here. But the system is getting faster. We'll catch the next one. Where was he headed?"

"Athens."

"Well, good work, thanks. Pass it down through the channels and send bulletins out to Athens and Interpol."

"Done already," Androulla answered.

Koniotis smiled—his first one of the day—and said, "You're getting more like Maria every day, Androulla. And that's a compliment. It won't be long before the two of you together will be so efficient and experienced that you won't need me around at all anymore."

"I don't think that day will ever come," Androulla answered. She smiled, and as she did so, the telephone on Koniotis's desk began to ring.

"Hello Koniotis? This is Mikhail Lukenov. I've learned some things that I think you should know. We need to get together in person. Soon."

* * * *

"I must be losing my touch," he thought bitterly, as he rose from his chair and strode over to the window. The newly constructed American embassy compound was still there, across the street. Irony of ironies to have that as a neighbor.

"Why wasn't I able to tell when we recruited the Filipino that he was a clumsy idiot? Such good placement, all he was able to pick up was that Munir Nahlawi and Suzanne Abu Hani were having an affair. Hardly news; she's been in every pair of trousers belonging to anyone in town who knows any secrets and who can't keep his hands to himself. He also reported that the visiting UN official was going to visit the Green Line the day before yesterday. Again, hardly a secret—or at least one that wasn't enough of a secret—in view of what happened to that group on Tuesday."

Mikhail Lukenov suddenly shuddered at the thought of the attack on the UN tour two days previously as he was regaining his son at the Vroisha monastery. He could not help but think of the airline brochures that had been left on the bodies at Astromeritis—the same marked brochure he had recovered from where his wife had disappeared at Soli. He turned from the window and returned to the desk in his office at the Russian embassy. He opened a drawer and pulled out the two airline pamphlets and a tourist booklet. Thus far he had not told the authorities about either brochure. One was from the Soli site; the other one was the one Uri had found at the monastery, the one that had been marking a page in the tourist booklet on the

127

Paphos District. The second one had not had "MB" marked on it in black marker as the one at Soli had been and, he had been told, that the ones at Astromeritis had been.

The page that had been marked in the tourist booklet had been about the well-known Ayios Neophytou monastery high in the hills overlooking the ancient cultural capital of Paphos. Lukenov had immediately sent his men to the Ayios Neophytou area, although he didn't think the terrorist band—and he was now beginning to think of the people who had snatched his wife as terrorists on a planned mission—would have tried to use Ayios Neophytou as they had the monastery at Vroisha. The latter had been a small, isolated complex. Ayios Neophytou, conversely, was a large, wealthy, and famous monastery that was a popular tourist attraction and had started out as a complex of hermit caves.

Lukenov didn't think the band would be so bold—or stupid—as to try to take over the Ayios Neophytou monastery itself as a hideout, but if there was still a complex of caves there, they may be planning to use those. Lukenov had his agents searching this area for evidence of the band for two days, but without luck. Perhaps it was time for him to pass what he knew on to Takis Koniotis. Koniotis was good, and he was trustworthy. Still, he had been avoiding the inspector's calls for two days, because he knew Koniotis wanted to grill him about what he had learned from Uri, and, more important, how he had learned where Uri was. Lukenov had no intention of handing over the in-place agent who had found Uri at Vroisha. Upon finding the boy, the agent had called Lukenov and stayed with Uri until the helicopter arrived. And then, at Lukenov's signal, he had faded back into the countryside, knowing that Lukenov would show his appreciation later—if only in being less demanding and critical of what the agent was producing in the godforsaken place he'd been sent.

The thought of Koniotis's name made Lukenov remember a couple of other tidbits the Filipino had passed on from the UN coordinator's dinner party. The information that Koniotis's wife; the American embassy Treasury agent, Paul Conte; and the new Canadian intelligence chief were going to Kantara today was of no import— although it did give a momentary jab of pain to Lukenov, as he could not help but connect it to the tragic family outing his wife and sons had taken on the Turkish side just four days previously. The related information—that Caitlyn Koniotis and Paul Conte might once have been more than just friends—was interesting and was worth salting away for possible use in the future.

And Lukenov had to admit that the discussion Eric Isaksen had forced about the reported training of terrorist groups in the mountains in both the Greek and Turkish zones had been useful. It had helped him make the connections to those who had snatched both his wife and, later, Isaksen. And it had helped him structure his countermoves.

Yes, the Filipino's information had been useful on the whole. But the man had bungled his access on his very first night of access. The embassy's other asset in the UN coordinator's resident, the Sri Lankan maid, had reported that the nosy *Simerini* columnist, Demetris Mattas, had warned Ingrid Bittmann that the Filipino was probably spying on her guests, and the Filipino had disappeared rather than facing off on the accusation.

Now the Filipino was less than useful. Now he would be a link back to the Russian embassy if he was found and grilled by

Bittmann or the Cypriot authorities. He was a liability now, and he had to be removed.

"But, first things first," Lukenov thought, as he reached for the telephone again. Irina was more important. And the demonstrated brutality of the terrorist band at Astromeritis and the Vroisha monastery and the failure thus far of Lukenov's operatives to track down the band indicated that time was too short for Lukenov to continue to play a lone hand with these brochures and the possible clue pointing to Ayios Neophytou. It was time to mobilize Koniotis's unit too.

* * * *

Caitlyn had almost called Paul Conte and canceled her inclusion in the trip to Kantara Castle on Thursday morning. She had felt that bad when she got out of bed. The excavation team had shown up as early as usual and were busy making a racket below her bedroom window—which did not help her discomfort or her disposition in the slightest. Takis had not come home last night, and it was unlikely he would come home longer than to shower, shave, and change clothes from now until he got the kidnappings under control. It was all just so awful. Caitlyn hadn't liked Eric Isaksen based on his own reaction to her, but she didn't wish him ill. She hadn't had time to meet Irina Lukenov at all, but she knew something of what she had been through in Grozny before coming here, and her heart went out to her and her boys if not to Mikhail Lukenov, who Caitlyn knew all too well.

When she had fixed a pot of tea—the flip flops in her stomach wouldn't permit her to even think of coffee—Caitlyn invited her friend and superior at the Cyprus Museum, Andriko Visiliou, who was supervising the excavations across the street, in for a cup. When she told him she planned to cancel out on the trip to the castle because she felt so poorly, he quizzed her closely about her symptoms and suggested that she first call Dr. Lambros again to see what she had to say. Visiliou knew Caitlyn had really been looking forward to the outing.

Caitlyn did as Visiliou suggested and was surprised that the doctor thought she should go on with the trip, because she should feel better later in the day and probably didn't have anything seriously wrong with her.

"We'll run some tests when you come in for your appointment tomorrow, but it doesn't sound like anything that would be affected negatively by going on your expedition. Just remember to take plenty of water and not to let yourself get dehydrated. And don't worry—but don't go doing any strenuous climbing either."

And Caitlyn had to admit that by the time Paul picked her up at the door, she did feel a lot better. Her excitement had grown, which evidently had pushed the pain to the background. En route to the Canadian high commission compound to pick up Ellen Larkin, Caitlyn had made Paul stop at the Bridge House Bookshop near the intersection of Grivas and Byron avenues and had bought a copy of *Enchanted Cyprus* so she and Ellen could read about the eastern side of the island as they drove up to the castle.

Paul had anticipated that they would have no problems at the Ledra Palace checkpoint, as they were driving in his Lancia sedan, with its green plates designating his diplomatic status. Diplomatic vehicles weren't stopped at the Greek checkpoint at all, and diplomats who were resident in Cyprus were listed with the Turkish Cypriot border guards and were checked, but not stopped. Caitlyn, of course, would have to go to the upstairs office at the Turkish checkpoint to obtain a day pass, but she should have no trouble doing so with her American passport in her maiden, non-Greek name.

As anticipated, there had been no trouble at the Greek checkpoint. Following that hurdle there was a drive of a couple of hundred yards through the buffer zone. The road here went past the entrance to the one-time five-star Ledra Palace Hotel, which had once been the center of social and business life in Nicosia and now was the home of the UN soldiers on duty in this sector. As they drove by, Caitlyn couldn't help but stare intently at the rambling five-story stone building with its mix of Arabic and British colonial architecture.

"If only these walls, bullet pocked from the Turkish invasion, could talk," she thought. Besides having been the congregating point of all those who were wealthy and powerful for many decades, the hotel had once been—and continued to be—the venue for the negotiation of the island's future. It was now the primary—and nearly only—place where Greek Cypriots could meet Turkish Cypriots, and then only during bicommunal meetings and events arranged by the diplomatic community. It was here that Takis and Safa Ziya met at least once a month, under the sponsorship of the British high commission, to cooperate in countering international crime affecting both sides of the island.

It was when they reached the Turkish checkpoint that Paul was afraid they had gotten themselves into trouble. He had pulled over to the side of the road so that he could take Caitlyn to the visa office for her day pass before they drove up to the crossing. However, as he got out of the automobile, a small sedan with Turkish Cypriot registration plates drove up to the side of his Lancia.

"Is this the vehicle carrying Mrs. Koniotis?" the driver of the sedan queried politely.

"Nuts!" thought Paul. "Someone has tipped them off and they are going to deny Caitlyn entrance because she's married to a Greek Cypriot."

There was nothing to do but admit that Mrs. Koniotis was in the automobile, of course. One did not argue with Turkish soldiers with guns, and there were Turkish soldiers aplenty at the barrier right in front of their car.

However, the man in the other sedan merely flashed them a smile and said, "The pass has already been arranged. Ms. Ziya assigned me to make sure that Mrs. Koniotis had no trouble on this trip. My name is Sami; I work for Ms. Ziya. I will be following you, but don't worry about me. Just go ahead and travel where you want and don't mind me. I just didn't want you to worry about the vehicle that will be following you."

"Why, thank you, Sami," answered Caitlyn with a warm smile. "That's very thoughtful of both Ms. Ziya and you. We will be going up to Kantara Castle. We may be stopping for a new minutes at Engomi and at St. Barnabas's tomb just inland from the ruins at Salamis, but we won't have time to stop at Salamis today."

It took them nearly two hours to reach Kantara Castle at the island's northeast corner at the end of the Kyrenia Range, where the long Karpas Peninsula juts out toward the underbelly of the Turkish mainland. Just before they hit the coast at Salamis Bay as they drove nearly due east from Nicosia, they did pass through and briefly stop at the ruins of the late Bronze Age city state of Engomi, center of one of the oldest civilizations on the island.

All that could be seen of the nearly 3,500-year-old site that once been one of the major Mycenaean trading cities of the eastern Mediterranean were the foundations of buildings below an escarpment that marked where the earthquake that had destroyed the city had raised the earth. But at this time of the year the site was beautiful, because the foundations literally became vases for a wide variety of colorful and fascinating wildflowers. It was hard to think that this had once been a busy metropolis of a resilient people—so resilient that when earthquakes forced them from this site, they moved closer to the water at Salamis, and when great earthquakes destroyed that long-time capital of the island in AD 332 and 342, they moved on to the present city of Famagusta, famous as the setting for the Shakespearean play *Othello*.

Immediately after leaving Engomi, they came upon the legendary tomb and former monastery of St. Barnabas, Cyprus's own apostle, who had brought Paul into the Christian fold. Now an icon and antiquities museum, this monastery provided Caitlyn and Ellen a contained, yet helpful exposure to the island's long and eventful history. St. Barnabas, who had journeyed to Cyprus with St. Paul, later returned to the island and was said to have been martyred in Salamis, from whence his body was spirited away and hidden along with an ancient copy of St. Matthew's Gospel. Many years later, as it was claimed, the saint and the copy of the gospel were found where a small chapel near the monastery now stands.

The three stopped near the chapel for a rest and drank some water. Sami was parked in the lot outside the monastery's door and saluted them when they had acknowledged his presence by waving to him. Caitlyn felt much better. She looked up toward the Kyrenia

Mountains where the hills started their descent onto the Karpas Peninsula. It didn't look like it could be a long drive from here up to Kantara Castle.

But she was wrong. It took them an hour longer to get to the castle, driving first along Salamis Bay and then, just before the little fishing village of Bogaz, turning back inland and following ever-narrowing roads up into the hills.

As they ascended—and between lingering moments of taking in magnificent views of the central alluvial Mesaoria Plain—Caitlyn read the history of the Kyrenia Range castles to Ellen. The chain of castles had been built by the Greek Comenus dynasty from earlier-constructed stone watch towers running along the spine of the Kyrenia range and later were embellished into crusader castles during the brief occupation by Richard the Lionhearted at the end of the twelfth century. Kantara was the eastern-most—and most remote—of these castles, now in almost total ruin since being taken from the French Lusignans by the Italian Venetians in the fourteen century. It was now primarily an isolated mountain-top perch for the occasional adventurous visitors who wanted to be able to see the whole northeast quadrant of the island and to catch a glimpse of the Turkish mainland across a forty-nautical mile stretch of the Mediterranean. This purpose alone had justified its existence.

When the trio reached the base of the castle, they immediately climbed the winding footpath to the castle's entry and paid their token fee for entrance. Sami pulled up to the parking area just about the time they reached the entrance. Rather than follow them, however, he walked back down the road to find a convenient place to relieve himself and have a smoke.

Sensing that Paul and Ellen would like a little privacy in this romantic spot and mindful that she had been told not to do any strenuous climbing, Caitlyn, guidebook firmly lodged under her arm, suggested that she take the easier route farther up in the castle—to count the 101 rooms legend claimed were here, she said—while the other two took in the view toward Nicosia in the southwest from a secluded niche in the western ward. Caitlyn climbed the more gentle gradient stairs to the central high tower, known as the Queen's Chamber, and, from there, she gazed toward the southeast over Salamis and Famagusta and opened her copy of *Enchanted Cyprus* to read more about the area.

It was thus that none of the three in the castle—or even the attendant at the entry gate—witnessed the death of Sami near the road below the cliff supporting the northeastern wall of the castle. As he moved into the brush beside the road and unzipped his trousers to relieve himself, one hand roughly wrapped itself around his neck and covered his mouth and nose from the back and another hand jabbed the blade of a long knife between the ribs of his back.

Having her fill of the view across Salamis Bay, Caitlyn walked over to the other side of the high tower and noticed that there was another, lower ward below her and to the northeast. She found a trail leading down through the rocks and wild flowers from the ruins of the tower and started working her way down to the lower courtyard, which was surrounded by the ruins of chambers abutting the outer castle walls.

Sometime later, when Paul and Ellen had reached a point where going any farther in their dalliance in the southwestern ward would have been a major embarrassment if Caitlyn, other visitors, or the castle keeper happened upon them, they became aware that too much time had elapsed without having seen or heard from Caitlyn. Motivated by the concern that she might have fallen on one of the steep, rock-strewn slopes and wrenched her ankle, they went in search of her in the higher castle chambers. But they didn't find her. Now panicked, Ellen returned to the castle entry to be told that the guard had not seen Caitlyn come back through there either. He joined them in the search, and before long, he called the others from the northeast ward. There, in the corner of one of the chambers, was the castle's postern gate—its emergency back door. Here there was evidence of quite a bit of recent foot traffic, and there, right beside the small opening that led out to a pathway down the cliff side that would have put fear into the heart of a goat, was a book. It was a brand-new copy of *Enchanting Cyprus*, and inside its front cover was a Cyprus Airline brochure, with the initials "MB" scribbled across the front in heavy black ink.

Shortly thereafter they found the lifeless body of the Turkish Cypriot policeman who had been sent to ensure their safety.

* * * *

Outside, the sunshine beat relentlessly on the red tile roof and searched mercilessly through the tropical gardens for vulnerable plants that could be withered. Inside, however, it was cool in the near darkness. The pair, both naked and firmly joined at the hips, were rolling around on the lush Oriental carpet at the foot of the huge bed. They seemed to be fighting for ascendency.

She was a wild woman when they did it this way, he thought, as he fought for leverage and lodged against the frame of the bed. She dexterously, without losing connection, turned just as he thought he had her pinned to the floor and wound up on top again. She seemed to like it best rough and on the floor—and in full control. At length he was totally spent and she let him rise. She lay there, propped against the bed frame, one arm trailing provocatively over her head and onto the mattress. She was panting, like a panther. Her violet eyes were flashing, also like those of a panther.

He left her and went to the bathroom adjacent to the bedroom. Her eyes darted around the room, always returning to the bathroom door. He had left the door open. When she saw that he had turned on the shower and had entered the enclosure, she quickly rose and quietly left the bedroom. She found the briefcase in the dining room. It wasn't locked.

When Alec reentered the bedroom, refreshed and ready for another bout on the floor, Suzanne, clothes in hand, dashed past him, planting a kiss on his nose while groping with her free hand in a movement that nearly doubled the British diplomat up in surprise, presented him with a dazzling smile, and closed and locked the bathroom door behind her in one swift motion accompanied by a giggle.

"Why, oh why," lamented Alec with a playful laugh, "did I have a lock installed on the inside of the bathroom door?"

* * * *

The sun was setting as Takis Koniotis mounted the broad marble front stairs up to his front door. The white jasmine vine was starting to bloom, its sweet fragrance already permeating the air. The museum's excavation team had already packed up and left for the day.

"Good," Takis thought. "I need a quiet nap on my own bed as well as a shower and change of clothes before I return to the department."

The Cyprus Airlines brochures Lukenov had given him from the Soli and Vroisha sites, although a mystery in themselves, certainly linked the Russian kidnapping with that of Eric Isaksen, and Takis tended to agree with Lukenov that these were politically motivated acts, probably by a group that could be classified as terrorists. The kidnapping of innocent women and international leaders and the murder of priests and peacekeeping soldiers certainly classified their activities as terrorism.

He was glad Lukenov had decided to voluntarily cooperate. That would make his unit's work easier, and they already were becoming better organized now that they had some idea what they were facing. He knew, certainly, that Lukenov must have hidden, illegal assets—agents—throughout the island and that the man Takis had seen with Lukenov's son at Vroisha surely had been one of these. But now was not the time to pursue this issue. He also was sure that Lukenov had scoured the Ayios Neophytou area—on the basis of what had been seen in the tour book—before reporting to Takis. But Takis would let that pass for now as well.

He now had his own people searching that area, and Takis was confident there would be a breakthrough within a matter of days. This was a small island, and no one could exist here long without attracting notice—especially not an armed band with two hostages. Of course, Takis had no idea how long he could keep control of the investigation. As he was leaving the office, Tenekides had called to say that the president wanted to talk to Takis the following afternoon.

Takis had the sinking feeling that this was the chop—that Tenekides had sold the unit and its investigation to the military.

Takis saw as he opened the entry door that the lights were off in the house and that it was silent as a tomb. That was to be expected, of course. It was a long way to Kantara and back, and Caitlyn no doubt had insisted that they stop and examine every sign of ruin—ancient, of course, Takis thought bitterly, not the ruins of buildings and people's lives that the Turks had caused when they invaded the island twenty years previously.

As he was opening the refrigerator door, the telephone rang.

"Hello, may I please speak to Mrs. Koniotis?"

"I'm sorry, she's not home. Would you like to leave a message?"

"Still not home?" an exasperated voice intoned. "Mrs. Koniotis does live at this connection, doesn't she?"

"Yes, but she's American." Takis couldn't think of anything else to say to justify Caitlyn not being here at the end of the workday. But the caller seemed to have accepted this as an explanation for the woman's absence. A Greek woman would always be home when her husband returned from work.

"May I ask who is calling? This is Mr. Koniotis. May I have her call you back when she returns?"

"Thank you, no. This is Phylaktis Baroutis. I'm a lawyer, and I need to talk with Mrs. Koniotis directly."

"Caitlyn isn't in any trouble, is she?" Takis asked, with growing concern. "I'm a policeman."

"Yes, I know who you are. No, no message. I will contact her eventually, I'm sure."

140

"She should be home any time now," Takis said right before he replaced the receiver and returned to the refrigerator, already lost in his own complex thoughts.

Unfortunately Caitlyn wouldn't be home any time soon, however.

* * * *

Caitlyn had been pushed and prodded westward, across the top of the Kyrenia ridge, toward the sinking sun, for more than three hours. She was exhausted and thirsty, and her nausea had begun to return. The people who grabbed and gagged her and half carried her from the back of Kantara castle had been cruel and uncaring—with the possible exception of one man, not more than a boy, really, whose expression seemed as frightened as hers must be and who occasionally supported her from a fall on the trail when any of the others would just have let her tumble.

She was scared and tired, but she also was angry. And a Spencer who was angry was not someone to take lightly. She had known in an instant that these must be the same people who had taken the Lukenov woman and Eric Isaksen. How could she have been so blind to the possibility that she, Paul, and Ellen could be likely candidates for kidnapping as well—self-identifying by wandering around in the Cyprus mountains, driving a diplomatic-plated car?

Where were Paul and Ellen? Surely they hadn't been killed. For a minute she thought she might be sick. But she hadn't heard any gunfire, and they had been on the other side of the castle from where her captors entered and exited when they grabbed her. And what about Sami? She hoped Safa would not be too hard on Sami. What could one man have done even if he had tried to help her? But how had they known that she was coming to Kantara? But they must not have known. She wasn't anyone special. She must have just been a target of opportunity in some sort of scheme to show the world that they could attack anywhere on the island.

She didn't really wonder much where they were taking her. They were moving in the direction of where the other kidnappings had taken place. But what were they approaching now? Why, it was another castle. That must be Buffavento Castle up there. Would they be hiding out near Buffavento Castle? The sun had just gone down over Morphou Bay, so it was logical that they were stopping for the night.

"Good," was her first reaction. "I don't think I could walk another mile." And to emphasize the point, she slowed down. This, however, resulted in a swift punch in the arm by the woman, who evidently was one of the group's leaders and who was trying hard to be the meanest, manliest member of the band.

"No stopping, Mrs. Koniotis," the woman barked as she pushed Caitlyn past the entry of the long, steep foot trail leading up to Buffavento. "The sun's gone down, so we can really start stepping out. Get a move on, or I'll do you right here."

The first shock that hit Caitlyn was that the woman could speak English. Up to now, the band had been speaking Arabic, and Caitlyn had felt some power, as she could speak and understand a little Arabic, and she assumed they didn't know that. But the second, and most debilitating shock then hit her. The woman had called her by her name! This was no capricious act. They knew exactly who she was and had planned to kidnap her all along.

Chapter Ten

This would never do. He would not be a part of this any longer. And even if he did decide to remain as the cover for the Hizballah operations in Beirut, the corpulent copper merchant, Nabil Jallud, who was operating now in Beirut under the name of Anwar Jabril, was now sure he would not survive the experience.

It had been bad enough when he was just providing a communications center for Ibrahim and his fighters. But now Ibrahim had brought a hostage into the shop and was keeping her, chained and gagged, in the small storeroom at the back of the store. Ibrahim said she was an Israeli spy who had been caught trying to infiltrate into Lebanon, but Jabril knew better. He was not the blathering idiot that he presented himself to be to the world. He read the newspapers, he made connections, and he knew that this was the wife of that Russian diplomat in Cyprus.

This must mean that his nephew, Ahmad, must have been part of the kidnap band in Cyprus. He must therefore be in grave danger from both the Cypriot authorities and the Hizballah band—and the Russians as well. The pear-shaped merchant was beginning to despair that he could do anything to help Ahmad—or even to help himself, for that matter. This was all far beyond his league. He wasn't below a bit of espionage or a great deal of thievery, but he was no murderer or kidnapper of innocent women.

Jabril had not, of course, let on to Ibrahim that he knew who the woman was. To have done that would have constituted sure suicide. He merely lolled his head to one side, produced one of his stupid grins, and congratulated Ibrahim on his "catch." He had not been stupid enough to ask what Ibrahim had intended to do with the woman. But, when Ibrahim told him they merely wanted to throw a scare into her and would release her in a couple days, Jabril knew that he himself was being marked for death. If Ibrahim was not willing to confide in him at least to the point of admitting the woman would not be released without ransom—and most probably would never be released alive at all—then Jabril knew he was being lied to and that his own usefulness to the Hizballah was coming to an end.

Ibrahim was across the street again at the coffee shop, and all of his fighters were off on some sort of mission. No customers were in the shop. Jabril went to the doorway and looked up and down the narrow street. There were no potential customers in sight. He went back to his desk in the office behind the shop and filled a cup with water from a thermos. Taking yet another look out beyond the shop and into the street, he then shuffled to the door of the storeroom behind his office. He knew the fighters made some effort to keep the woman fed and to give her water and to walk her to the tiny, stinking bathroom on a regular schedule. But he needed to talk to her to find out for sure that she was the Russian missing from Cyprus, and he needed for her to trust him. At least he needed for her to say something, so he could determine what language she spoke—Russian or Hebrew. And she had been so quiet. Even when they had taken the gag away to feed her, Jabril had not heard her utter a sound. Perhaps if he showed some small kindness to her, she would speak to him—if she wasn't so deep in shock that she couldn't focus.

The storeroom was dark. The woman was huddled back in the corner, among some rolled-up carpets. He purposely made noise as he bustled in, so she would be aware of his presence. But she didn't move. "She must be asleep," he thought. "Oh, Allah, the Magnificent, do not let her be dead. Not here in my shop, and at least not until I've managed to figure out how to get out of this situation."

But now that his eyes had become accustomed to the darkness, he could see that she was not asleep at all, but was staring at him, her eyes big, but listless. He dug down for his most benign, grandfatherly smile and started toward her, holding the cup of water before him. But then he sensed a movement to his left from beside the shelving. Not all of the fighters had gone off.

In a swift movement of self-preservation, Jabril changed his smile to one of teasing malevolence, saluted the bound figured with the water, and slowly drained the cup down his own gullet. The figure to his left settled back into the shadows.

As Jabril turned to the door, however, he encountered Ibrahim, who was staring at him with deep contemplation.

"I needed to get some more supplies from the storeroom, and I could not help but tease the Israeli bitch," explained Jabril with as much bravado as he could master.

Ibrahim gave the merchant a long, hard look. At length, he said, "Speaking of supplies, we are about out of food. Go to the market and buy some more."

145

Jabril gratefully and swiftly moved to scurry past the terrorist band chief, who kicked at the merchant's ankle as Jabril passed him and sent him stumbling through his office and out into the shop.

"And I don't want to see you coming into the room with the prisoner again—ever."

Jabril didn't even stop to take money from the till for shopping. He allowed the momentum of Ibrahim's kick to carry him out of the shop and into the street, down which he waddled as quickly as his little legs would carry him. At the first corner down near the Holiday Inn Hotel and the cornice, Jabril turned toward the right and back into the teaming city. However, at the next corner, when he should have turned left toward the market area, he turned right again. At length he reached his destination.

Jabril stood outside the forlorn-looking, obviously nearly deserted Russian embassy for a long time before knocking on the big double doors. From this point there would be no turning back. And he could not see how his nephew, Ahmad, could be saved if this step was taken. But he could not see how either Ahmad or he himself could be saved in any other way. And this was certainly the only hope for the Russian woman.

It was growing dark before Jabril managed to leave the embassy. It had taken him much longer to convince the Russians that the missing diplomat's wife was here than he had anticipated, and then it had taken even longer for the embassy to contact Nicosia and for Jabril to strike his deal. He only had time to scurry through the market and pick up some necessities before returning to the shop. He would use credit for his purchases, although he now knew he would not be in Beirut long enough to pay his bills. He would have to weave a ponderous tale for Ibrahim about having met friends and having frittered his time away at a coffee shop. He would undoubtedly be beaten about a bit, but Ibrahim would believe his story. Jabril had gone to great pains to make Ibrahim believe he was a mindless idiot. And Jabril was banking that he hadn't outgrown his usefulness to Ibrahim just yet.

Nabil/Mehmet/Anwar Jallud/Tosun/Jabril was no fool. He had wriggled out of many hopeless situations before now, and he had every intention of surviving this one as well—if Allah allowed. One more day, and he would be gone, regardless of what happened with the Russian woman and Ibrahim.

* * * *

Safa Ziya was standing in the window of her new office—the office that had gone with her recent promotion to the position of chief investigator with the Turkish Cypriot police department—the office that actually had a view. She was watching, without actually seeing, the traffic snarl in central Attaturk Square of the Turkish sector of the old city of Nicosia, a scene that was being softened by the red glow of the early evening warming the southern slopes of the Kyrenia Range. It was a good thing, she thought, that she now had an office to herself. She could not bear the thought of her former office mate seeing her cry, as she was now doing.

She was disconsolate. Her friend Caitlyn kidnapped. Her long-time colleague and friend Sami dead. her promise to Takis to keep Caitlyn safe in the Turkish zone ashes. All because she had not fully acted on her intuition.

When Paul Conte and Caitlyn had first mentioned at the UN coordinator's dinner that they planned to visit Kantara Castle today,

Safa had experienced a twinge of premonition that something bad might come out of the excursion. It had been more than professional courtesy that had prompted her to pledge protection for Caitlyn while she was visiting the Turkish side. When she learned the reason behind the Russian embassy search around Soli and heard of the attack on and kidnapping of the UN official Erick Isaksen, Safa assigned her best detective to escort Caitlyn and her companions on their outing. But Safa knew now that she should have counseled Paul Conte not to make the trip at all, and she could kick herself for not having done so. Or she should have arranged for more guards, even though how she would have wrangled that, she had no idea. She guessed it had merely been national pride that had prevented her from acknowledging that perhaps she could not prevent a terrorist operation in the Turkish zone.

She wiped the tears from her eyes and turned back to her desk. Her assistant, the usually indomitably cheerful Tansul, was filling the frame of the outer doorway, with tears freely flowing down her own face. The two spent several minutes consoling each other. It was so hard to accept that Sami was gone. Untimely death—especially by violence—was still a highly unusual event on either side of the island. Cyprus, on the whole, was safer than most other countries.

But Safa couldn't mourn like this for long—and Tansul fully understood that. Both of them had to get back to work on tracking the terrorists down. And they had to free Caitlyn Koniotis and avenge Sami.

Safa pulled Paul Conte and Ellen Larkin out of the police red tape that could have drowned them at worst and could have kept them pinned down for hours at best and promptly sent them back to the

Greek side to inform Takis Koniotis and to set off alarms with the UN and Greek Cypriot authorities. She asked Paul to cut through the red tape of the other zone as well to ensure that daily meetings at the Ledra Palace Hotel could be set up between her and someone from the Greek Cypriot International Investigation Division so that the division of the island would not be an impediment to tracking the terrorist band down and bringing its members to justice. They had already used the cover of the buffer zone in their operations, and Safa was determined to take that advantage away from them.

Although right now Safa didn't know how she would be able to face Takis, she hoped that he would be the Greek Cypriot official she would be meeting. She realized, however, that he might not be in any condition to carry on with his work, and she knew she could work nearly as well with his deputy, Maria Solonos.

One last detail to pin down right now. Safa picked up the telephone and called the police chief. In addition to requesting that the Turkish army be asked to go on alert in the Morphou area, she asked for special police details to start up into the Kyrenia Range from all points and to fan out around the Green Line south of Morphou. These terrorists had struck in the mountains twice—making use of both of the island's mountain chains—and had not been far from the mountains for the attack on the UN tour. They probably were most comfortable operating in that terrain. If they were on their way back to the Greek side, that most likely would mean they would work their way toward the west across the top of the Kyrenia Range and then move across the open ground in the Morphou area and through the buffer zone to reach the Troodos Range on the Greek side in the southwest.

If they were moving down the Kyrenia Range, they would not have had time to get out of the mountains on foot as yet. She could have related this to the Turkish army and asked them to go up into the mountains, but she didn't want to endanger Caitlyn. The Turks were mean fighters. They would fire first and check for hostages later, no matter how important the hostages were. She would instruct the police patrols to locate and report but not to attempt to apprehend. After she put this into motion, she would have to decide what the next step should be when the band was located.

But, after having talked with the police chief, and before deciding her next step, she had one other call to make—to Sami's newlywed wife. This was going to be a long, stressful night.

* * * *

It was young Russian embassy code clerk Andrey Chizkov's very first week of work in Athens and his very last day on earth. This was his first overseas assignment. He was thrilled at the freedom from Russia, which had continued to make him feel controlled and isolated despite the many reforms of the past couple of years, and he was ecstatic at having his very own Fiat to drive around the Greek capital—at least for however long he could avoid a collision with an aggressive Greek driver—which would be any Greek on the road.

Andrey had been very impressed by his job—handling, coding, and decoding all sorts of hush hush messages for the large intelligence contingent in the embassy. He had been told that in years past—before the end of the Cold War—Athens had been a hub of international espionage and that embassy personnel such as himself had had to watch their personal security carefully. It was only in the last year, in fact, that the embassy's three code clerks had been permitted to move about the city on their own.

As he shifted down in gears and jockeyed successfully with a Mercedes for a lane change in the late-afternoon rush hour, Andrey reveled in the new freedom from the embassy shuttle service. He should not have been nearly as happy with the change in policy, however.

As he was idling behind a long queue of vehicles at a stoplight, several motor scooters passed by his window, barely missing his rearview mirror. The last one by, passing his window just as the light changed, seemingly was not so lucky. Andrey heard a hard thump at the side of his fiat just as he was reaching for the gearshift. He started to roll his window down and to turn to curse the clumsy cyclist, only to be facing a flashing pistol.

The Russian embassy's duty officer was on the bloody scene almost as fast as the Athens police were. As the police were primarily absorbed in unsnarling traffic around the small Fiat, the embassy official had time to examine the interior of the automobile closely. He could not help but see the airline brochure that was lying on top of the body, which had been pushed over onto the passenger seat by the force of the bullets. The blood patterns showed that the brochure could only have been tossed into the car after the shooting.

Upon closer inspection, the brochure—from Cyprus Airways—was revealed to contain a crudely written note in poor English. The intent of the note was clear, however. It demanded ransom and a shipment of arms in exchange for the release of the wife of the Russian diplomat in Cyprus.

The embassy official looked around. No, none of the Greek policemen had seen him pick up the brochure. He thrust the pamphlet into his pocket, only slightly concerning that he was getting fresh blood all over his pocket lining. He had been briefed on who the kidnapped Russian diplomat's wife was—not to mention the importance of the Russian diplomat involved. The same could have happened to his own wife. And it could just as easily have been he himself as the young Chizkov dead in this Fiat. Pity, but he would have to leave Chizkov for now. He had to get back to the embassy immediately.

The Russian embassy duty officer faded back into the crowd, as unnoticed as he had been when he arrived. Thursday evening, late in the rush hour, was not a good time for a murder in the center lane of a busy Athens street.

* * * *

It was well past dark when the terrorist band ended its journey at a quiet cul-de-sac in the hillside retirement community of Leonides Village on the slopes above Paphos. Higher, at the rocky top of the hill, was the Ayios Neophytos monastery complex. The four retirement villas that the terrorists had taken over were off to themselves, at the edge of a relatively new complex of homes that were being built for retired Europeans, mostly Brits. The houses were accessible to the main road up to Ayios Neophytos via a small dirt road as well as by an oiled road that connected them to the rest of the housing complex.

Two of the houses had not been occupied, their owners obviously off to their home countries for a spell. The retiree couples in the other two villas had been disposed of without trouble. None of the four families appeared to have developed any active friendships in Cyprus as yet. The people Abdul had sent on ahead to secure this hide-out had intercepted no telephone calls or attention from nosy neighbors since they had taken up residence.

The trip from the Kyrenia Mountains had both confused and infuriated Caitlyn. After passing Buffavento Castle, on the peak of the mountains above the artists' village of Bellapais, on foot, the band had continued westward, across the top of the range. Caitlyn knew they would have to come down to the road between Nicosia and the northern coastal harbor town of Kyrenia, and she hoped they would attract attention there as they tried to cross the road over the pass. She also knew it was a hell of a long haul from Kantara down to the end of the range and then, presumably over the Morphou plain to the buffer zone. Takis had told her the band seemed to be working out of the Paphos District foothills of the Troodos Range. If they were headed there on foot and they had not killed Paul Conte and Ellen Larkin back at Kantara Castle, Caitlyn was confident the terrorists would be apprehended a long time before they made it to the buffer zone.

This hope was dashed, however, when the band came down into the pass linking the capital with the northern coast. On the eastern side of the road in the pass, there was a picnic grounds that was used, primarily on Sundays and holidays, by Turkish Cypriot families escaping the heat of the lower ground. As the band descended into the area, Caitlyn saw that there were two green-plated diplomatic cars and a van, also with diplomatic registration, parked at the upper end of the picnic grounds. Caitlyn's first reaction was that teams from the embassies had driven up here to intercept the terrorists. But then she realized, in horror, that the terrorists were moving directly toward the vehicles. They somehow had possession of diplomatic vehicles.

Caitlyn was forced into the van. One of the sedans, filled with terrorists, who had taken their camouflage fatigues off to reveal shorts and T-shirts and had stuffed the military clothing into the vehicle's trunk, was pulling out of the picnic area, pointed toward Nicosia, as she was gagged, tied up, and forced into the back of the van and pushed down on the floor. The van left next, with the other sedan presumably waiting for several minutes before it started off.

Caitlyn knew, from the rhythm of the slower movement, when the van crossed the buffer zone at the Ledra Palace crossing. With its diplomatic tags, the vehicle encountered no trouble negotiating either the Turkish or Greek checkpoints or the UN zone.

They didn't let her off the floor of the van for the subsequent two-hour drive, but she could tell by what she could see through the van windows above her—the occasional mountain slopes and cuts through the mountains, which turned from reddish dirt-colored to sandy soil—that the van must have traveled down to the southern coast on the main Nicosia-Limassol highway, around the six roundabouts of the Limassol bypass motorway, and then on, westward, and through Paphos and back up into the hills.

As she was hauled out of the van—painfully hauled, as the ride on the floor of the van had truly been a jolting experience and she fought nausea the entire distance—she got a glimpse of the lights of Paphos down on the island's western coast before she was hustled into what appeared to be a very pretty little stuccoed, red-roofed villa.

Caitlyn was pushed through the living area of the small house and into a dark, shuttered back room, which must have been some sort of guest room. Her gag and bonds were ripped away, and she was thrown onto a small bed. The door was slammed and she was alone.

But she quickly found she was not really alone. Although the window shutters were closed—obviously secured from the outside—glints of light from a street light filtered in through the shutters' slats. There was movement on and a moan from another bed that paralleled the one she had been tossed on. She sat up on the side of her bed, her legs in the narrow aisle between the two beds. The figure loomed before her, hand clutching at hers, a scruffy face with glittering eyes staring into hers.

"Anna, Anna? Is that really you? I knew you wouldn't desert me."

Caitlyn had found Eric Isaksen—and he obvious was so disoriented that he thought she was his deceased wife.

* * * *

Takis Koniotis was, of course, devastated when Paul Conte reached him, told him that Caitlyn had been kidnapped, and produced the tour book with the Cyprus Airways brochure insert. But he did not react as The Asp apparently had expected. Takis didn't blame Conte for the snatch, and he certainly didn't blame Safa Ziya and her office for having been unable to prevent it. He placed the blame squarely on the terrorist band that had taken Caitlyn. He perfectly understood why they had done it, and he immediately redoubled his resolve to catch them and free the hostages rather than folding under the pressure and withdrawing from the case.

The use of the Cyprus Airways brochure as a link between the Irina Lukenov and Eric Isaksen kidnappings had not been released to the press as yet, and Paul Conte had not heard of the connection.

Thus, although the American diplomat strongly suspected that Caitlyn's kidnapping was linked to the earlier cases, he had no idea that the evidence he brought back with him—the airline pamphlet—had clearly—and purposely—established the connection.

"The grabbing of Lukenov's wife and Isaksen were obviously motivated to make an international news splash," Takis told Paul. "Caitlyn's kidnapping just as obviously is designed as a tweaking of the nose to me and to cripple the investigation of this band's operations. I'm supposed to be so wrapped up in concern and grief, I'll wager, that I'm not supposed to be able to function. Well, I won't oblige them. Caitlyn probably would not have been taken at all if I had gone on the Green Line tour with Isaksen and Herodotou as I was supposed to have done. From the terrorists' perspective, the attack on the UN tour was probably an especially sweet operation—grab a UN official while, at the same time, killing the interior minister, the commander of the UN troops in the western sector of the buffer zone, *and* the person who would be the chief investigator of these crimes. It's insidious. It also means that someone close to the inner workings of the Cypriot government and the diplomatic community is passing on information to the terrorists. What do you think of that theory, Paul?"

"I'm afraid you must be right," answered Conte in a weak voice. The man looked as if he would be sick.

* * * *

Caitlyn more than just looked sick. her nausea had finally gotten the best of her, and she had had to hurry to the bathroom. Luckily this small bedroom came with facilities attached.

"It would be awful to have to tell one of these gorillas that I was pregnant and had to be given access to the bathroom down the hall on demand," she told herself.

"Pregnant. Yes, I've let myself deny it too long. I'm sure that this is my malady—just a slight touch of pregnancy—and that this is why Andriko, whose wife has had three children in the last four years, and Dr. Lambos did not seem all that concerned by my bouts of nausea."

"Well, I certainly wanted to be pregnant, but I never would have wanted to be so in this context. If these people find out about my condition, there is no telling how they will take advantage of it."

Caitlyn sat back on her bed and sipped water from the glass she had found on the sink in the attached bathroom. Her first several moments in the room had been so strange. She had not been surprised to find Eric Isaksen here. If anything, she was surprised she hadn't found Mrs. Lukenov here as well. But, when he had mistaken her for his dead wife, she had almost lost her own sanity.

Caitlyn had known nothing about Anna Isaksen or about her death. When Isaksen bear-hugged her and rocked back and forth, murmuring words of endearment to Anna, Caitlyn was thrown for a loop. He had quickly recovered, however, and had profusely expressed his embarrassment and apologies. Luckily, Caitlyn was quick-witted enough to sooth him and to talk him back to sense in as gentle and nonthreatening a way as possible. It would not help at all for the man to remain in a protective fantasy world or for there to be an insurmountable barrier of embarrassment and dislike between the two; it would take their combined effort and intelligence to survive this situation.

When Isaksen was once again lucid, Caitlyn claimed she was exhausted, which was anything but a lie, and suggested that he too try to sleep and that they discuss their predicament further when they had been rested—if they were still here then. She wanted to give him time to compose himself and to reassert his dignity before they moved any further in their forced relationship.

Isaksen went to sleep almost immediately and didn't waken when the door to the hallway opened and a slight figure entered the room. Caitlyn withdrew to the corner of her bed in a defensive reaction, but she relaxed a bit when she saw that it was the young man who had been the only one of the band to show her any compassion during her forced march from Kantara to the Kyrenia Pass, just below St. Hilarion Castle.

The young man had brought some food and a thermos, which he put on the floor next to the door. When he looked up, Caitlyn could see in the light from the hallway that he had a worried expression on his face, and the shy smile that he offered to her when he saw she was watching him almost gave her the impression he was as much a hostage in this situation as she was.

Suddenly the light from the hall was blotted out by another figure that had appeared behind the young man. It was the rough woman terrorist Caitlyn had heard someone call Widad a couple of times during the march. Her hair was down. Caitlyn would never have guessed that it was so long and glossy from the way the woman had pinned it up under her beret in the mountains. She was wearing only a man's rumpled shirt, which came down almost to her knees in front, but which was cut high at the sides. From what Caitlyn could glimpse at the side cut and through the thin material in the backlighting, it was quite obvious the shirt was the only covering on the woman's body.

"He wants the woman now, Ahmad," Widad said in Arabic with a leer at Ahmad. "It looks like you have been displaced."

Caitlyn more or less got the gist of the words the woman had said based on the limited Arabic she knew, but the concept of what the woman was talking about confused her and she assumed she must not be understanding what was said clearly. But she did experience a sharp, visceral stab of fear and panic, even if she could not quite identify the source.

The young man—apparently named Ahmad, if she could trust her understanding of what Widad said at least that far—took on a look of fright that equaled Caitlyn's.

"Yes, yes, I'll bring her. I have to take him his whisky first. He told me explicitly to bring him whisky after he had done with you."

"You bring the whisky; I'll bring the girl."

"No, no," Ahmad responded immediately, his voice wavering from even deeper fright than he had exhibited before. "He was quite explicit about what he wanted. I knew he would want the woman directly after his whisky. It's all arranged. You know you will only make him mad if you go against his wishes. Didn't he say he was finished with you when you left him?"

Widad gave Ahmad a long, searching look of suspicion, but she then turned and flounced off.

Ahmad looked sick and listless as he gazed pleadingly at Caitlyn one more time and slowly closed the door.

Caitlyn was beginning to process the meaning of what Widad had said when she first came to the door. The woman's near nakedness had Caitlyn figure it out. For the first time since she had been kidnapped, Caitlyn felt that the bile rising in her throat resulted from stark fear rather than the early stages of pregnancy. For many minutes, her eyes darted around the room in search of escape, refuge, or defense. She would not let herself be subjected to this. She would rather die.

But she had others to think of now. Surely she had to survive as best she could for as long as she could. She was so confused. Perhaps she should awaken Isaksen. No, he had enough burdens of his own without having to share hers as well.

Seconds dragged on to minutes, which turned into hours. They had forgotten—or neglected—to take her wristwatch. She could maintain context as long as she had her watch. Why hadn't Ahmad come for her? After two hours, she began to hope that he was not coming for her. And when the third hour had passed and no one had come, she built up the courage to move to the door and to eat some of the food Ahmad had left. The thermos had been filled with coffee, which was now cold and bitter. But no coffee Caitlyn had ever tasted before had been this good. Then, exhausted, she returned to the bed and fell into fretful sleep.

As she slept, Caitlyn had a vision of women gathered around her in a mist, shielding her with their cloaks as the sound of hoof beats grew louder and she heard the babble of men's voices—speaking Arabic in raucous tones. The women were huddled over her, and Caitlyn looked up and seemed to recognize them all, even though they were clothed in guises that marched back through history, to the very beginning of time—and the figure that seemed most familiar to her seemed to be that of her deceased friend Eleni Piccard, who lifted a finger to her lips and

160

smiled a reassuring smile. In the space inside the gathered cloaks, Caitlyn felt the silkiness of a diaphanous scarf swirling about her head. And, despite the eerie semidarkness under the cover of the cloaks, she could get a sense of it—a scarf Eleni had given her, a scarf which had blown away from Caitlyn's shoulders and floated into the open grave as they were lowering Eleni's casket into the ground. As the women huddled together, the hoof beats grew fainter, as did the sounds of the men's voice, and Caitlyn realized that Eleni was murmuring to her, telling her everything would be all right.

Calmed now, Caitlyn's fitfulness lifted off her and she descended into a deep, merciful sleep.

Chapter Eleven

In the wee hours of Friday morning, Maria Solonos rushed down to police headquarters in the Greek sector of Nicosia. She was very upset. Not only had her good friend Caitlyn been kidnapped, but Maria had not been reachable when the news of the kidnapping had been reported to the police department. She knew the International Investigations Department must be in turmoil without Takis Koniotis's leadership, as he surely was so distraught over his wife's disappearance that he was not already busy planning countermeasures. Maria was doubly concerned that she had not been there either to console her colleague or to get the new angle of the investigation on track.

She had been with Demetris Mattas at his flat all evening and into the night, and it was he who had been informed of the kidnapping, through his paper—but only when the two had exhausted their lovemaking and he had returned the telephone receiver to its hook. Demetris was a slow-paced, methodical lover, who tried to keep both himself and Maria on the edge of ecstasy for as long as possible. And, as he was constantly receiving telephone calls at home in conjunction with his newspaper political satire column, the only way he could make love as he wanted was to disengage the telephone.

As it was, the telephone started to chime insistently as soon as Maria left his bed for the bathroom.

"She's what? Been kidnapped. Is this the same . . . ? Hold on; I'll be there in fifteen minutes."

He considered briefly just leaving—or maybe just leaving a note. But then he came to his senses. He went to the bathroom door.

"The call was about Caitlyn Koniotis, Maria. She's been taken on the Turkish side. Maybe the same band as the others. One of Safa Ziya's assistants was killed. I'm going, but you'd best cut the shower short too."

He heard the moan and his shower curtain being nearly jerked off its rod, but he didn't linger longer. He threw on some clothes and was halfway to the door before Maria rushed out of the bathroom, but, even in the rush to leave, he stayed long enough to tell Maria what little he'd been told. She was picking up the receiver to his telephone as he left the flat to pick up the threads of the story in his own way. He never tried to use Maria to get a story. He knew she would leave him the first time he made such an effort, and he would not risk that. He fully recognized that Maria was the best thing that had ever happened to him.

For a brief moment as she was pulling on her own clothes, Maria felt guilty about not having given Demetris's telephone number to the department receptionist as a regular contact number when she could not be reached at home. She was a grown woman. Everyone probably knew she had boyfriends—lovers. Then she gave up the guilt with the realization that even if the department had Demetris's telephone number—and someone in the department was willing to call a newspaper reporter—the receiver had been off the hook and they could not have contacted her.

She reached the department within ten minutes and pushed her way into the division's central squad room with every intention to start barking orders and getting the new investigation rolling. But, as she entered the room, she saw that most of the detectives were already there and on the move—in an orderly and organized fashion. Takis was in the middle of the activity and obviously was in full control of the action.

Takis saw Maria immediately and was able to see the conflicting expressions of apology, worry, and concern forming on her face. But he cut off whatever thoughts she was forming to say in the way of concern for Caitlyn and for not having been available sooner.

"Ah, good, Maria. You've caught up with us. No, you don't need to say anything. And, no, I'm not all right—as I'm sure you know and appreciate—but I need to stay busy and to remain focused on getting her back, safe, as soon as possible."

"Right," answered Maria, as she took her jacket off. "Where do you want me to start?"

"You can start by reading these reports on the operation. At some point you'll need to take over the control of the investigation on the headquarters end. I can't stay cooped up in here. As soon as we have an indication where to start searching, I'm gone. We have three helicopters and a National Guard team waiting for a target."

"All right," responded Maria. "I'll be ready to take over here as soon as you have to go. Is Androulla around?"

"She's checking on one of my hunches. These kidnappers are operating on both sides of the island. See in the report there? See the references to the Cyprus Airways brochures in the report there? My guess is that these are not Cypriots—that this is some sort of international terrorist band, possibly sent here for training in keeping with the various reports we've been receiving and now spreading its wings to try out actual operations. The new background database at the airport pulled out the name of a terrorist the other day who had come and gone. I've asked Androulla to bring us all the information the database had on this man's entry and exit cards. Whatever is going on, I think it's bigger than Cyprus."

"How do you figure that?" Maria asked. She wasn't really laying down a challenge. Takis was incredibly good at this, so she wasn't questioning his reasoning. It was just that she usually was able to keep up with him, and he seemed to have taken a leap of assumption here that had left her back in the weeds.

"I keep dwelling on why they took Isaksen and killed everyone else on the tour, including the UN forces commander. Isaksen was on his way to try to broker some sort of important deal in the Middle East. Logic tells me his kidnapping—and maybe the Lukenov woman's as well—has something to do with where he was going and what he was working on. Cyprus was just a rest stop for him." And then as a young man entered the room and bid for Takis's attention, "Yes, what is it, Costas?"

"It's just coming in now, sir," answered the clerk who kept track of the communications machines. "It's a fax from the Athens police. There was an assassination there yesterday evening of a Russian embassy employee."

165

"Yes, I vaguely remember hearing that on the radio on the way over," said Koniotis. "What about it?"

"The Athens police just received an anonymous telephone call claiming to reiterate its demands for money and the publication of a manifesto in return for the release of Mikhail Lukenov's wife. The police said it was a strange call, because the caller seemed angry that there had been no response to the first demand that he claimed had been left with the body of the Russian embassy clerk. But the police say they don't know anything about a first demand."

"Lukenov's wife? Athens?" mused Koniotis.

And when he turned to Maria, she said. "OK, you're right. Probably something connected to Isaksen's mission to the Middle East."

And then he turned back to the approaching senior detective and said, "Androulla, where had you said the flight the terrorist Faris Sukkar took was destined?"

"Athens," she answered, as she reached the circle of detectives.

"Does the information you've brought say where he came from when he first entered Cyprus?"

"Cairo."

Takis thought for a moment. "I think we've found a link— thanks to the records we seized from the Petrou Travel Agency, that clearing house for travel for Palestinian terrorists we quietly rolled up last year, and thanks to our new database system at the airport, I think we know who made that telephone call in Athens as well as who assassinated the Russian embassy clerk. Faris Sukkar."

And then the instructions started to fly: "Androulla, start searching the database for entries on the days around Sukkar's arrival in Cyprus of anyone else who might be on our watch lists. Concentrate especially on flights from Cairo, but that may not be too helpful. The band more than likely came here from separate destinations. They probably don't know, however, that the Petrou Agency kept good files and that we now have those files. And, oh, yes, for each suspected hit in the database, including Sukkar, trace the airline files to see if we can find out who issued their tickets."

"Who issued their tickets?" queried Maria as Androulla hurried off.

"Yes, maybe we can find out who these types of people went to after the Petrou Agency was shut down. Maria, could I leave it to you to call the Russian embassy here and make sure they know about the ransom demand in Athens for Irina Lukenov?"

"Certainly. Oh, Takis, Costas is waving at you again. It looks like you have a telephone call."

Takis returned from taking the call, excited. "That was Paul Conte. He's on his way over to pick me up. He and Safa Ziya have arranged for me to meet up with her on the Turkish side, near Morphou. They haven't found the band yet, but she's sure they haven't broken out of the Kyrenia Mountains and onto the plain in the Morphou area. And the Turkish Cypriot police should have finished scouring the mountains by the time I get over there. They are going to let Safa and me work directly on the operations."

A car horn sounded, and Takis quickly departed.

* * * *

167

"Now that's strange," thought Maria Solonos, as she put the telephone receiver down. They had put her directly through to Mikhail Lukenov at the Russian embassy, and she told him about the ransom demand for his wife as gently and tactfully as she could. And he had seemed neither surprised nor concerned.

It was understandable that the information might not have come as a surprise to him. The information on the ransom demand had probably reached him via the Russian embassy in Athens as fast if not faster than her own police unit received it.

But Lukenov didn't ask any questions about what was going to be done from here, nor did he offer any information or help of his own. Up to now—and from the time Lukenov called Takis to share his son's story on tracking the terrorists to the Vroisha monastery and to reveal the information about the airline brochure clues—Lukenov had been cooperative and as concerned that his wife be found by the Cypriot authorities as the police division had been. But now he acted as if he didn't need the help of the Cypriots.

"Is Irina still in Cyprus? Has she been moved to Athens, perhaps, and Lukenov knows that—and knows the action has moved to Greece?"

Maria called a detective over and asked him to check on whether the Russian embassy people were still out in the field with the Cypriot police units. The answer to that question provided what she thought was the answer to her other questions. The Russians had all pulled out of the search groups more than an hour previously. Lukenov knew more than he was revealing—and more than the Cypriot police knew.

But, although Maria may have been correct in her assumption of the effect, she was not correct in her assumption of the cause and the new venue. Lukenov had, indeed, received both the Athens police report on the "reiterated" ransom demand in Athens for his wife's release and the separate, better-informed report from his own colleagues in Athens on the original demand, folded into a telling Cyprus Airways brochure and left on the body of the embassy's code clerk.

But he hadn't been fooled or deflected. He had already received information that revealed the use of either Athens or Cyprus as the focus of activity as being mere ruses. No, he had to look elsewhere for Irina. And he and his men could handle this terrorist band on their own from here. The authorities would not be brutal enough in putting this insult down. The Russians always kept the incidents of terrorism on Russian interests down by taking brutal revenge for every single infraction—just as the Israelis did. No, he knew where Irina and the center of this operation was now, and he and his men would take care of the situation on their own and in their own way now—in Beirut.

* * * *

It was early afternoon and Takis had returned to the police office on the Greek side and was sitting, tired and dejected, in his office as frenetic activity continued in the outer central squad room.

He, Safa, and Paul had come up blank in their short vigil at the foot of the Kyrenia Range near Morphou. Shortly after he and Paul reached Safa's side, the last report came in from the hunting parties in the mountains that neither the kidnappers nor Caitlyn had been found. There had been traces of the band having moved across the Kyrenia ridge and down to the Nicosia-Kyrenia road pass near St. Hilarion Castle, but there had been no trace of them having moved farther along the ridge.

"Chances are," he thought, "they went down to Kyrenia and took a boat." Although how they might have circumvented the heavy surveillance of the waters surrounding the Cypriot coast was beyond him.

By the time the Friday morning sun had come up, Safa had managed to arrange for a Turkish army helicopter to take the three of them up and they spent the rest of the morning methodically searching the mountain range themselves from the air.

As disappointed as he was, Koniotis had been very grateful to Safa and the Turkish Cypriot police for letting him come across and join the search and to Paul Conte for setting it up. He now didn't have to trust the efforts of others—and, notably, of people he had been trained not to trust—that they were doing their best to find his wife. He had seen from first hand that they had given the search their utmost effort and that they had shown genuine concern. He would never forget what Safa and his fellow Cypriots in the north had attempted to do.

He thought back to the only other possibility he could think of pursuing from the Turkish zone side—that the band had managed to reach the coast undetected and unchallenged and boarded a vessel and slipped away. If so, they must have headed straight to the Turkish mainland coast, as the coastal patrols of both zones had been quickly alerted to the situation. The only other explanation was that they somehow had reached safe haven on the Turkish side and out of the mountains. It was hard to accept that they could have slipped through the ground patrols and reached the Greek side on foot—across a UN-patrolled and mined no-man's-land.

On a final, weak hunch Koniotis asked Safa Ziya to have the records of the registration numbers of automobiles crossing the Turkish checkpoint at the Ledra Palace Hotel over the past two days compiled, with special attention given to those crossing into the Greek zone after the time of the kidnapping at Kantara Castle. He'd have whatever records the Greek checkpoint scrutinized too, but as the Greeks claimed there should be no border there at all, they didn't carefully record all of the license numbers as the Turkish Cypriots did. Ziya promised to pull these records on a priority basis and to get the information to him at the meeting Alec Stuart had arranged between them at the Ledra Palace Hotel the following afternoon.

As Koniotis now sat in his office processing in his mind the events since the previous afternoon, his eyes growing heavy from stress and the lack of sleep, Maria popped her head into the door, a new look of concern on her face.

"Takis, Caitlyn's supervisor, Dr. Visiliou, is on the phone and says he needs to talk to you."

"Could you handle the call, Maria? I know Andriko wants to commiserate with me and I appreciate that—do tell him so, please—but I have to focus on getting Caitlyn back. Talking with her friends about the situation right now won't help get that done."

"He knows that, Takis. I think you'd better take this call. He has information you need to know."

Maria was quite right, although Dr. Visiliou's information didn't help the situation at all.

171

"I won't waste your time in telling you how sorry and concerned my wife and I are, Takis—but, of course we are—and I'm sure you know that. I wouldn't have called just to say that. I'm only calling at a time like this because there is something you need to know." Visiliou plowed right ahead without waiting for a response. "I got a call from Caitlyn's doctor today. Caitlyn was supposed to go in for medical tests this morning, and Dr. Lambros called me as soon as she heard the news about Caitlyn—she had tried calling you, but you weren't at home and the department switchboard wouldn't put her through to you there. Under the circumstances, I'm sorry to have to tell you this, Takis, but Dr. Lambros is fairly certain Caitlyn is pregnant."

* * * *

The British high commission's intelligence chief, Alec Stuart, was sitting at the Garden Café in the mid-afternoon sun in what functioned in reality as the governmental center of Nicosia. The old, nondescript House of Representative building and the national hospital complex were behind him; the municipal theater and, beyond that, the Paphos Gate into the old city and the edge of the Turkish zone at the most narrow buffer zone point on the Green Line, flowed off to his left; and the Cyprus Museum faced him directly across the street, lined at this time of day with several tourist buses that illegally, but effectively blocked the road to free-flowing through traffic.

His agent in the Russian embassy's administrative section had just vacated this table as Stuart arrived. The paper the agent signaled would be passed today had been left right where Stuart expected it— between the folds of paper napkins that were kept in a plastic glass on the table of the outdoor café. Having ordered a brandy sour and looked around quickly and professionally to ensure he was not being observed, Stuart took a napkin out of the glass and placed it, accompanying note face down, on the table in front of him. When the drink was delivered, the spy chief flipped over the napkin and stared down at his drink—and at the message now pinned to the table by the base of the brandy sour glass.

"Lukenov's goons have been ticketed to fly to Beirut tomorrow. Wonder what that means. Must be important, or the agent wouldn't have taken the risk of a special and direct message exchange."

This had been quite a day for intelligence gathering, Alec told himself. Just before being summoned to this meeting, he received a report from the agents he had combing the Paphos area for information on the group that was kidnapping important foreigners. The report had included some very interesting information on activity near the plush retirement community on the hillside below the Ayios Neophytos monastery. It would be somewhat ironic if everyone was expending their energies scouring the caves around the old monastery and the terrorists were actually holed up in luxury villas just below.

Alec was drawn in two directions. He very much liked Caitlyn Koniotis and, so, wanted to help Takis rescue her. But he had a professional responsibility concerning this terrorist group. There may be more important issues afoot. There were issues afoot that went far beyond Cyprus. It should be obvious why they took Isaksen away, presumably alive, but killed the rest of those on tour with him in the buffer zone; Isaksen was tied up with peace talks in the Middle East. He decided he would pass on what he knew to the authorities, but not until he was sure of what it was safe to tell them—and that it didn't compromise his own interests. Before leaving the office he had put the report in his briefcase to work on further at home. He had decided he'd deploy more of his agents in place in the Paphos region later in the evening to dig out more useful—and corroborating evidence of terrorist activity that just shouldn't be going on here.

A tourist bus rolled right up on the sidewalk next to Stuart's table in a cloud of blue smoke and began disgorging a group of chatty and minimally clad tourists, who were being herded directly into the Garden Café. Stuart swept the napkin—and note—that were under his brandy sour glass into his open briefcase, downed his drink, signaled for the waiter, and looked at his watch. No time to go directly back to the office now. He had an assignation at the Averof Street house. His legs grew wobbly and the juices started to flow at the mere thought of the tryst that was to come.

* * * *

Despite the repeated, ever-harder psychological body blows Takis Koniotis had been taking in recent days in the deepening "Cyprus Airways brochures" kidnapping case, he could not collapse. In fact, he faced an appointment with the republic's president this very afternoon, and he was not sure that this was not to be the knockout punch. Chances were better than even that the police chief and acting interior minister, Zenon Tenekides, had convinced the president to turn this particular investigation over to the defense establishment and perhaps even to close down the International Investigations Division altogether.

Although Koniotis would fight tooth and nail to keep control of this investigation—to the point that he might end up being fired today, which would not deter him in the slightest from continuing his search for his wife by any means available to him—he had to admit that the government would not be unreasonable if it didn't permit him to head an investigation that involved the kidnapping of his own wife. But then the kidnappers would have won their specific objective in snatching Caitlyn in the first place—to get him off the case just as they had already effectively removed the strong interior minister, Ioannis Herodotou, from the equation.

But regardless of whether or not the president took Takis off this case, it would be a dire mistake to close down the International Investigations Division. What was happening now in Cyprus was proof enough of this. However, Koniotis would face that prospect when he met with the president.

Shortly after Dr. Visiliou telephoned Takis went home and showered and shaved and changed into a clean suit. He then drove back toward the west on Grivas Avenue, turned south on Dem Severi Avenue, and headed out of town. Just before reaching the circle where the growing city of Nicosia met the edge of the old town of Strovolos—and subsequently swallowed that village up—he turned left into the drive up to the presidential palace. Across the avenue, the new, white-marbled Foreign Ministry building towered beside the old, British colonial-styled, ochre-colored stone and red-tile roofed ministry building. Beyond the palace and across the circle were the treed grounds of the prestigious English School.

Takis and Zenon Tenekides sat uncomfortably outside the president's office a good twenty minutes before they were ushered in. Neither man seemed to want to make either eye contact or small talk, and this only served to make Takis more morose at the prospect of what was to come.

The president's visage gave no hint of how bad the situation was as the two men entered the room and walked down the maroon runner to the foot of the chief of state's desk. He was smiling, but, as the Turkish Cypriot leader Rauf Denktash well knew, a smile from this man gave no comfort.

"It's good of you to come, Mr. Koniotis," the president said as he held out his hand, first to Tenekides and then to Takis. "I know the circumstances are not the best. I am gravely concerned for Caitlyn, and we will not fail in any effort and expense to bring her back to us safely."

Takis cringed a moment at the president's use of Caitlyn's given name and at the realization that his wife, now famous for her archaeological work here, knew more important people in his own country than he did. But at this moment, he didn't begrudge her a friendship with the most powerful political force in Greek Cyprus. It could only help to bring her back.

"You're too kind, thank you," Takis responded in a soft voice.

"I know this isn't a good time—and I'll perfectly understand if you wish to withdraw into seclusion—"

"Here it comes," Takis thought. "The ax." And to stave this off if he could for as long as he could, he quickly interjected, "Please, Mr. President. I couldn't just stand by in these circumstances. It simply isn't in me. Please, for your friendship for Caitlyn, let me stay on the job. I know that Caitlyn—"

"I'm quite glad to hear that, Mr. Koniotis," the president interrupted in turn. "Because I can't think of anyone who can bring this to a quick and satisfactory conclusion better or quicker than you can—even with the pressure you understandably are under. And you can maintain leadership in this investigation if you wish. In fact, that will be completely your call if you accept the request I have that brought you here today. I would like you to take over as the national chief of police."

"Excuse me?" Takis muttered. He knew he hadn't heard this correctly. He turned and looked at Zenon Tenekides, who was now acting in the position it sounded like Takis was being offered for signs of surprise or distress. But Tenekides looked quite calm—he even was smiling slightly.

Seeing the shift in Takis's eyes, the president plunged ahead. "I wish you to take over the police chief duties. Then you can handle these kidnapping cases however you see fit. And don't worry about Zenon here. I have already asked him to take over the duties of interior minister upon the unfortunate death of the incumbent."

Shortly thereafter, Takis left the presidential palace teeming with mixed emotions: relief, elation, determination, and a renewed sense of responsibility and the need to move at full speed. His only stipulations, both quickly granted, indeed one already approved, were that Maria Solonos was to be the new chief of the International Investigations Division and that Takis would be permitted to directly supervise this one last investigation.

When Takis pulled his Jaguar out of the drive of the presidential palace and turned its nose north on Dem Severi Avenue for the straight, ten-minute shot into town and to police headquarters, it was with a new determination and a confidence that he and his people would now gain the upper hand. In particular, he was convinced now more than when he had his hunch earlier in the day, that a combination of the information available in the airport and

Petrou Travel Agency databases and from Safa Ziya's check of the recent buffer zone crossings would go far in cracking the backbone of this case. And how did the terrorist band—unless it was able to infiltrate the city and diplomatic community at will—know when and where to strike? There was a key there someplace. Maybe that was what Maria could concentrate on.

* * * *

Alec Stuart barely had time to open the front door of his Averof Street mansion and to cross the threshold, when the door was slammed behind him and he, in turn was pushed up against the doorframe. Suzanne Abu Hani, decked out in a short, black net negligee that was almost completely transparent and accompanied only by a tiny G-string, sandwiched Alec tightly between her own body and the heavy wooden door. He dropped the briefcase where he stood, his surprised and slightly painful expression stifled by her parted lips and searching tongue. His knees turned to rubber and his legs involuntarily bowed in reaction.

By this time, however, Alec had recovered from the unexpected assault and decided to take charge. Smoothly pulling her up by her armpits and lifting her legs with one arm, he shuffled into the lounge. He dropped her full length on the sofa, and, as she was regaining her breath, he stood boldly before her, slowly stripping off his shirt. He momentarily towered over and very close to her, almost menacingly.

Suzanne's eyes slitted with pleasure as she watched Alec's excitement grow. She reached up for him to guide him into her, but he roughly pushed her back down on the sofa with one hand, fiercely ripping the negligee from her body with the other. She laughed huskily as he forced her legs apart with his knees.

Sometime later, as Alec contentedly whistled down the hall toward the shower off his bedroom, Suzanne slipped out into the foyer and quietly snapped open the latch on the brief case he had dropped by the door.

As quiet as the snap of the latch on the case was, however, it was clearly detected by Alec's highly sensitized hearing as he entered the shower, and he immediately identified the source of the sound. In an instant his whole comfortable world snapped as well.

Chapter Twelve

Once more Takis Koniotis's hunches were ringing true. In the early morning hours of Saturday, the first matches between the terrorist name list that had been seized from a Nicosia-based travel agency some months before and the travel databank the International Investigations Division had recently established at Larnaca International Airport and the Limassol port began to fall into synch. The port was chosen as the second location for the installation of the expensive technology because arrivals via tourist ships constituted the second highest number of foreign nationals entering the country. However, even the port received only a small fraction of the number of foreigners that arrived in Larnaca by air in wave after wave of holiday tour flights.

This left the newly designated international airport outside Paphos, on the western tourist coast, uncovered for now. But the police were working on establishing data collection points as fast as possible there as well. In the meantime they weren't telling foreign travelers either that Cyprus had a sophisticated traveler tracking system at Larnaca and Limassol or that the traveler who wanted to hinder detection could still enter and exit the country through Paphos. Of course, foreign visitors could not enter first into the Cyprus Republic from the Turkish sector via the Ledra Palace checkpoint at all. However, anyone who wanted to enter Cyprus illegally need only have access to a boat and not be too susceptible to seasickness. The Mediterranean's third largest island had many miles of unguarded coastline, even though the numerous coastal guard ships steaming in the vicinity made this a gamble.

Koniotis was half dozing, half thinking, feet on desk, a cup half full of tepid coffee suspended dangerously in midair, when Androulla burst into the office. Maria Solonos, perched on the only other chair in the room, was half-heartedly trying to make larger, neater piles of the stacks of papers on floor and desktop within reach of the chair—although she was also principally deep in thought. The rising morning sun, ricocheting off the wall off the workspace of the Homicide Division in the wing adjacent to this one, was trying to invade the room. Rather than providing a cheery atmosphere, however, it served mainly to reveal the heavy dust in the air.

"Takis, we've got some matches from the Larnaca databases on possible terrorist infiltrators," Androulla started off, but then she stopped, in embarrassment, and looked nervously from Koniotis to Maria. "I'm sorry, Chief Koniotis, Ms. Solonos. I guess I was too excited about the information to remember the change in positions here."

"No problem, Androulla." Koniotis warmly responded. "It will always be 'Takis' for you. But I suppose you should give your report to Ms. Solonos now. I will listen in."

"And it continues to be 'Maria' for both of you as well," Maria said with a smile. "And, Takis, you started out leading this investigation, and I know you have a big stake in it, so you will continue to get the reports and call the shots until you decide otherwise."

"Fine with me—but anything else coming in at this point that doesn't seem to be connected to this investigation is yours. What do you have, Androulla?"

"We looked on the tourist agency list of PLO splinter group travelers, as you requested. And we've come up with four others from the list who arrived in Larnaca within several days of the arrival of the known terrorist, Faris Sukkar. Three men, Mamluck al-Turk, Isam Kuraydi, and Salem Qazzar, arrived the same day Sukkar did, the first two from Beirut and the third from Amman. Two days before that, a woman—Widad al-Ghabra—arrived at Larnaca from Paris. And, most interesting of all, the day after the woman arrived from Paris, another man, Abdul Mustada, arrived from Marseilles by ship at Limassol port."

"Marseilles seems to ring a bell, but I don't know why," Koniotis mused. "But, why do you say the ship arrival is the most significant?"

"Precisely because Marseilles rings a bell with you," returned the detective. "Although we already had the added information that this Mustada person arrived on the *Arsinoe*."

"The Piccards again?" Koniotis asked in surprise at the mention of the flagship of that family's shipping line.

"Appears so. The connection of Marseilles and one of the Piccard company's ships rang a bell for us too." Only months previously one of Takis's investigations had uncovered a drug running operation between Cyprus and Marseilles masterminded by the French ambassador to Cyprus, using the shipping company managed by his Cypriot aunt, Eleni Piccard—Caitlyn's mentor in Cyprus.

"So," Androulla continued, "we dug a little deeper and we came to an even more interesting connection between all of these terrorists than that they arrived within days of each other and all were listed by their apparent true names in the Petrou Tourist Agency files."

Both Koniotis and Solonos leaned forward in their chairs. Androulla, looking like the cat who swallowed the canary, continued: "The Piccard family owns more than just the shipping company and the hotels and export handicraft business Eleni Piccard controlled here. Among their holdings is a travel agency, the Thisbe Travel Agency. Our check with the shipping line revealed that Mustada was ticketed through this agency—and, surprise, surprise, our research into all the others we've already identified showed they were ticketed through Thisbe as well—all from the agency's Beirut office."

Maria whistled softly. "So, it looks like the Piccards walked in to take some special travel accounts when we rolled up the Petrou agency. Weren't Eleni Piccard; that French ambassador, Jacques; and Nora Petrou all wrapped up together, Takis?"

"That's right—although Eleni's connections resulted in no more than a wrist slap for her. But at the time we didn't see any possible connection between either of the Piccards and the Petrou Travel Agency. They seemed to have been entirely different threads that had found themselves in the same piece of cloth. I think we'd best review our notes on the earlier investigation after we've tracked down this terrorist band. It looks like we have turned over another very interesting rock. I'll leave this angle of the investigation to you, Maria.

Just let me know if and when you find it folding back into the main investigation."

"Thank you Androulla," both Koniotis and Solonos said almost in unison, signaling that she could withdraw and continue with her digging. But she stood her ground.

"There's something else I thought you'd want pinned down," she said and continued when she had their attention again. "We have exit data only on Sukkar. The others haven't exited with the documents they used for entry, and we now have the Larnaca and Limassol security systems primed to pick them up as soon as they present their documents anywhere."

"Great work, Androulla. Many thanks," praised Koniotis warmly, as the telephone the desk rang.

It was Paul Conte. His arranged meeting this morning at the Ledra Palace Hotel between Koniotis and Ziya had been approved, and he was on his way by to pick Koniotis up.

"Carry on, Maria," said the new police chief, as he rose and moved to the door.

"Just one thing about our job changeover, Takis," Maria broached delicately. "Could we have someone come in and start boxing your old files up to send upstairs? Tenekides has already had his things shipped over to the interior ministry, and I've always wondered something about this office."

Koniotis raised his eyebrows and took on a quizzical expression as the new chief of the International Investigations Division finished her thought. "Your office has always been so untidy that I've long wondered what covered the floor beneath the stacks of old files—what color your floor tile was. If this is my office now, I'd like to know. Couldn't we go ahead and start the switching of offices?"

Koniotis roared with laughter—the first moment the thought of Caitlyn being held captive was not shrouding his every thought—and then walked through the door, calling out: "Adreas, Loris. Your new chief has an unpleasant and dangerous project for you."

* * * *

Meanwhile, across the city's old Venetian walls, in the Turkish Cypriot sector of Nicosia, Chief Inspector Safa Ziya was also making progress on the investigation that would more than justify the time she would spend in going to meet Takis Koniotis this morning on neutral ground at the Ledra Palace Hotel.

She had passed the list of registration numbers for vehicles crossing the Ledra Palace checkpoint around the time of Caitlyn Koniotis's kidnapping to the American embassy's small office in the northern zone the previous evening. These were to be passed to Paul Conte, who, in turn, was to hand them over to Takis Koniotis for inspection. Taking what she had promised to do with these registration numbers one step farther, she, herself, had the vehicle registration numbers matched with the drivers' and passengers' document numbers—taken from either an embassy identification card or a passport—compiled overnight and was just now putting the list, which she had found quite interesting, in her briefcase for review at the coming meeting.

As she was closing her briefcase and rising from her desk, her assistant, Tansul, appeared at the door and breathlessly announced that the switchboard downstairs was even then trying to figure out how to get an overseas call—the caller said he was phoning from Damascus,

Syria, and was afraid the connection wouldn't hold for long—transferred up to Safa's office.

The telephone buzzed, and Safa, filled with curiosity, picked it up.

"Miss Ziya?" queried a hesitant voice in excellent Turkish from far down the telephone line. "Hello? This is Nabil Jallud. May I please speak with Inspector Safa Ziya?"

"This is she. I'm sorry, the connection is not very good. Who did you say you were?"

"Nabil . . . . Mehmet Tosun. I am a merchant. I once had an antique shop near the Turkish checkpoint in Nicosia."

"Ah, yes," answered Ziya. "I remember you. The last time I heard about you, you and your nephew were being pursued by a murderer across the country. We were afraid you both had been killed. Obviously, you managed to evade death. Are you preparing to return to Cyprus? The man who was after you is dead and that case has been satisfactorily closed, but we do have some questions that need to be cleared up concerning your knowledge of that man's activities and about some artifact smuggling activities. And your nephew. We need to know if he really did witness the murder of an American art collector at Othello's Tower in Famagusta. Is your nephew there? Is he well?"

"No, he isn't here—and I don't know if he's well. I'm afraid he may not be . . . that he might be in danger. That's why I'm calling. I'm not planning to return to Cyprus, but I think I do have some information of interest to you in a current investigation and, in return, I need some help from you concerning my nephew."

As Nabil Jallud—for a change a succinct and deeply concerned uncle rather than an unctuous con artist—began to unravel his story, Ziya grabbed a pen and sank back down into her desk chair. She would be late to the meeting with Takis now, but she hoped he would wait for her to arrive. This would explain so much of what was happening.

* * * *

Manuel, the Filipino houseboy who had been hiding in his friend's flat and who had not returned either to the UN coordinator's villa or to his own squalid room since the night of the dinner party for Eric Isaksen, disappeared into the kitchen as his friend opened the door to the Russian.

For a considerable time at the door, the Russian and Manuel's friend argued about whether Manuel was at the flat and whether the Russian would turn over the money to anyone but Manuel. Manuel's friend insisted he didn't know where Manuel was and would not learn about how the money was to get to Manuel for several days. The Russian, however, who was making every effort to see past Manuel's friend and into the flat, said he couldn't give the money to anyone but Manuel. At length, the Russian opened his satchel to prove he had, indeed, brought a large amount of cash—the money Manuel thought was due him for agreeing to spy for the Russian embassy on the UN coordinator's activities. This maneuver got the Russian into the flat, but Manuel still didn't appear, and the argument concerning his whereabouts continued to rage.

After several more minutes, the Russian produced his trump card—two airline tickets, one that he said would get Manuel to

Frankfurt, Germany, and other that would get Manuel's wife all the way from Manila to Frankfurt.

This did the trick. Manuel rushed out of the kitchen area and reached for the tickets.

What followed was an anticlimax, at least in the short term, and, if Manuel had had much intelligence, he certainly would have been suspicious. Of course, if he had had much intelligence, he probably would not be in the bind he now was in.

Upon the appearance of Manuel, the Russian changed tack, handed the satchel and airline tickets to Manuel straight away, and quickly backed out of the door and scurried down the steps.

Manuel and his friend were too busy in their excited, wide-eyed exploration of the satchel to bother to go to the window and observe the departure of the Russian. If they had, they probably would have seen the two men walk briskly toward the entrance to the flat, and they would have had at least a moment or two to prepare for what followed.

* * * *

Takis Koniotis had, indeed, waited in the Treaty Room of the Ledra Palace Hotel past the appointed hour to be sure he could meet with Safa Ziya. In addition to wanting to tell her of his promotion and that she probably would be doing most of her liaising with his replacement, Maria Solonos, from now on—which he didn't think would upset Safa—he wanted to tell her of the breakthrough they were making in identifying the members of the terrorist band. He now was confident that they were, as previously suspected, a combat group of terrorists from some Middle East organization, who probably were put here to train in the mountains and then to start conducting operations that would draw attention to and further the interests of their parent organization.

Conte having stepped away to check in with his embassy, Takis stood, alone, in the empty, cool and damp, stone-walled room and walked over to the huge fireplace and laid his head against the stone mantle. The inaction—the minutes of waiting for Safa to arrive—was tearing him apart. As long as he was busy, on the move, relentlessly closing in on those who held his wife, he could hold the despair and frustration at bay—or at least force it to the back of his mind. Alone, in this dimly lit room, with its windows bricked up as a barrier to bombs being tossed into the center of negotiations on the island's future, he felt like he was in a tomb—and his fears for his wife's safety weighed heavily on him—on him, who was expected to have nerves of steel.

But then, just as he was about to scream out and beat his head on the mantle, she was there. Safa Ziya had finally arrived, and he could push the monsters to the back of his mind again. They both had information to share, which, when melded together, helped clarify the situation significantly and which, if the two police organizations had been forced to continue working separately, probably wouldn't have been too helpful.

With the information Nabil Jallud, calling himself Mehmet Tosun, had given her on the telephone, Safa Ziya was able, not only to confirm Koniotis's theory of the purpose of the terrorist band but also to put a name both to the organization behind the band and to the band itself. Jallud had told her that the band had been dispatched from and was controlled—or had once been controlled—by the fundamentalist terrorist group, the Hizballah, in Beirut—a group that

Isaksen had said was not pleased with the possibility that his mission to the Middle East could arrive at an accord that didn't favor the Hizballah.

One of the sinking feelings Koniotis was getting was that perhaps the band in Cyprus wasn't under the control of a central, politically sophisticated organization anymore, though. Even if the seizure of Isaksen—and possibly even a Russian—could be rationalized, if the effect a group was seeking was focused elsewhere in the region, why had they gone to pains to kidnap Caitlyn? Maybe the control on the band was loose at best; maybe it had been sent here for secret mountain training but had decided to engage in operations on its own. Cyprus had always been treated as neutral ground before. If these operations were part of the intentional planning of one of the mainline terrorist groups, all of the rules were being changed, and Cyprus was being put on the firing line.

Returning to a discussion with Safa, Takis learned that Jallud had also cleared up the significance of the Cyprus Airways brochures that were being left at the scene of operations.

"It relates to the name the band has taken on for itself. What are the initials that have been scrawled on the brochures?"

"MB," answered Koniotis.

"And what is the symbol of Cyprus Airways? It appears in stylized version on its brochures," Ziya continued.

"The mouflon. The mountain goat-like animal that is only found here on Cyprus."

"Right. MB. The band is calling itself the Mouflon Brigade, and it has been leaving us its calling card. Although it's toying with us; it wants to stake a claim on its operations."

"I remember this merchant who called you—the one we knew as Mehmet Tosun and who disappeared from the island. How does he know about what is happening here?"

"That's why he called. He and his nephew—the one who witnessed that murder of the art dealer from Boston—eventually made their way to Beirut, where they were forcibly suborned by the Hizballah. The nephew, Ahmad Jallud, was made to come here as part of the terrorist brigade because he could speak Turkish and had grown up in Cyprus. The uncle has passed the information to us in return for our promise to try to get the boy away from the band alive. But more important than any of this, Takis. The uncle told me that Irina Lukenov was spirited away from Cyprus altogether and is now being held prisoner elsewhere. He was about to tell me where when the line was cut."

"Yes, now it's beginning to fit," said Koniotis. "She may be in Athens. That's where the most recent operation seems to have been, and that's where the ransom demand for her return originated. But, then, maybe not. Maybe that's just a ruse and she's being held somewhere else altogether. Maybe Beirut, where Jallud and his nephew were taken up into this situation, or—where did you say he was calling from?"

"He claimed he was in Damascus, Syria. We don't really have sophisticated enough telephone equipment to pin that down."

"Yes, maybe Syria. But not likely. The Syrians are trying to wipe the Hizballah out. Tehran would be a more likely place—they're playing all of the sides—if not Athens or Beirut. But we can now be fairly certain she's no longer being held in Cyprus. And I wonder if

191

that means Isaksen . . . and . . . Caitlyn are . . . did Jallud say anything about—?"

"No, I'm sorry, Takis. He didn't."

Takis fought back tears of frustration threatening to bubble up in his eyes and returned to his former line of reasoning.

"It seems logical that Irina Lukenov isn't still in Cyprus. Not just because Jallud has said she's someplace else, but also because Mikhail Lukenov himself seems to have lost interest in searching for her in Cyprus. I had no idea why he had changed when he first called his searchers back to Nicosia, but that makes sense now. He appears to have found out as well that Irina had been moved out of the country."

But then Takis's stomach began to churn as his thoughts returned to what this might mean for where Isaksen and Caitlyn were too. Mercifully, however, Koniotis was not permitted the time to worry that concern for very long, as on this cue Paul Conte hurried into the room and announced, "Takis, you'll need to come back right away. The suspect you identified, Faris Sukkar, tried to return from Athens this morning. He's being detained at Larnaca airport."

Koniotis shot out of his chair and toward the door, his thoughts now focused on Sukkar but with enough presence of mind to throw profuse thanks over his shoulder to Safa Ziya for her information—and her help. He had grown up to believe there was nothing good in any Turk. But Safa Siya was something else. Takis could never again completely believe what had been programmed into him.

"No, wait, Takis," Ziya called at his retreating back. "There's more you should know."

"Can't now. I'll have Paul start setting up another meeting as soon as possible, but I've got to get to this Sukkar guy and see what we can pry out of him."

"But, it's about Caitlyn."

That stopped Koniotis dead in his tracks, and he turned back to his colleague.

"Did you have a chance to look at the registration information you requested that I collect from the Turkish Cypriot checkpoint?" And when Koniotis shook his head in the negative, she continued. "The most interesting information I gleaned from my own cursory research into this is that several hours after Caitlyn was kidnapped at Kantara Castle, three vehicles from the Syrian embassy, filled with people who had crossed over on diplomatic visitor's passes, passed from the north to the south. They had entered the Turkish side early the same morning."

Koniotis looked grim, quickly voiced his heartfelt thanks, and was gone. And as he left, he threw Syria back into the mix on what the source of all of this might be.

Chapter Thirteen

Just about the time Manuel and his friend realized there was something funny about both the money in the satchel and the airline tickets Manuel had been given, two men surged into the room. The Russian who delivered the satchel (purposely) failed to close the door completely when he left, and Manuel and his friend were so absorbed in the contents of the satchel that they hadn't bothered to close and lock the door either—although this would have only given them a couple of seconds of respite anyway.

The two burly, mean-looking men had equally mean-looking pistols in holsters at their waists. They immediately demanded to know which of the two was Manuel and, after Manuel's friend quickly provided that information, the friend was invited to go back to his bedroom for a while, and their attention was concentrated on Manuel.

Once having gained the bedroom, Manuel's friend was out of the window, down the side of the building, and three streets away in a flash. If he had stayed around, he would have seen his friend being hustled down the entry staircase and into the waiting automobile below—and it would have been his last view of his friend for all time.

Manuel was taken straight to Larnaca airport and bundled onto the next flight out, which, fortunately for the Filipino, was headed for the barren, remote—but very wealthy—city of Doha, capital of Qatar, where the need for trained domestic servants was so acute that such as Manuel could land a job while waiting in the immigration lounge and without the hassle of having to have a visa to enter the country.

Lukenov had put the kibosh on the quick and dirty solution because he couldn't gauge the backlash possibilities. The fast shuffle solution had resulted from the Russian embassy's cleverness in convincing a highly sensitive and accommodating Immigration Police Division—albeit through one of the UN-affiliated agents rather than directly from the Russian embassy—that Manuel was a particularly embarrassing illegal alien who needed to be disposed of as quickly and quietly as possible. That he was documented to work for UN Coordinator Ingrid Bittmann was acknowledged by the Cypriot intermediary the embassy sent, but the immigration police were told—and had no reason to doubt, considering their views of foreign women—that the UN coordinator had been using Manuel for informal bedroom duty more than for serving guests in the dining room. The intermediary said that the arrangement had gone sour, that Manuel was threatening to go to the press, and that the UN coordinator would like the man off the island posthaste and without fanfare. The intermediaries had noted the embarrassment to Cyprus of recent charges the Philippines consul had made in public on the treatment of Filipino domestics on the island, and the immigration officials became more than happy to help.

As they watched the flight to Doha take off, the two immigration policemen were feeling quite satisfied they had done their country and the UN coordinator a great service in getting rid of useless scum without publicity or unnecessary red tape. They were, perhaps, half right.

* * * *

The cloaks were lifting up and away from her—and the early fingers of sunlight were reaching in to her from between the trees of the glade. The women— her protectors from down through the ages—were drifting away from her, swirling the cloaks around their bodies and fastening clasps at their necks. A smiling Eleni was standing at the edge of the glade, her eyes fixed on Caitlyn's, telegraphing calmness and assurance—and counseling patience. Caitlyn blinked her eyes and when she opened them again, she was alone.

When Caitlyn blinked her eyes again, soft light was filtering into the room through the barred window. Eric Isaksen was still asleep on the other bed. Caitlyn laid her head back on the thin and lumpy pillow and breathed in a shallow rhythm, not wanting to wake the elderly man. She drifted off into half sleep. When she was fully awake again, she realized that the house had been quiet for some time. Eric was sitting on the side of his bed, watching her, and when she too sat up, as silently as she could, they spoke across the narrow aisle between the beds in whispers. They decided that most of the band must be away. Caitlyn fervently hoped they were not off on yet another operation that would result in another hostage. She knew Takis must be frantic with worry, but she also knew that being able to work directly on her rescue would keep him focused and from despair. At least it was a mercy, she mistakenly thought, that he didn't know she was pregnant as well.

After his first night of confusion, Isaksen had been both lucid and comforting. He wasn't at all the cold, disdainful man he had appeared to be to Caitlyn at the UN coordinator's dinner. She now knew, from the torrent of sometimes humorous, sometimes poignant stories he had been telling her about his life and experiences—all related, she knew, to helping them both from stewing about their plight—that he had initially reacted to her the way he did because she had painfully reminded him of the wife he had dearly loved, tragically lost, and sorely missed. They soon were fast friends, and she could not stop herself from thinking ironically that, except for the conditions in which they had been thrown together, these would have been among the most interesting, mind-expanding, and rewarding days she had ever experienced.

Just about the time Caitlyn had gotten up the courage to try to open and peek out of the door into the hallway to see if, by chance, a miracle had been rendered and they had been abandoned and were actually free to go, the door opened before her and the young man who had been kind to them entered.

Caitlyn had not seen him since the first, terrifying night she spent in this room, and she had found she had been worrying about him for no rational reason she could think of. After all, he was one of her captors, just like all the others. But, no, she had to admit that he was not like all of the others.

He had brought a plate of food with him and stood very close to them both, plate in hand, and quickly whispered some instructions. He said his name was Ahmad, that he had been forced to run with this

197

band because he had grown up on the island—on the Turkish side—that most of the band was gone, that the only other guard who was here was asleep in the other bedroom, and that they should immediately and very quietly follow him through the house and to safety. Ahmad then urged the two toward the door, but Caitlyn put her hand on his forearm and, in an insistent whisper, said she had to know what happened that first night and why they had not come for her. Ahmad's eyes filled with tears, and he hung his head in shame. In that instant, Caitlyn fully understood what had saved her that first night, and she started to say something comforting and grateful to the young man.

However, before she could get any words out, there was a stumbling noise and the sound of an obvious curse in Arabic from the hallway.

The young man called Ahmad did an astonishing thing. He turned the plate over toward himself so that the food splattered down the front of his shirt. Then he gave a shove to both of the hostages toward the beds and loudly exclaimed, "So, I'm sorry, Your Highnesses, that our food in this five-star hotel does not satisfy you. Perhaps if you miss this meal, you will appreciate the next one."

He flounced out of the room and started up a jabbering conversation with his comrade in the hallway, which surely covered the plight of both of their misfortunes to be here playing babysitter to a couple of spoiled snobs while the rest of the band was off having fun somewhere.

Caitlyn sat down heavily on the bed, and although she tried to look composed, she could not keep back a sob of frustration. Isaksen sat down next to her, enfolded her in his arms, started a gentle rocking motion, and began yet another of his stories: "This reminds me of the time Anna and I were on a safari at the wildlife park outside Nairobi, and we were served boiled snake for breakfast. Now, this was probably considered a real delicacy in that part of Kenya, but . . ."

Caitlyn calmed down almost immediately—partly because of the distracting story Eric was spinning for her, but more because she remembered back to the dream she was having before Ahmad opened the door to her prison. Eleni, in her dream, had signaled to her it would all be OK. And that was all the strength Caitlyn needed. Ahmad's arrival had just been a sign that Caitlyn and Eric were not alone and forsaken.

* * * *

Mikhail Lukenov sat in the uninviting upper-floor cafeteria of the uninviting main terminal of Larnaca International Airport and watched with satisfaction the two burly immigration policemen watch with satisfaction from the nearby outside observation platform the departure of Manuel for Doha. At least this particular plan seemed to have gone well, Lukenov thought.

The planning of the main chance—the liberation of his wife in Beirut and the very public punishment of her Hizballah captors—was not going as well. The five "enforcers" he was sending out on the scheduled 2:20 PM MEA 262 flight to Beirut were not gone yet, and it was already nearly 4 PM. When the small, inadequately staffed Russian embassy in Beirut learned from an informant that Irina was being held in a shop there near the waterfront, Lukenov immediately pulled his people back from the search parties in Cyprus, took over the planning of her liberation in Beirut, and was sending his own men to accomplish this task—with as much noise and bloodshed among the Hizballah as possible.

He was careful about the flight booking of his men, so as not to draw attention to his operation. The embassy travel office booked all five separately through different travel agencies, and they all arrived for airport check-in separately and at different times. They were even dressed differently, so it didn't look like they were all traveling for the same purpose. Everything swiftly and flawlessly organized, and, yet, here—or rather, there, down in the departure lounge—they still all sat waiting for the plane to take off—and with each minute that went by, they were finding it harder and harder not to reveal that they, essentially were all Russian goons cut from the same cloth.

The plane was also sitting there, out on the tarmac, serviced and ready to pull up to the jetway. Something was wrong, and these men had to get to Beirut very soon. The deadline on the ransom note that had been left at the assassination site in Athens was quickly approaching, and Lukenov took the threats of the Hizballah very seriously. He could punish the Hizballah regardless—but he wanted his wife back, safe.

Lukenov looked at another man at a table not far away and signaled ever so slightly. The two met in the upper-floor men's room, and Lukenov passed on a terse instruction and returned to his table. Several minutes later, the other man returned and the two just happened to find themselves standing next to each other out on the observation deck.

By flashing his credentials in the right place, the other Russian embassy official had found out that MEA 262 had been grounded because there had been a bomb threat against the plane. The inspection of the plane was just about completed, and the passengers were expected to be boarded within half an hour.

A bomb threat? Could it be a coincidence? But Mikhail Lukenov had not remained alive because he believed in coincidences and did not take all necessary precautions. He issued another string of orders and returned to the cafeteria line for another cup of terrible coffee.

The other embassy official descended the stairs, went out into the parking lot, and quickly talked with three drivers, who, in turn took out their airport passes, clipped them to their breast pockets, and started fanning out toward the tarmac beyond the terminal building.

This precaution turned out to be one of Lukenov's better thoughts of the day, for at that precise moment, a figure in camouflage gear had just finished clipping through the wire fencing at the southeastern end of the main runway, just where it met the Mediterranean, and was carefully crawling through the scrub alongside the runway, across the concrete runway strip from the airport complex. It was slow going even though the fully loaded experimental B-300 Light antiarmor weapon he was hauling only weighed nineteen kilograms. The rocket launcher, which was certified effective to a 400-meter range was still officially listed as in the developmental category by the Israelis, but it had been deployed in the Lebanese theater for over a year.

The documentation the man carried—as insurance—also identified him as an Israeli. His name on the documents was Joseph Berkowitz, and he had an Israeli passport in his pocket in that name showing he had entered Cyprus from Tel Aviv the previous evening. The entry slip in his passport listed his contact address in Cyprus as the heavily barricaded Israeli embassy at 4 Gryparis Street in Nicosia. His only job while in Cyprus was to knock MEA 262 out of the sky— along with the Russian goons it would be carrying.

He proceeded to concentrate on this job forty minutes later, as MEA 262 came roaring down the runway toward him and lifted slowly into the air. With the newly developed, heat-seeking B-300, the large passenger airplane was almost impossible to miss at this distance and angle. And, since this particular weapon was outfitted with the augmented HEFT—a High Explosive Follow-Through round, which blows a hole in its target with the first charge and then sends a secondary charge through the hole and into the target's interior, there wasn't much hope for MEA 262 and its passengers.

Except that, just after the man lifted the B-300 to his shoulder and pressed the trigger of the weapon, one of the Russian embassy drivers blew two very neat holes in the back of his head. The recoil from the head shots caused "Berkowitz" to drop the angle of the B-300 just as it fired, which resulted in the weapon's heat-seeking rocket locking onto a nearly full fuel truck sitting in an isolated spot on the tarmac across the runway as its target of first choice. The resulting fireworks were more visually impressive—and gave the Russian embassy driver plenty of time to melt back into the landscape unnoticed—than even the hit on MEA 262 would have been. But the human carnage quotient was very disappointing.

* * * *

Takis Koniotis drove up to the front of the airport just as Mikhail Lukenov was crossing the road to the parking lot. They both gave surprised looks, and Koniotis noticed that Lukenov looked a little defensive. Also, he saw the diplomat exchange looks with his driver—

who gave a curt nod—that Koniotis found much too suspicious. But the new national police chief had several more important matters facing him at this instant than grilling Lukenov about what he knew about this terrorist group that had prompted him to withdraw from the search for his wife within Cyprus. Maybe Lukenov knew something about Caitlyn's whereabouts as well and just wasn't sharing that information.

Yes, he would have to put some pressure on Lukenov. The Russian should quite easily be able to understand Koniotis's frustration over the kidnapping of his wife. They were in exactly the same boat. Lukenov just didn't look as worried about that as Takis felt.

But first, he had to interrogate the detained terrorist suspect, Faris Sukkar. Chances were very good that Sukkar had been part of both the kidnappings of Irina Lukenov and Eric Isaksen and the assassination of the Russian embassy employee in Athens.

No, unfortunately that couldn't be first now that he was the national police chief, Koniotis thought bitterly. The fuel tanker fire had been both spectacular and frightening from the distance as he drove between the large salt lake and the Mediterranean-bordered airport complex. He first had to check what that was about and see if he was needed.

But that didn't turn out to be the real "first thing" he did as he entered the airport terminal. With a bank of telephones being the first thing he saw as he entered, on impulse he walked over, slipped his telephone card into one of the public telephones, picked up the receiver, and dialed the number of the Syrian embassy in Nicosia. Identifying himself by his new title, he asked to be connected through to Ambassador Munir Nahlawi, only to be talking to the ambassador's wife, who said Nahlawi had been out of town for three days. She was evasive, however, about the ambassador's specific whereabouts and whether he was in Cyprus or abroad, and she claimed not to know anything about the visit of a large group of off-island Syrian diplomats or about the use of embassy vehicles to go into the Turkish Cypriot sector and back. The follow-up call to the embassy's chargè met with similar evasion and an uncertainty when the ambassador would be available to talk with the chief of police.

"Well, you can tell Ambassador Nahlawi that he should be prepared to talk directly to the Cypriot foreign minister on Monday morning and be ready to answer some questions concerning possible Syrian embassy support for terrorist acts in Cyprus."

This sobered the diplomat up considerably, but it didn't give Koniotis all that much satisfaction—nor did banging the receiver down on the telephone.

He then started off to begin the interrogation of Sukkar, but that was destined to be put off yet again. When he identified himself at the airport police office, a worried-looking official told him they had just found a body and a rocket launcher—the probable source of the fuel tanker fire—out near the runway and that, since the identification they found on the body was that of an Israeli national, the airport police were in immediate need of his guidance.

Koniotis called Maria Solonos in Nicosia and told her she and a crew needed to get down to the airport on the double to take up her first investigation as International Investigations Division chief, and he then turned to looking at the body and contents of the dead man's clothing.

"Much too obviously Israeli," Koniotis concluded at the end of the search. "This has all the markings of a setup. Have fingerprints ready for the Nicosia crew as soon as they arrive and tell them they need to check the prints as soon as possible through the Israelis—not telling them specifically what we have here—and Interpol."

"Now I wonder what he really was after. I doubt he was out there to sink a fuel vehicle. I wonder what his real target was. And I wonder who shot him and why. And I wonder how Mikhail Lukenov fits into all of this."

Turning to the chief of the airport police, Koniotis said, "Please have a list of all planes that departed and left within fifteen minutes of the explosion of the fuel tanker—I want to know where they were bound for—and I want to see their passenger manifests."

And, as he moved down the hall for his first dance with Faris Sukkar, Koniotis thought half aloud, "With Lukenov having been there, I wonder whether this really is a totally new case for Maria, or whether it is just another worrisome wrinkle of the antics of the Mouflon Brigade."

Chapter Fourteen

MEA 262 landed in Beirut from Larnaca several hours late after nearly no time in the air late that Saturday, although very few of the disgruntled passengers on the aircraft realized how lucky they were to have survived the flight at all.

The airplane had been buffeted by the air waves from the explosion of the fuel truck on the Larnaca tarmac and all had heard the explosion. But the pilot of the MEA 262, with the cockpit crew being the only ones on board who could see the flames below, had quickly assured his passengers over the sound system that everything was fine—that they had just hit an air pocket at the same time one of the fighter planes from the airstrip at the nearby British sovereign base at Akotiri had broken the sound barrier. If he had suspicions about why the fuel vehicle had burst into flames, he was keeping these suspicions to himself. As it was, he held his breath for nearly the entire thirty-minute, sixty nautical-mile trip from Cyprus to Lebanon.

The five Russian agents from Cyprus merged again immediately after having cleared customs and were met and swept away in two automobiles to the Russian embassy. After a short, but intense briefing at the embassy, the five and a guide descended via three separate routes on the copper and souvenir shop near the Beirut cornice that was supposedly owned by Anwar Jabril.

The street was deathly quiet. No one was about and the coffee shop across from the souvenir shop was closed, its tables turned with tops toward the establishment's windows in an apparent effort to keep the table tops dry in anticipation of a late-evening rain. The street was entirely too quiet. But this section of the city was not frequented by the guide from Moscow's embassy in Beirut and the men from Cyprus had never been to Beirut before—so their suspicions were not aroused.

A small alleyway, hardly large enough for a grown man to pass through, ran down the eastern side of Jabril's shop. Four of the Russians disappeared down this alleyway, being careful that they could not be seen from the shop's interior, and they fanned out in two different approaches to the back of the shop. The two Russians who had approached the shop from the west stopped just short of the front of the souvenir shop and hugged the wall, almost within reach of the shop's glass front door. Two of the men who had entered the alley continued down the side of the building, turned to the left, and crouched beside the shop's rear door. The other two Russians deftly climbed up the side of the building and swung around to the balcony that ran across the front of the shop on the floor above.

At a prearranged signal from the mission leader on his handheld radio, the Russians stormed the building from three different directions. Those who crashed through the front jumped in opposite directions and hit the deck as they entered. If the noise from the breaking glass of the panels slid across the front of the shop at night had not been enough to surprise and alert the Hizballah terrorists in the back of the building, the sound of two bodies skidding through copperware, on one side, and pottery, on the other, would have done the trick. The entry of the rear-guard team, splintering through the flimsy wooden back door, and the crash through the glass window above into a storeroom filled with porcelain dishes only added to the noise, a noise that was designed to immobilize the terrorists for the brief moment it would require to obtain the upper hand in the attack.

But the Hizballah terrorists weren't immobilized, and the Hizballah terrorists didn't seem particularly surprised. There was no evidence anyone was there at all. But there, there in the light of a flickering candle, back through two doorways and near the back of the building, the mission leader, who had been one of the pair who had come through the front door, could see something or someone. He lifted his assault rifle and started to squeeze the trigger. But in his night-vision targeting scope he obtained enough of a sense of familiarity with the target to stay his hand. He checked his firing but did not lower his rifle.

The figure was moving ever so slightly in the bonds that kept it pinned tightly to a chair. The mission leader circled cautiously around the room, motioning both the man on his right and his other comrades who were appearing from other areas of the building to remain where they were.

Yes, as he moved a bit closer, he became sure they had, indeed, found Irina Lukenov. The figure had a blanket thrown over its head, but the clothes he could see on the figure matched the description the searchers had been given of what the Lukenov woman had been wearing when she first disappeared. He reached over and lifted up the edge of the blanket, but just as he was at the point of a positive identification, he tripped the wire and the explosives under the woman's chair carried her, the Russians, and millions of bits and pieces of the best souvenirs Lebanon had to offer up into the sky over Beirut.

It had been the Hizballah operations chief Ibrahim's special plans for the merchant Anwar Jabril, whose real name was Nabil Jallud, that had led to the destruction of the Russians. Ibrahim had never found out for sure for himself that Jallud had betrayed the whereabouts of Irina Lukenov to the Russians, but he had gotten a telephone call from the brigade in Cyprus the previous morning that tipped him off that the Russians had stopped searching for the woman there and had booked a team on a flight to Beirut. This had clicked with the disappearance of Jallud the night before.

It had been customary for Jallud to take off at midnight after he had gone to Friday prayers and to spend much of the rest of Saturday, from the previous midnight to Saturday noon or later, playing cards and drinking with some of his old cronies several streets away. He sometimes didn't reappear at his shop until Sunday, leaving his not-too-bright woman shop assistant to watch over the shop.

If Ibrahim had not decided it was time to dispense with the services and suspicions of the irritatingly obsequious and stupid merchant and hadn't sent one of his men to check on Jallud and to waylay and make his killing look like a street robbery when he was returning from his weekly outing, Ibrahim may not have made the connections that told him the Russians were coming to Beirut and probably knew precisely where the woman was being held. The assassin had not found Jallud with his cronies, and he had been told that Jallud had even been missing from the Friday prayers.

The conclusion had been obvious. Jallud had betrayed the Hizballah, and the Russians sent to rescue the woman needed to be seen as getting her killed instead—as an example that the Russians weren't smarter than he was.

There was only one loose end in this part of the operation, Ibrahim thought, as he watched the first brigade try to contain the inferno across the street from his vantage point from inside the barricaded coffee shop. They needed to track Jallud down. This had all been just an off-the-cuff exercise by The Asp, anyway, so there was nothing lost in the short term by the loss of leverage of the hostage. But Jallud had betrayed them, and he must die. His nephew, who was with the band in Cyprus, must die as well, of course, but that had always been the plan. He could rely on The Asp to take care of that. But Jallud. Jallud was his. They had someone in the Russian embassy. They would have to start finding out where Jallud had gone.

* * * *

It was meant to be déjà vu all over again. She spent the day on the black sands of Pissouri Beach. When the afternoon sun had reached its peak, she retreated to the same first-floor of the Colombia Pissouri Beach hotel room she had taken before and popped into the shower. And, as she heard the rustling outside the veranda door, she wrapped the thin negligee around her body and turned her back to the sun. But there the similarity ended.

With a rough, painful jerk of her shoulder, Abdul spun Suzanne around to face him. She was used to this form of foreplay. She was momentarily nonplussed that he was fully clothed, but, ever adaptable, she reached down and unbuttoned his trousers with one hand and went trawling with the other.

With one swipe, The Asp knocked Suzanne's hands away while he shoved her back onto the bed. Recovering quickly, Suzanne gave a husky laugh, scooted farther up on the bed, threw aside her negligee, and opened her legs wide in invitation.

The Asp just stood there, hands on hips, obviously not interested.

For the first time that afternoon Suzanne began to feel fear. Abdul was a wild, crude animal. There was no doubt about that. But she had always been able to control him with sex. She had always been able to control any man with sex—at least any man who was a man. What was wrong? What had changed? And what might Abdul do to her if she couldn't drive him crazy with lust?

"Is he dead? Did you do it?" The Asp demanded.

"No, not yet. Don't look at me that way. I'll do it. You know I'll do it. I just haven't had an opportunity. besides, they wouldn't like that in Beirut. He's part of the network. Why, anyway do you—?"

"I have to answer to him here in Cyprus. I shouldn't have to do that. I should be head of the Cyprus operations."

"Ayman head the Cyprus operations."

"No, you husband controls far more than that. Cyprus itself is of little concern to him."

Suzanne tried a different tack. "You don't want me to get caught, do you? Where would you be without the information I've been giving you? What's the matter? Come here."

In an effort to change his mood, she cupped one of her breasts in one hand and slowly ran the other hand down and across her belly.

No effect. "And do you have information for me now?" was all he said.

"No, I'm sorry." She sat upright on the bed, within easy reach, teasing him. "No, not true, there *is* something. Your fighter who was captured reentering the country. He's been moved to Nicosia, but I don't think he's said anything yet. He's Lebanese, so they have to let my husband know what's going on. I understand he's tried to commit suicide a couple of times."

"We must see that he succeeds," said The Asp grimly with a faraway look in his eyes.

"I'm working on that," Suzanne answered, trying to please the terrorist.

"I want to know how he was detected coming into Cyprus. Work on that too."

There was no question that it was a command rather than a request.

"What else have you learned?" he continued.

"I've not had the opportunity to gather anything else. I can't be seen as withdrawing from my social duties. Call me late tomorrow. I'll plan on being home by midnight. Ayman and I have been invited to a reception at the presidential place before that; Koniotis is scheduled to be there in his new capacity as police chief. By then I hope to have had the opportunity I need. In any case, I should be able to pick up more information at the reception."

"See that you do. I would hate to lose one as beautiful as you." And at last Suzanne saw the rising spark of desire that she had expected to see as a full raging flame when he first entered the room. With a swift motion, he wrapped both hands around her head, lacing his fingers through her flowing hair, and pulled her to him. But, when she was finished and reclined on the bed in anticipation of the next event, he buckled up, turned, and was gone, back through the veranda door.

Swiftly descending the latticework by the service court, The Asp moved boldly to his four-wheel-drive sedan—or rather to the sedan he had liberated from one of the elderly couples of the Leonides Village villas above Paphos. He didn't seem to care if he was being observed, as he roared away from the coast and turned west on the highway leading to Paphos. And, as a matter of fact, he *was* being observed.

Willie Hamilton, the star political reporter of the *Cyprus Mail* was an expert at surveillance. He had watched the whole performance from the edge of the beach road with his binoculars. He had figured a few things out—by sifting and analyzing succeeding events through the double-angled view that the observations of the servant Manuel and of he himself had provided at the UN coordinator's fateful dinner party. Two and two had added up to Suzanne Abu Hani as having passed information to the terrorist group that had kidnapped Eric Isaksen and Caitlyn Koniotis. And one look at The Asp had convinced Hamilton that he had seen the actual linkup—a far more insidious political linkup than that of the sexual act his binoculars had revealed to him.

Hamilton managed to tail the sedan in his red Morris Mini all of the way through Paphos and up into the hills, through the small villages of Emba and Tala to the Leonides housing estate. When The Asp pulled into the retirement village, Hamilton continued on up the slope as if he were going to the nearby Ayios Neophytos monastery.

213

But on the hillside overlooking the retirement villas, Hamilton parked his Mini over the rise and walked back to the edge of the road, where he looked down into the complex.

The sedan he sought was pulling up into a cul-de-sac of four darkened villas in the southeastern corner of the complex. His quarry got out of the sedan and went into one of the houses. Hamilton put his binoculars up to his eyes and moved closer to the edge of the road, searching for signs of activity around the four houses. As he did so, his foot hit something soft, but large, and Hamilton pitched out over and down the slope.

* * * *

As Maria entered her new, larger—and clean—office thanks to the efforts of the special demolition team, the telephone rang. Takis Koniotis was standing at one side, staring out of the window, apparently admiring the scarred and fissured wall of the Homicide Division next door. The telephone didn't faze him a bit. He was lost in thought. He hadn't managed to extract any information from the terrorist Faris Sukkar as yet. Koniotis was more convinced now than ever that Sukkar was responsible for the killing of the Russian embassy clerk in Athens. If so, he must be one of the senior members of the band. Sukkar had been brought to Nicosia on Koniotis's instruction, although almost no one had been told of this, and Takis went into the cell to interrogate Sukkar nearly every hour. The man was tough as nails. He had already tried to commit suicide more than once, and the constant questioning did not seem to have taxed him overly much as yet. But he was one of the keys to this case, one of the only keys Koniotis held—and he *would* break.

Maria picked up the telephone and listened for a short while. She voiced her thanks and replaced the receiver.

"Takis," she said, and then, when he didn't respond, she raised her voice. "Takis, you'll want to hear this."

He turned, no longer lost in thought.

"That was Androulla, calling from the lab. They've just finished comparing fingerprints on the body at the airport with those from the Interpol records. It seems I still don't have a case of my own. The supposed Israeli who was shot in the rocket attack is one of our terrorists in the band here in Cyprus. We now know where Isam Kuraydi is."

"Somehow it all fits," Takis said in a flat voice. "I've just about figured it out, I think." And he turned back to the window.

* * * *

Willie Hamilton painfully got up and brushed himself off. He hadn't fallen far down the embankment and was just dazed. He still held the binoculars in his hand. He jiggled them gingerly and was rewarded with an ominous tinkling sound.

"Damn."

He wondered what he had tripped over. It didn't take long to find out. He pulled himself up the incline he'd fallen down and in the brush at the edge of the road he found a man's body. Hamilton, a former British army officer who was unaffected by the sight of death, rolled the body over.

"Dead at least a day; throat cut," he thought. "Wait, I know this man. I've seen him with someone. Yes. Alec Stuart. I've seen him with Alec Stuart."

And then Hamilton remembered his own purpose for being on the hillside. He stood and put the binoculars to his eyes. One of the lenses was still intact. He panned over the cul-de-sac below. Nothing. Not even the sedan his quarry had arrived in. But he heard a car. On the hillside above him, moving up past the Ayios Neophytos monastery, on the overland road to the distant town of Polis on the isolated northwestern Chrysochou Bay. It was too late to follow.

But why had whoever had been in the car stopped at the villa below? This was very near the area they had been searching for the band for days. Hamilton somehow knew that those four villas figured in the equation. He returned to the Mini and drove down toward the cul-de-sac. There didn't seem to be any activity there. Parking the automobile on a nearby street, he cautiously approached from the rear of the villa the man had entered. When Willie was sure all was still quiet, he entered the villa through the open patio doors. No one was there. He looked through at the rooms. In the smaller of the two bedrooms, he picked up a distinctive, familiar scent. Caitlyn Koniotis. Her own intriguing perfume.

"She's been here. I'm sure of it. But where is she now? And what do I do now?"

A more intense search of the house revealed that he had not initially been correct. Someone *was* still there. To be precise, two someones. When he reached the stairway in the kitchen leading down to the small basement heating room, Willie was hit with that old, sickening battlefield stench of death. He momentarily feared he had found Eric Isaksen and Caitlyn Koniotis, but his grim inspection revealed the remains of an elderly couple. "The owners of the villa, no doubt."

216

Hamilton returned to the lounge, took out his ever-present flask of brandy, and drank down two hefty slugs.

"What a mess they left this room in," he thought in a purposeful effort to redirect his attention from the cellar. He picked up a wine bottle from the floor in front of the sofa and set it on a side table. "Pity it's empty; it's a good vintage. Too good for the pigs who have been living in here."

But he couldn't divert his thoughts from reality for very long. Up until now he had pursued this story on his own. But these people obviously meant nasty business, as evidenced by the body on the hillside and the two in the basement, if one discounted those who had been killed during the kidnapping operations. Up to now this had primarily been just another story, albeit one of his more dangerous assignments, and up to now he had not shared what he found out with the authorities—as was his usual method of operation.

But in the brief moment when he thought it was Caitlyn Koniotis who was dead down there in the basement, the full import of the situation hit him. Once before, not long ago, he had kept what he knew about a developing story to himself and it had almost gotten him killed. It had been Takis Koniotis who had swept in and saved not only him, but his wife, Ginger, as well. And, when both he and Ginger could have been prosecuted for their involvement in the case, Takis Koniotis had kept them out of the courts.

No, this time he would go no further. This time he would call in Takis. He leaned over and picked up the telephone. But, in accomplishing this maneuver, he had to turn to face the entry door. In sudden shock, he realized he was not alone. The hand holding the receiver froze in midair.

* * * *

The next telephone call was for Takis. Alec Stuart was on the line and was insisting on talking to Takis and only Takis. He had not heard from the agent he placed near the Leonides village site, and he was worried. He decided he'd gone long enough—probably too long—in not telling Koniotis how he knew what he knew, although he saw no reason to reveal how long he had known it. Koniotis was too energized by the information to ask. Thanking Stuart profusely for the lead that the band of kidnappers might be holed up in an isolated section of the Leonides Village complex, Koniotis began making telephone calls of his own, ordering up helicopter support and mobilizing men.

Koniotis was already out the door when the third telephone call came through. A worried Maria Solonos caught up with him in the parking lot to let him know they had just been informed Irina Lukenov probably had been killed with explosives—along with those who were trying to rescue her—in a Beirut shop. They couldn't identify anything as human remains yet, but the Russian embassy in Beirut had acknowledged what had been planned in the way of rescuing Irina, and the Hizballah in Beirut was already publicly gloating over the explosion. Koniotis asked Solonos to try to keep the connection between Irina Lukenov and the Beirut bombing out of the Cypriot media for as long as possible.

Koniotis had already pieced together what was probably in the works in Beirut. This situation revealed two very disturbing and frightful facts to Koniotis, facts that spurred him on to try to find the terrorists and their hostages as soon as possible. Not only were the terrorists ruthless in their disregard for and use of their hostages, but also someone with very good connections was supplying the brigade with vital information. They had known where to strike to obtain useful hostages, and they had known a Russian team was going to Beirut and when and by what means. If he could maintain limits on who in Cyprus knew Irina Lukenov was already dead, perhaps some slipup would lead him to the source of the information.

He briefly talked with Maria before he left for the helicopter pad. He was going to try to get to the Paphos area in time, but she must stay behind. Hers was perhaps the most important job now. She had to find out who was passing information to the terrorist band and stop up the damaging leak.

Unfortunately, neither Koniotis nor Solonos were in the office to receive the fourth telephone call, or that important question would have been answered.

* * * *

Willie Hamilton slowly put down the telephone receiver, as the *Simerini* columnist Demetris Mattas walked into the room.

"How long have you been here, Mattas?" Hamilton growled.

"Longer than you have. And longer than the man who left before you arrived. But not, apparently, as long as the man you found dead up on the road. I have been watching this house for most of the day. It seems my leads paid out just as yours did, but, alas, not in any more timely fashion than yours did."

"What have you seen?"

"Well," the columnist answered, "although I've been cooling my heels on the hills above for much longer than you did, I didn't really see anything more than you did. The arrival of the man in the automobile down at the house and you in the Mini up on the hill road were the first action I saw here. And then I watched you tumble down the hill and climb back up and the man drive off. And if I wasn't such a decent fellow and had not been concerned whether you had hurt yourself, I would now be following the other man and would be closer to the story than you are. Then I watched you discover the body on the hillside and then come down here to the house. I suppose no one else is here?"

"No one who could help you with your column, certainly," Hamilton responded dryly—and then took another swig from his brandy flask to counter the dryness.

"And, so, where does that leave us?" Mattas asked sweetly, as he settled down on the arm of an overstuffed chair.

"Well, I've decided it's time to call in the authorities," answered Hamilton firmly. "I owe it to both Takis and Caitlyn—not to mention whoever belongs to the bodies in the basement."

Mattas lifted his eyebrows, but he stayed on the main course. "Don't let me stop you. And if you get through, let me talk to Maria Solonos as well."

But they did not get through to either Koniotis or Solonos, although another detective took the information, noted to Hamilton that Koniotis had just received the information from another source and was on his way, and told Hamilton to stay where he was.

Willie did not tell the detective about Suzanne Abu Hani being the link to the terrorist band. The involvement of an ambassador's wife made the whole issue very sensitive. He didn't want Mattas to hear that part of the information—both because both newsmen knew they were still competing for a story and because Hamilton knew that Mattas had once been involved with Suzanne himself. And Hamilton also wanted to save this important information for Koniotis's ears alone. He knew Koniotis would be angry—justifiably angry—with him for not having reported the information hours ago, and Hamilton wanted to have a significant peace offering to deflect the police chief's ire.

As Hamilton replaced the receiver, Mattas stood up, yawned, stretched, and sauntered toward the door.

"Hey, where are you going?" Willie barked. "The police told us to stay here until Koniotis arrived."

"Point of order," Mattas countered. "The police told *you* to stay here. You didn't even mention to them that I was here as well. And, as it happens, this wasn't my only lead. See you later."

Hamilton rose and followed Mattas out of the door. "Sorry, Mattas, but where thou goest, I will go also. What other lead?"

"The man you were following took the road toward Polis. This wasn't the only place I was told the terrorist band could be holed up. One of my informants told me the police found out that three Syrian embassy vehicles crossed the checkpoint both ways the day Caitlyn Koniotis was kidnapped, and there hasn't been any better theory I've heard on how the band got out of the Kyrenia Mountains and back on the Greek side without being detected. And another one of my informants told me the Syrian ambassador, Munir Nahlawi, and several Greek Cypriot businessmen have frequently been seen going up into the mountains around the Kykko monastery—near a Troodos mountain village named Chakistra. Chakistra, significantly enough, is not far from Vroisha, where the band hid out after grabbing the Russian diplomat's wife."

"So, we're going up to Chakistra to see if that's where our mystery man has gone and to see if he links up with Syrian ambassador?" Hamilton asked, with the excitement of the chase in his voice. He presumably knew better than Mattas that there might be a link. He knew there already was a link between the terrorists and Suzanne Abu Hani—and that there was a love-nest link between Suzanne and the Syrian ambassador.

"Well, at least *I'm* going up. I've got a four-wheel drive vehicle, which will be required to reach Chakistra from this side of the mountains. Your old Mini won't even get close."

This set up yet another mystery for Takis Koniotis when the helicopters descended into the Leonides Village complex. Where had Hamilton gone, and why was his Mini still here, parked just one street over from the four houses the terrorist band had abandoned? With the number of bodies the police found around the area, it was clear the band had been here—and, although, not finding Hamilton among them, Koniotis feared for the little bull dog, who Koniotis couldn't help but liking.

This fear was not misplaced. When Mattas and Hamilton reached the Chakistra area very much later that night, they split up to search for signs of the band. It was Hamilton who found what they were searching for first, although Mattas had come within sight of Hamilton in time to see him being marched off into the mountain forest at gunpoint by no less than Syrian ambassador Nahlawi himself.

A distraught Demetris Mattas—now, as Hamilton had experienced hours before, in full realization that this was not a game and that he was in deeper trouble and graver personal danger than he could ever have imagined he would be—did make it back to his vehicle undetected. But his nerves were clearly shot as he tried to drive up to the Kykko monastery to link up with the asphalt road that would bring him down to the police station in one of the larger mountain villages—Pedhoulas or Prodomos. For that reason, he hadn't made it much past the peak on which the monastery was perched before he took a curve at too great a speed and crashed over the side and down the isolated mountainside.

* * * *

Faris Sukkar had expected the detective to come to his cell again long before now. He feared that man fiercely. He knew that his fear must be so strong that the interrogator surely could smell it on him. He also knew that the last woman they took—the woman with the blond hair who seemed so calm and in control even though she was nauseous much of the time—was the policeman's wife. This gave the detective added power over him. He knew that Cypriots normally were not brutal, but they prized their families highly. Sukkar knew what *he* would do if he got his hands on someone who held *his* wife hostage, and he expected the detective to let loose and tear him limb from limb at any moment.

Many times over the past day he had been on the brink of telling the detective all. It was at these times he desperately looked for some way to kill himself. He was dead already; his body just didn't know it yet. Either these Cypriots would kill him, or he would be returned to Greece and they would kill him—or, worst of all, the Russians would get hold of him and kill him. But, no, the worst of it was that he could never go back to his comrades even if he were to escape. They too would kill him. And rightly so. He had failed in his mission, and they could never trust him again even if he managed to return.

But he still could not understand how he had failed. How had they managed to pull him out of the immigration line at Larnaca? How did they know his true name? He knew his forged documents were good—and they had gotten him in the country and back out again before without incident. If he could do nothing else but get to his comrades one more time to warn them about the danger at immigration control, he then could die in peace.

What miracle had prevented the detective from coming in again this evening? Sukkar knew that if the detective had come again this evening, he could not have held out any longer. And there were no avenues of suicide left to him here. They had stripped him and his cell of everything he could have used. He even had failed to eat his supper—it was still sitting on the table by the door—with the thought that he would starve himself to death. But that was silly. That would take too long. No, it was probably hunger that had weakened his resolve. Perhaps if he ate he would regain the strength he needed to resist the detective's relentless interrogation. Perhaps it was a sign that he had not come back again this evening.

Sukkar shuffled over to the table by the door, picked up the bowl—no utensils had been provided—and went back to the pallet on the floor. He shoveled one mouthful from the bowl and then another. Before the second mouthful had gone done his throat, he began to gasp and choke. The guard, who had been watching everything through a two-way mirror in the door, had the iron door open quickly, but Sukkar was dead before his head hit the floor.

Chapter Fifteen

One of the most beautiful and peaceful views to be had in Cyprus is that from the heights of the village of Dhrousha. Located in the center of the least-visited western quadrant of the island, Dhrousha occupies the highest point of the Akamas Peninsula. Standing in one of the high meadows of the village, with its buildings made out of native fieldstone and roofed with twigs and looking to the east over a valley of small, walled family plots where the cultivation of grapes and almond trees predominated, one can take in one of the most unusual sights of Cyprus—mile upon mile of pine and cedar trees planted on the western slope by the former British colonial administration in an effort to reforest an island that had lost its lush forests centuries earlier to foraging sheep and goats and to the navies of various Mediterranean sea powers. To the west, across Lara Beach, with its natural giant sea turtle hatcheries, stretched the blue Mediterranean. But the most breathtaking view of all was directly northward, across the ancient city state of Polis and over the semicircular Chrysochou Bay.

It was to this scenic village of Dhrousha that the Mouflon Brigade had taken their "guests," Caitlyn Koniotis and Eric Isaksen, when they hurriedly left the enclave of retirement villas in Leonides Village, a half hour's drive to the south. They chose Dhrousha for its view, but not because they were sightseers.

The band's second in command, the woman, Widad, was in quite a quandary when they discovered the Canadian agent spying on the houses at Leonides Village. Before he died, they forced him to tell them who he represented and that his whereabouts—and, more important, theirs—was known to the Canadian high commission in Nicosia. He said his boss in the high commission wasn't planning to pass what they knew on to the Cypriot police until he reported back on what he was able to learn about the band and the location of its hostages. But Widad couldn't be sure he was telling the truth. In his place, she would have lied about how soon searchers were expected to arrive.

Widad could see the necessity to move on immediately, but The Asp wasn't here. He was off on the southern coast meeting his informant, that snooty slut, the Lebanese ambassador's woman, and he had told the band to stay where they were. But The Asp *had* set up contingency plans, the not-overly-clever Widad reasoned to herself, and this *was* an unexpected development. So, the decision was to move and to take the higher ground, from whence the band could see any approaching force, rather than moving on down to the seaside where they eventually had planned to go.

Leaving the prearranged clues, an empty wine bottle on the floor in front of a sofa in the lounge, Widad and her comrades roughly seized their two hostages, squeezed into the three sedans they had stolen and parked close to the sides of the villas, and drove up the hill, past the Ayios Neophytos monastery and onto the road northward toward Polis.

The main road to Polis passed below and to the east of the hilltop village of Dhrousha. Upon reaching the area, the three sedans took different routes up to the town. Two of the sedans drove through the center of the little village from different angles and part way down the western slope. One sedan parked off the road almost within the town center with its narrow streets and tightly compacted buildings. The other one drove a bit farther down the hill and pulled off onto a stone wall-enclosed plot of mature almond trees.

The third vehicle, a van that was transporting the two hostages, had driven around the base of the hill and was approaching the village from the west. Nearly half way up the slope it pulled off the road and over to three derelict buildings, built almost into the hillside, which had been abandoned since their Turkish Cypriot owners had fled to the northern zone in August of 1974 and which now were used mainly as sheep crofts in the winter months. This site had been spied out as a likely retreat months earlier when The Asp had arrived in Cyprus for the first time.

He had come with two other terrorists who had been assigned to help protect the interests of the travel agency in Nicosia that had laundered bank accounts and arranged travel for the Palestinian terrorist organizations of the region. Several foreign intelligence agencies as well as the Cypriot parliamentarian stepson of the agency's owner had begun to sleuth out the agency's operations and the three terrorists had come to Cyprus to kill a few nosy people.

The other two terrorists had died when they killed the travel agency owner's stepson. He himself had barely gotten away from the temporary flat they rented before the police raided it. He had retreated to the western part of the island, over the Troodos Mountains. It was there that the kernel of a plan to bring a band of terrorists back to this region and to train them for mountain operations had been born.

Caitlyn and Eric were pushed into one of the huts, the one at the greatest distance from the dirt road. One of the terrorists went into the hut with them. The others divided themselves between the two other buildings and waited.

They didn't have to wait for too long before The Asp caught up with them. He had no trouble finding the huts. He had located and added these huts to the list of hideouts in the first place.

Well into the evening, when the Dhrousha villagers could be counted on to be concentrating on their dinners, The Asp sent Widad up to a tavern near the hotel to make the telephone call to their headquarters. The unusual presence of a nicely appointed three-star resort hotel in such a remote village was part of the reason The Asp selected the area as a possible hideout location. Placed here to take full benefit of the spectacular views, the cool breezes during the summer, and the promise of solitude, the presence of the Dhrousha Heights resort hotel meant that the mere presence of a stray foreigner or two would not set off alarm bells in the village's closely knit society. Thus, Widad could move up the hill and into the village with confidence that she would be taken as just one more of the strange tourists who had found the Dhrousha heights Hotel.

But all of the The Asp's careful planning had gone for naught, for dreamy-eyed Dora Makromali, who had come down to the grape vineyards to watch the moon play on the far-off Mediterranean and to spin in peace fantastic plans of becoming a famous dramatic actress, far from the harsh voices and limited imagination of her parents, had seen the band arrive. Although it wasn't unusual to see foreign tourists roaming around the small village, it certainly was unusual to see several vehicle loads of scruffy-looking foreigners converge on deserted huts from several different directions and hide behind broken doors and shutters as quickly as possible.

Regardless of how unusual it was, however, Dora didn't go off immediately to pass her observations on to her parents. Her parents had stopped listening to her and her fantastic dreams a long time ago. No, she wouldn't tell her parents. She'd wait and tell her favorite teacher—the one who encouraged her to dream of becoming a famous actress. Yes, her teacher would listen to her. He wouldn't say she was only making it up to make herself appear more important than a poor Dhrousha villager could ever hope to be.

* * * *

Demetris Mattas was one lucky motoring accident statistic. Although he careened off the mountain road into a forested valley on his pell-mell retreat from the Cedars Valley mountain village of Chakistra, his four-wheel-drive vehicle had come to rest on the roof of the mountain retreat of a leading Limassol restaurateur. Even more luckily for the newspaper columnist, the restaurateur had, firstly, just happened to have decided to spend the night with his mistress at the mountain home, far from the prying eyes of his wife, and, secondly, had not recognized the author of the "Under the Grapevine" column, which had jabbed him and some of his fellow Limassol seafront restaurateurs only two months previously for selling doctored white fish as Russian salmon.

If the roof-top arrival of Mattas's vehicle had not diverted the attention of the restaurant owner and his paramour so effectively, Mattas would not have survived the night. He suffered multiple fracture and, most seriously, internal bleeding from a head wound, in the plunge. The quick actions of those who found him and their fast trip to the clinic in Pedhoulas saved his life.

As it was, Mattas had been unconscious when they reached Pedhoulas, and the doctors thought it would probably be days before he would be awake again and in any condition to speak.

One of Pedhoulas's police officers arrived at the clinic quickly, notified of the accident by the clinic's night receptionist. Fortunately, the police officer was very professional; unfortunately, the restaurateur, once he had made sure Mattas was brought to where he could get medical attention, wasn't at all anxious to parade around in the limelight of Pedhoulas square in the company of his mistress.

The mistress didn't seem to be shy, however, She was fully and vociferously responding to the police officer's questions, as her lover crept around in the shadows behind him, trying to pretend they hadn't arrived at the clinic together.

"He kept saying words like 'terror,' 'Willie,' 'Hamilton,' 'killed,' 'serious,' and 'Kate something or other.' And I kept saying, 'I know you're scared, honey, and that this is serious, but we'll get you to the hospital on time.' That's my Despo for you. He always comes through."

Buzzers went off in the police officer's brain, as Despo tugged at the woman's sleeve and tried to get her to be quiet. The officer had already gone through Mattas's identity cards and seen that he was a political newspaper journalist; he knew that Willie Hamilton was a political reporter for the *Cyprus Mail* as well, and he had just spent three of the last five days in search around the caves near Ayios Neophytos for a band of terrorists and for Caitlyn Koniotis, the wife of the new chief of police. He made the woman repeat the words that Mattas had kept saying, and then he ran off to the telephone on the nurse's desk.

Despo moved his girlfriend off toward the door in an effort to escape as quietly as possible. But he couldn't resist making the correction as they reached the door: "Syrian. the man kept saying something about 'Syrian,' not 'serious.'"

"Yeah, now that you mention it, that was what he was saying. Something about a Syrian. We should go back and tell the officer."

"Oh, no, we've had enough public exposure for tonight," Despo answered firmly, as he swept her out of the clinic door. "You're going down to Limassol in a taxi right now. I have to go back to the house with the police. But I want you out of it now—and quickly. And no talking with reporters when you get home, either."

"OK, sweetie. Maybe I'll just call your wife." And then, when Despo's face had lost all of its color, "Just kidding. But it was fun, now that I know the guy will be all right. Now I'll know what to say if my friends ever asked if the earth had ever moved for me."

Despo just stood there, looking bewildered.

"I'll say 'no, but the whole house shook one night, and I met a dreamboat too,'" and she disappeared into a Mercedes taxi and blew Despo a kiss as it moved off toward the southern coast.

* * * *

Maria had been over every aspect of the movement of the suspected terrorist Faris Sukkar from Larnaca airport to the secluded

231

prison cells in the basement of police headquarters and of the care and feeding of the prisoner up to the moment he died. It was a fast-acting poison that did him in. The coroner had said that someone had put poison in his last meal. But that was not possible. Maria herself had supervised the preparation and delivery of all of the meals sent to Sukkar's cell. Only two other people had been involved in the process, and they were among her most-trusted associates. Only five senior members of the division, including Takis, had had contact with Sukkar since he left Larnaca airport, and only those five had known where Sukkar had been taken.

With the exception of the Lebanese embassy. As Sukkar had been traveling on a Lebanese passport, the police had no choice but to notify their consular officer both that Sukkar had been arrested and that he had been brought to Nicosia. The consular officer had visited Sukkar in his cell—the police couldn't keep him away without going to higher authority than Takis Koniotis to approve the total isolation, and Koniotis had seen informing the Lebanese embassy as a lesser problem to expanding the knowledge of Sukkar's whereabouts within the Cypriot government. At least then they would know where the problem was.

And that was exactly what Maria now knew. No, after going over all of the details, the only explanation was that only the Lebanese embassy had been given the information on Sukkar's presence in the Nicosia police department building and that only the Lebanese consular official had had access to Sukkar to put the poison in his food. The last meal had been delivered to Sukkar before the official had visited him, but the prisoner did not touch it until just before he died.

Maria spent more than a half hour trying to get the Lebanese consular on the telephone. No one was at his home, and the Lebanese embassy was closed up as tight as a drum. The people there who Maria had talked to on the telephone had refused even to acknowledge that the person who had come to the police department with the credentials of the Lebanese consular official worked for the embassy. Her attempts to contact Ambassador Abu Hani were also thwarted.

"The ambassador has not told us where he is tonight—he is not in the residence. And since he has no important appointments tomorrow, we don't know when he will return to the embassy."

Maria had tried to scare whoever she was talking to at the Lebanese embassy with obstruction of a murder investigation, but the caller blithely played the diplomatic immunity card. She could see that she was getting nowhere, but she also knew something the caller didn't know.

"Damn right he has an important meeting in the morning," Maria screamed inwardly, as she slammed the telephone receiver down. "It's the same meeting I'm going to. And he's going to answer a couple of pointed questions when he gets there."

* * * *

"Got the bastard. He's in Damascus." Ibrahim, the Beirut Hizballah cell leader, had received the information he sought through his agent in the Russian embassy.

"You can't get away from us that fast, Nabil Jallud, my fat little friend. He must have made a deal with the Russians. Saved his own hide—or so he thinks—and abandoned his nephew in Cyprus. Well, when they call, I'll ring the death knell for the nephew. And you,

Jallud, I know of just the person to take care of you. You will die like the Russians did. But not nearly as fast or as painlessly."

Ibrahim moved toward the back of the coffee shop, his new unit headquarters. But, before he could get to the special telephone to make his call, it rang. And before he finished his conversation, he forgot all about putting out the contract on the Lebanese merchant who had betrayed him. Fortuitously for Jallud—at least for the time being—the information and request that Ibrahim had now received had already knocked all intent to issue a kill order for the merchant.

After hanging up, he headed straight for the corniche and for the fishing vessel he had used for his previous shopping trip to Cyprus. As the vessel steamed away from the Beirut waterfront, Ibrahim remembered—too late to put them into operation—the plans he had made for both of the Jalluds.

"No matter. The slimy merchant's fate can hold for a day or two, and now I can have the pleasure of dispensing with the nephew myself."

* * * *

"But we've got to find out where Mattas has been," Koniotis repeated stubbornly. "Too many lives are depending on finding out where he was with Hamilton. The editors at both of their papers have admitted the two were investigating the Mouflon Brigade story. It may not be too late for Hamilton, and they must have stumbled on to Caitlyn and Isaksen as well. But why was he coming through the Troodos if the band is over on the Paphos side of the mountains? Why didn't he just come around the good road along the coast? Could it be that he was afraid he would be intercepted? Damn, We've got to find out where Mattas has been."

"You keep saying that, Takis," Androulla voice with concern, "but we can't find out what Demetris Mattas knows until he's conscious. That could not be for several more days."

"Maybe we need him to be conscious, and maybe we don't. Androulla," Koniotis directed with authority as he lifted the receiver on the telephone in Maria Solonos's now very neat office, "I want you to call the police department in Pedhoulas. I want all of Mattas's clothes up here within two hours—bagged so that they are intact as he wore them, and I want sweepings taken from his vehicle and any dirt that's on his tires, and I want them here at the same time. Send a helicopter up there, if necessary. And, yes, I know it's in the middle of the night."

Androulla looked confused, but Koniotis shooed her toward the door with a wave of his hand. "I'll explain latter; just get it set in motion now."

He lifted the telephone receiver and rang a number. A groggy Paul Conte picked up on the third ring.

"Paul, this is Takis Koniotis. I need your help. Willie Hamilton has disappeared. I think he found Caitlyn. Demetris Mattas was with him, but he has had an auto accident and is unconscious. It's a long shot, I know, but wasn't it noted at the UN coordinator's dinner the other night that one of the guests, a British agronomist named Peterson or Paterson, could tell where someone had been by the residue on their clothes?"

A still-somewhat disoriented American diplomat grunted a short assent and added, "Patterson. John Patterson. I think that was his name. He's in Famagusta—on the Turkish side."

"But didn't he say he'd worked extensively on this side in years past and had included Cyprus in his studies and writings because of uniqueness of the island—that it's made up of two plates of earth with quite different compositions jammed together?"

"Yes, I think I remember that. He and Caitlyn had quite a conversation about that at the dinner."

Koniotis explained that he was having Mattas's clothes and the sweepings of his vehicle sent down to Nicosia and asked Conte if he would, first, go to the Turkish outpost at the Ledra Palace border crossing—which was closed to vehicular traffic at night—and call Safa Ziya. She should be asked to try to track Patterson down while the materials were being collected and brought into Nicosia. And then Conte, if he would, should deliver the materials to Ziya at the crossing when they had arrived.

"I know it's a long shot, Paul. But I've got to do something. I can't just sit here on my hands waiting for Mattas to regain consciousness."

"I understand, Takis, and I'll be happy to do it. I've been frustrated that there hasn't seemed to be anything I could help with. Anything with the remotest chance of leading to Caitlyn has to be tried. I'll leave immediately."

Paul's quest went a lot quicker than he thought it would. He didn't have to track Patterson all of the way to Famagusta. As soon as he got to the Turkish side, he called Safa Ziya.

"John? He's right here, Paul," Safa responded as soon as Paul had spilled out in a torrent of words who he needed—and why. "I can have him at the Ledra Palace center as soon as the border opens in the morning."

Paul was so overwhelmed with his good fortune that he didn't give a thought to why John Patterson would be at Safa Ziya's flat in the middle of the night. Even if he'd been in the frame of mind to consider it, he probably wouldn't have believed either of the two would have been doing what they were doing when he called.

* * * *

Ginger Hamilton was nearly finished applying her face for the night crawl, when she was telephoned and informed that her husband had apparently been taken by the same terrorist band that had seized Eric Isaksen and Caitlyn Koniotis and that there was some specific fear that he had been killed in the process.

She woodenly hung up the receiver and returned to her artistry. To the extent she thought at all about Willie for the next thirty minutes, it was in unconsciously but functionally moving him from the present to the past imperfect column of her long list of husbands—some dead but some just escaped. Ginger was a professional when it came to the state and/or act of matrimony—and what came afterward, whether separation by death or divorce.

Having put the last touch to the mascara on her eyes and having fluffed her sunny, bottle-blonde hair one last time, she rose from her throne, turned out the lights lining her shrine, and tripped down the stairs of the Strovolos flat and out to her baby-blue BMW convertible.

Within minutes she had reached the top of Byron Street where it met Grivas Avenue and was driving down the tree-lined street to the museum square and the Paphos Gate into the old city. She drove through the gate, the north wall of which was in the Turkish zone, the south wall in the Greek zone, and the road itself under UN control. Once inside the gate, she veered to the right, following the road—the Holy Cross Catholic church, with its front door in the Greek sector and its back door in the Turkish zone was almost directly in front of her. She drove the familiar route as if she was on automatic pilot.

Almost immediately, she passed the old Lusignan crusaders' hall, the Kastellian, and then turned left at the Pallas movie house, which featured slightly pornographic films in search of an audience of young, bored UN soldiers from the nearby Ledra Palace Hotel barracks. Within two blocks she stopped and parked in the narrow street, barely leaving enough room for automobiles to pass, and walked through a door and up the stairs, entering the Apollo Nights club, yet another but very different attempt to attract UN soldiers.

Ginger came to this club often, as did a few other matrons of similar degeneracy. Some of the best-looking men in Cyprus could be ogled in this out-of-the-way nightspot. The fact that the men were gay detracted a bit from the experience, of course, but Ginger sometimes was in the mood just to window shop and be bitchy.

She went straight to her usual table, one of those abutting a runway-like platform with small, flashing lights lining each side. She ordered her usual drink in a monotone voice and sat staring straight ahead toward the runway. Usually she spent a good deal of time scanning the other clients, valuing and judging what she saw and occasionally fantasizing in an "only if . . ." vein. But tonight she appeared to be focused. She was looking ahead at the runway, intently.

At length the loud music transitioned into a bump and grind melody, and one of her favorites, a hunky, long-haired Swede wearing only a gold loop earring and a tiny, glittery thong brief, gyrated in slow motion down the runway. He stopped occasionally, slowly and rhythmically squatting in front of an appreciative patron, who usually inserted a one-pound note in one of the thin bands holding his costume in place. He performed this familiar maneuver now before Ginger—knowing that she always was good for a five pounder, although she almost always handled more than the string of his thong in the process. But on this night she didn't respond. She just continued staring through him. After a few attempt to gain her attention, the dancer swiveled back up to full height and moved on down the runway.

The music changed mood again as the Swede undulated back up the runway and disappeared through a curtained door. Ginger fell forward on the table and began to sob uncontrollably.

Several patrons at nearby tables came to her and tried to find out what the matter was. No answer; she just continued sobbing, her newly created face melting and streaming down her cheeks and wrinkled neck.

It was a Dane named Horst who took the initiative to look into her purse for identification and an address. He found two addresses. One was in the village of Lefkara, an hour's drive to the south, in the foothills of the Troodos just before the Nicosia-Limassol motorway reaches the southern coast and veers off to the west.

"Not a chance," the Dane thought. He wasn't driving an hour into the country for an old dame tonight. But the other address was in Strovolos. And there were keys on a BMW chain. He had seen the old lady in the nifty BMW convertible before.

Half out of concern and half from itchiness to drive a BMW convertible, Horst helped Ginger out to her automobile. She was still crying, but the loud sobs had subsided. She still wasn't talking, however.

When they got to Strovolos, Horst parked the BMW in the square in front of the block of flats that matched the address on Ginger's driver's license. Announcing that she was home and that he hoped should would feel better soon, he got out of the automobile and slowly started moving down the street in search of a taxi stand. He looked back at the vehicle. She hadn't moved. She just sat there, looking down at her lap, the tears streaming down her smudged face.

Horst returned to the BMW and helped Ginger out of the automobile and up to her flat. He sat her down on the sofa and walked toward the door. She was hit with a wracking sob, which brought Horst back to the sofa. He sat down and took her in his arms. They sat in that position for more than an hour. She didn't try anything funny, and he certainly had no intention of trying anything funny. But for some reason he couldn't leave her. He had no idea what had caused her to break down, but she looked so vulnerable, and he kept thinking back to his own mother. If she was ever in such a state, he could not imagine just going off and leaving her.

In time, the sobbing and the quaking stopped and Ginger began to breathe evenly. She had gone to sleep. Horst gently lowered her head to the pillows against the arm of the sofa and lifted her feet to the other end of the sofa. He then looked around for the woman's purse. Opening it, he rummaged around inside for her billfold, which was stuffed with Cypriot pound notes. Thinking again of his mother, he took only enough for cab fare back to the club, turned and covered the woman with a blanket, and clicked the door to the flat behind him as he left. If he hurried back, maybe the hunky Swede would have waited for him at the club.

Chapter Sixteen

The atmosphere outside the old Ledra Palace Hotel in the mid Monday morning sunshine had taken on all of the trappings of one of the major intercommunal peace conference negotiations or treaty signing sessions that had dignified the rambling stone complex, with its Moorish architectural embellishments, for more than a hundred eventful years.

Those driving in from the Greek side of the border, past the residence of the Greek ambassador—set defiantly within sight of the Turkish-held wall of the old city, through the Greek checkpoint, and then past the German embassy's Goethe Institute, were forced to pass two banks of media reporters. Those of the Greek Cypriot media hovered around the raised slow bump at the Greek checkpoint, waiting for the appropriate automobiles to slow down as they passed the checkpoint so that questions could be hurled at diplomats and detectives, snapshots could be taken for the morning editions, and video footage could be collected for the evening news.

Having passed this gauntlet with its relatively polite and a bit diffident newshounds, those coming from the Greek section were faced, almost immediately, with a tougher challenge. The more hard-nosed representatives of the foreign media entered the buffer zone itself and stationed themselves directly in front of the entry gate to the hotel's front courtyard. Having established this beachhead, those attending the morning's session could not avoid a more persistent and pointed face-off, as they had to leave their vehicles at this point to enter the Ledra Palace Hotel. The mere presence of the foreign press marked this as an extremely unusual and important conference—even for the building, which had seen a great many peacekeeping sessions.

The embattled division of the island of Cyprus had been going on for so long that the daily developments of the Cyprus Issue were only front-page news in Cyprus itself. But this session was different. It had leaked out that this was to be the ultimate "war council" for tracking down the terrorists—the "Mouflon Brigade"—that had been operating in the region and that had delivered spectacular events not only in Cyprus but in Greece and Lebanon as well. This had become the focal point of world interest for today—and perhaps only for today, given the fickle nature of public interest. So, for today, at least, the foreign press corps, which was present in major force in Cyprus but with the mandate to cover other regions from a Cyprus safe haven rather than covering Cyprus itself, did not have to catch a flight on short notice to cover the primary regional story of the day. The game was right here.

First to arrive from the Greek sector were the British high commission political officer, Alec Stuart, the formal sponsor of the regular meetings between the Greek Cypriot and Turkish Cypriot police departments, and Ingrid Bittmann, UN coordinator and formal chief officer over facilities within the buffer zone, which included the Ledra Palace Hotel. The reporters concentrated on Ingrid Bittmann rather than Alec Stuart, who was an old drinking buddy, but an acknowledged tight-lipped old drinking buddy. But they were light on Bittmann, keeping their powder dry for more important game, and let her off with a couple of leading questions that allowed her to emphasize the importance of the kidnapped UN official, Eric Isaksen, to world peace and to appeal to his captors for his good-will release based on the fact that he had been on his way to Lebanon at the invitation of the Hizballah to help reach a total cease-fire in Beirut.

The next arrivals, the new Police Department chief, Takis Koniotis, and the new chief of the International Investigations Division, Maria Solonos, were the main targets for the reporters. Not only was Koniotis presumed to hold all of the information that was to be had on the status of the investigation and how far its tentacles spread beyond Cyprus, but his wife, an American national, was one of the hostages as well. But, although the reporters got some premium visual coverage of a handsome, but determined and stony-expressioned detective and concerned husband, they couldn't get a single comment out of Koniotis. Solonos was only slightly more helpful, promising to hold a press conference on the investigations at 4:00 PM that afternoon in the Police Department auditorium. Time enough for most of them to file for the evening broadcasts and for the next morning's editions. But Solonos was a new player for them. They couldn't provide assurances to their editors that they would have a story to roll until they had worked with Solonos long enough to know whether she would be helpful or evasive in a news conference.

The later, almost simultaneous appearances of the Lebanese and Greek ambassadors were very interesting and were taken as confirming the reports that the assassination of the Russian embassy clerk in Athens and the rumored bombing of a group of Russians in Beirut were related to the exploits of the Mouflon Brigade here in Cyprus. Some of the rumors had even held that the first person captured here, the wife of the Russian embassy political officer, Mikhail Lukenov, had been killed in a Beirut bombing and that the whole operation was connected to the Hizballah. If so, this would fold everything back on the mission of another one of the hostages, Eric Isaksen, who had been invited to come to Beirut under the protection of the Hizballah. This would then invite speculation that either there were rifts within the Hizballah leadership, just as rifts had appeared in the Palestinian movement some years before, or the Hizballah was playing a very dangerous and convoluted political game.

If the reporters could have gotten to Ayman Abu Hani, the Lebanese ambassador, they could have queried him closely on these significant issues. But, unfortunately for them, the Greek ambassador's automobile had driven up a fraction of a moment earlier, and they were all being held captive to an impassioned speech on how this would all have been avoided if the occupying Turkish army had withdrawn from northern Cyprus. Amid this barrage, Abu Hani managed to slip past them and halfway up the hotel walk—a considerable distance beyond the zone in which the press was permitted to operate—before the reporters realized who he was.

The media were exhausted from the lecture from the Greek ambassador and, thus, were a bit off guard a few seconds after he'd finished when the lone diplomatic-plated automobile traveling into the buffer zone from the Turkish checkpoint pulled up to the entryway. The vehicle was driven by Paul Conte, a political officer with the American embassy. Conte was not an unexpected attendee, as the foreign journalists knew that he helped arrange bicommunal meetings between the Greek and Turkish Cypriots. But they might have invested more interest in him if they had known that he had been on the Turkish side to deliver evidence connected with the Mouflon Brigade case to a forensic expert in the Turkish zone for analysis or that this evidence had involved two of the journalists' own local— well-known and highly respected—colleagues, Willie Horton of the *Cyprus Mail* and Demetris Mattas of *Simerini*.

As Conte maneuvered as close to the entry gate as the horde of reporters would permit, Ellen Larkin of the Canadian high commission and Safa Ziya, the chief investigator for the Turkish Cypriot police, stepped out of the vehicle. The journalists went straight for Ziya, who was probably better known and more highly respected as a criminal investigator internationally than she was in the small, remote, and unrecognized northern Cyprus zone.

Even though Ziya had not been fully prepared to encounter reporters before entering the Ledra Palace Hotel—there had been none at the Turkish Cypriot checkpoint; indeed, most Turkish Cypriots were not following this case at all—she handled herself well. Taking a strictly nonpartisan stand, which the foreign journalists found both refreshing and rare in their experience of talking with either Greek or Turkish Cypriots, Ziya said that Cyprus was a peaceful and gentle island at heart and that the use of the island by the forces of international crime, whether motivated by politics or economics, would be combated by the combined efforts of the Greek Cypriot and Turkish Cypriot authorities. She went on to say that, in addition, both Takis Koniotis and his wife, Caitlyn, were personal friends of hers and that every effort would be made by the Turkish Cypriot authorities and by Ziya herself to track down the terrorist band and to release all of the hostages safely.

Although the journalists got some very good quotes from what she had to say, she refused to be drawn out on the specifics of the case and firmly walked away as soon as Paul Conte had parked the car in the narrow lane that now ran between checkpoints and past the hotel's entry gate. After parking, he joined up with Ziya and Ellen Larkin again. No one bothered to ask Larkin any questions. In truth, very few of the journalists even knew who the well-scrubbed, perky, girl-next-door type of woman was—and they would have been shocked to have been informed that she was the Canadian's chief intelligence agent on the island, that she had been with Caitlyn Koniotis when the archaeologist was kidnapped, and that she was very good at her job.

With the escape of Safa Ziya and the American and Canadian diplomats up the walk to the hotel, the vigil of the journalists was over until everyone emerged from the Ledra Palace Hotel once again. Although they didn't think it was the end, and the prolonged presence of Alec Stuart in the hotel's portico and the anxious glances he devoted to his wristwatch and to the road leading to the Greek Cypriot checkpoint seemed to confirm their belief that more interlocutors were expected.

At length, however, looking worried, Stuart gave up his vigil and entered the hotel. The journalists, in turn, settled in for the wait, discussing the case among themselves and composing in their individual heads what would go into the individual media accounts of the situation.

The journalists would have been very interested to know who had been invited and had not shown up. Firstly, had they known that Mikhail Lukenov had been invited to the conference and hadn't come, the rumors that his wife was not dead and was no longer being actively sought would have gained credence. And, if they had known that the Iranian ambassador had been expected in vain, they would have worked even harder on developing the Hizballah connection, the only possible link to the case of Iran being Tehran's assumed control of the Hizballah movement in Lebanon.

And they would have been just as interested to have learned who *had* shown up to the conference but had cleverly eluded both the Greek Cypriot and the foreign journalists. The front entry into the Ledra Palace Hotel from the short, tree- and derelict mansion-lined avenue running between the two checkpoints was not the access that the UN troops for this sector themselves used to enter the hotel, which served as their barracks. There was another road leading off a small circle near the Greek Cypriot checkpoint that led to the large parking lot behind the hotel. Although this road was closed to general traffic and was guarded with a checkpoint of its own, diplomatic-plated automobiles were usually granted entrance when their occupants could prove they had a meeting scheduled in the hotel.

The Syrian ambassador, Munir Nahlawi, had gained access to the back of the hotel via this road. He was attending this meeting with great reluctance, but he was expected to show up and did not want to draw suspicion to himself. He also wanted to know what they knew. If he had checked with his embassy this morning and had learned that Takis Koniotis was specifically looking for him, he probably would have cleared out of town—and maybe away from Cyprus—by now.

But he thought there still was time and opportunity to cover his own activities. However, to be safe, he was entering from the back to avoid reporters—and, not incidentally, to provide an escape route if that became necessary.

* * * *

The Treaty Room of the Ledra Palace Hotel, venue of innumerable negotiations and cease-fire and treaty agreements since the British colonial period, was a study in extremes. Designed to be an elegant and airy setting for the large private dinner parties of the rich and famous among British colonial social circles throughout the Middle East, the room was dominated on one side by a huge stone fireplace. Across the room from the fireplace was a false façade of columns supporting Moorish arches beyond which were located three large window doors facing the front of the hotel. Windows dominated a third wall, opposite of which were accordion doors, which, when opened, doubled the size of the room. The walls had once been covered with brocade with stone trim work, and once the carpet undoubtedly had been one of the finest and largest Orientals that could be obtained.

Now, however, the bullet-hole pock-marked hotel having been a focal point of the fight for this strategic sector of Nicosia in the 1974 Turkish invasion and since then having been the home of several generations of rough and rowdy UN peacekeepers, the hotel and the Treaty Room itself had been stripped to the bare necessities. The stone fireplace remained, but the coat of arms of Richard the Lionhearted, one-time owner of the island, that had been embedded above it was gone—undoubtedly long since removed as a hated symbol of British colonialism. The walls were bare stone and slightly dingy, the carpets

249

were barely functional and threadbare, and the furnishings—folding tables arranged in an open square and utilitarian chairs—belied the continued use of the room by high-level national and international officials for important conferences.

In addition, the original airiness of the room had disappeared—not in the wake of the 1974 invasion but during the anti-British resistance period several decades earlier. Although the large windows once looked out over sunny gardens, they had long since been bricked in. The purpose was not to maintain the attention of the many generations of negotiators who had used the Treaty Room on the political business at hand, but to protect them from the bullets and bombs of fanatics while they were trying to achieve their settlements—or, more likely, while they were trying to avoid doing so to their country's advantage.

When all of the investigator and diplomats Koniotis had invited to this review and planning session had been accounted for—and the whereabouts and intention *not* to attend of the Iranian ambassador and the Russian political counselor having been marked—Koniotis invited all to sit around the table and proceeded to provide a detailed—if not wholly complete—review of the investigation into the activities of the Mouflon Brigade.

The review covered the kidnappings of Irina Lukenov, Eric Isaksen, Caitlyn Koniotis, and William Hamilton and the deaths of the Cypriot interior minister; the Argentine Un contingent commander; the Orthodox monks at Vroisha monastery; Safa Ziya's assistant, Sami; the elderly couples at the retirement villas near Paphos; the Russian embassy clerk in Athens; and Irina Lukenov and several Russians in Beirut. It also included the attempted firing on the MEA airplane at

Larnaca airport and the death of the perpetrator of that act as well as of a suspect who had been arrested who was connected with both the terrorist band and the assassination in Athens.

Koniotis loosely indicated how all of this fit together and pointedly—while both he and Maria, who had reviewed ahead of time what he would say, watched the Lebanese and Syrian ambassadors for their reactions—noted that they had identified many, if not all, of the terrorists. He did not, however, provide specific information on how they had obtained the names of the terrorists or that one of the band members was someone they wanted to protect.

Neither did he specifically identify the embassy whose vehicles probably transported the terrorists and his captured wife across the Ledra Palace checkpoint, although he flatly stated he knew which embassy was involved, and both he and Maria were staring straight at the Syrian ambassador when he provided this discussion. He also flatly said that their review of the death of the terrorist concluded that he only could have died at the hands of the embassy consul who had visited him—but he didn't identify the embassy that was involved. Of course everyone in the room knew without the need to identify it.

Much of the information was new to nearly everyone around the table, especially the disclosure that Irina Lukenov had, indeed, been judged to having been killed in the Beirut bombing, the most recent information on the disappearance of Willie Hamilton, and the insidious nature in which it all fit together as threads of one, internationally controlled, series of operations. Munir Nahlawi and Ayman Abu Hani were particularly quiet and pale. Ingrid Bittmann asked which embassies had been implicated and how the police knew that Hamilton had been kidnapped by the terrorist band.

251

"Good questions, Dr. Bittmann," Koniotis answered. "As for the latter question, Hamilton wasn't alone in his search for the terrorist band. Demetris Mattas of *Simerini* was also there, saw Hamilton get taken, and escaped without he himself having been seen. He then was involved in an automobile accident and was only able to pass on a bit of what he saw before he lost consciousness. But he should regain consciousness soon and be able to tell us where Hamilton was captured and who captured him."

Koniotis quite purposely did not reveal that it probably would actually be a couple of days before Mattas regained consciousness.

Munir Nahlawi, the Syrian ambassador, nearly collapsed under the table, a movement that didn't go unnoticed by anyone in the room.

"As for the other questions, they lead to many other questions that we should raise and cover here," Koniotis said mildly, "so perhaps we should take a short coffee break before we go further. Ambassador Nahlawi, you don't look well. Can I get you a cup of water—or coffee?"

"I'll just help him down the hall to the men's room," Ingrid Bittmann interjected. "He looks like he needs to pat some cold water on his face more than he needs a cup of coffee."

While she helped Nahlawi to the door and was followed by Paul Conte and Safa Ziya, Koniotis turned toward two UN soldiers who had been on guard in the room and asked one to go to the hotel's main entrance and the other to the hall entrance to the back parking lot that was just outside the door into the Treaty Room.

"Mr. Conte and Ms. Ziya seem to have taken the situation in hand and are keeping an eye on the Lebanese and Syrian envoys, but please try ensure that neither envoy leaves the hotel during the break.

You can't detain them, of course, but you can raise the alarm to the rest of us that they're trying to leave."

Unfortunately, these precautions were not sufficient for the need. Conte and Ziya had not been following the ambassadors at all. Ziya was sending Conte off via the front entrance to go back into the Turkish sector to check on John Patterson's tests on the clothing and automobile scraping that had been brought to him the previous night. And, after seeing the Syrian ambassador to the men's room down the main corridor, past the entry lobby, Ingrid Bittmann had gone on to the ladies' room. The UN soldiers *did* ensure the ambassadors didn't leave by the two doors they had been asked to guard, but there was a third door with access to the rear parking area—the door leading to the swimming pool area.

* * * *

Munir Nahlawi made only one stop on his way to Paphos airport to catch the afternoon flight to London. He let the Lebanese ambassador off at his home. Nahlawi knew about the new traveler-tracking systems at Larnaca airport and the Limassol port and passed this information on to Abu Hani. This was not the only reason he had chosen to leave via Paphos airport, though. If the authorities expected him to leave this quickly, they would be looking for him at Larnaca. Of course they could hardly expect that he could react this fast. As a matter of fact, he already had his ticket on the flight from Paphos, which had been obtained in another name. He had decided to leave on that flight anyway. He had already gotten too deeply involved, and he didn't want to be around when—and if—they found Willie Hamilton.

Ayman Abu Hani also quickly planned and put into motion his scheme to escape. He had not planned to use any of the major exit points either. He knew it would be hard for an ambassador to leave by any of the normal routes. Besides, unlike the Syrian ambassador, who had an ugly wife who paid no attention to business, Abu Hani couldn't leave his own beautiful, knowledgeable—and heavily implicated—wife here alone if he left. He thus knew it would take time for him to find her, time that could be effectively used by the Greek Cypriot authorities to close the airports and Limassol port to him.

As he gathered up some clothes and his most sensitive papers, Abu Hani started calling around to locate Suzanne. She wasn't at home, or at the embassy, or at the Hiltonian Club. But why make more telephone calls, he thought. He knew where she would be. He went down to the garage and threw two suitcases into the trunk of a nondescript Japanese-model automobile with regular yellow registration plates. He was well away when the police and a foreign ministry official arrived ten minutes later.

* * * *

Takis Koniotis had not had a long time to brood over letting the two ambassadors slip out of his fingers. Detaining them would have been a long shot anyway considering the diplomatic immunity they both enjoyed. After realizing they were gone, he ordered, through the authority of an embarrassed Ingrid Bittmann, a thorough, but unsuccessful search of the hotel and its grounds. The guard at the checkpoint at the rear of the hotel had confirmed his fears. The two ambassadors had left together in Nahlawi's embassy Mercedes a half hour earlier. Koniotis barely had time to radio in a bulletin on the two, however, before his attention was diverted by an excited Paul Conte.

Paul returned to the hotel, the British agronomist John Patterson in tow, with what he had thought would be earth-shattering news, only to find the discussion session in complete disarray in the wake of the unscheduled departure of Abu Hani and Nahlawi before Koniotis could grill them on this neutral ground about their evident implication in the case. Patterson had been able to cross the checkpoint into the UN zone by prior arrangement made by Safa Ziya.

After being briefed about what had transpired in his absence and commiserating with Koniotis, Conte got straight to the point.

"You've got to hear this firsthand, Takis. Patterson has examined the materials you sent over and thinks he may have something interesting. But he doesn't want to go out on a limb on his findings."

Everyone turned their attention to the diminutive, diffident agronomist.

"What did you find?" asked Koniotis, trying to keep any signs of impatience from his voice.

"Well, a lot of dirt samples, of course. It would take weeks to track those down, of course—"

"We don't have weeks, John," Safa Ziya interjected gently but firmly.

"I appreciate that, certainly," Patterson said nervously, wiping his hand on his trousers. Then he took a couple of plastic bags from his pocket.

"That's why I concentrated on these two samples. Maybe you can help identify them. The first is tufts of animal hair. The hair had clung to Mattas's trouser legs in strands, as if he had picked them up by moving through an area of low brush."

"I'm not sure how that would help; we have goats and sheep all over the island," responded Koniotis.

"That's what seems strange about this. When I was in China, I worked closely with wool production and became quite familiar with the properties of both goat and sheep wool. This hair seems to be from another animal altogether. Similar to both a sheep and a goat, but something else completely. I've never seen anything like it."

Maria started to say something but then went into a pensive attitude along with everyone else.

"The other sample is more straightforward," Patterson continued. "Do you have any stands of cedar trees around? I found slivers of cedar wood from the cuffs of the trousers as well as from samples taken from the floor of the vehicle."

"Cedar trees. Yes, there are a few around, but I don't know about a whole stand," Koniotis answered. He was thinking hard on the question. He wanted answers to appear.

Maria Solonos burst out: "Cedars Valley. It fits, Takis. It fits everything. Cedars Valley. That's where we have a large stand of cedars and that's where the mouflon are—the tuffs of goat-like hair. But hair from some other strain of goat—a mouflon. The Mouflon Brigade. Don't you get it?"

"Of course!" Koniotis exclaimed.

"Cedars Valley? Where's Cedars Valley?" queried Alec Stuart dumbly.

"Mouflon? What is 'mouflon'?" asked Patterson at the same time and just as dumbly.

"Cedars Valley is located in just about the right spot for the terrorist brigade and for Mattas's escape route," answered Koniotis. "It's in the Troodos, beyond the Kykko monastery from here, and not far from the buffer zone at Soli, where Irina Lukenov was kidnapped;

it's not far from Vroisha, where she was taken; it's in the mountains above Paphos; and the road that leads up to it from Nicosia is the road on which Mattas had his accident."

"And mouflon?" Patterson persisted.

"That's almost what I was going to say when you were talking about the wool samples," Solonos spoke up. "The mouflon is a nearly extinct cross between a mountain goat and a sheep. It's only found on Cyprus, and its protected preserve is in the Cedars Valley. That could explain the hair sample you couldn't identify. It also could explain why the terrorist band took the name 'Mouflon Brigade' and have used a Cyprus Airways brochure as their calling card. They are taunting us. The airline uses an stylized image of a mouflon as its symbol on the tail of its airplanes. You're a wizard, Mr. Patterson!"

Safa Ziya beamed at John Patterson with pride, and John Patterson beamed back at her with an entirely different, deeper emotion.

* * * *

After Koniotis and Solonos left the Ledra Palace Hotel to set a search of the Cedars Valley into motion, Alec Stuart departed directly for his Averof Street hideaway. he more than half expected Suzanne Abu Hani to be there, and, in his expectation, he wasn't disappointed. On the whole, however, he was not at all pleased.

He knew that he had to have a confrontation with the vixen. He knew she had been spying on him, and it did not take much imagination to figure out what she had done with the information she gleaned from his briefcase and his telephone conversations. He felt the right fool, and he was coldly angry.

His was an anger that he had not revealed to anyone since he realized what she had been up to and how she had prostituted herself just to obtain information from him. He knew what he was capable of, and he knew that he had to be careful in this confrontation with her. It would not help anyone if he killed her—at least not before he got some of his own back and before he found out where what *she* knew could lead him.

She was already in bed, waiting for him. She was as beautiful and as enticing as she had ever been. She also was quite naked and invitingly open to him. No woman had ever made love to him as well as she did. That had made it all the more bitter for him when he found out she had only made love to him to use him. He walked over to the side of the bed, fists clinched, willing himself not to crush her lovely face with one punch. He started to speak—to accuse, to condemn, to start the interrogation. But she had risen to him and covered his lips with hers and started her familiar, expert games with her fingers.

"Just one more time. One more time for me. She owes me this," Stuart kept repeating to himself in his mind, as he was being peeled of clothes and was pulled down onto the bed and top of her.

He was cold and brutal, more like a monstrous and wounded, rutting animal than a long-time lover. And, perversely, she loved every stroke of it and, in fact, slapped, bit, and prodded him into two renewed assaults after he spent his initial wrath and his energy. In the end, he fell back onto the sheets, thoroughly exhausted, unable, he thought, to move another muscle.

Suzanne must have thought so, as well, because just as Alec was turning away from her on the bed, she reached under her pillow and a knife flashed at Stuart's neck. The trained British commando saw the flash in a mirror, however, and instantly twisted away from the threat, receiving only a slight nick on the shoulder. He reached out and caught her by the wrist, twisting it cruelly so that she screamed out in pain and dropped the knife. Her knee shot up and caught him in the groin, doubling him up in pain. But in the same movement, he rolled off the bed and onto the floor. He was quickly back up onto his knees and pulling at the drawer of the night stand. The pain was intense, but so was his anger.

Suzanne searched fruitlessly among the sheets for the lost knife. When she saw that Alec had recovered, she launched herself off the bed and ran toward the French doors she had left ajar for just such an exit. But Alec had the revolver out of the drawer and was only a couple of feet away from her when he fired off all six rounds.

Instead of explosions, the firing of Alec's revolver only produced clicking sounds. She had removed the shells from the gun. Both antagonists, breathing heavily, looked around the room with darting eyes in search of a weapon. Suzanne was the first to find one. The brass lamp connected with Alec's skull with an ugly crunch, and he went down for the count, his head wound bleeding profusely into the beautiful Heracat Oriental carpet.

There, she had done it. She had killed him as Abdul had ordered. Now she could return to Abdul.

She quickly put on the clothes she had folded so neatly and placed on the terrace outside the window and hurried through the garden to the gate.

But, as she opened the gate and started out onto the street, she was confronted with two blazing, accusing eyes. Ambassador Ayman Abu Hani had found his wife.

* * * *

Two hours later Abu Hani and his crew were steaming out of the Larnaca yacht basin and into the Mediterranean. Destination home. Beirut was less than sixty nautical miles away. Just two days before, in preparation for just such a need, the ambassador had his yacht moved to the Larnaca port from its usual mooring at the Sheraton hotel Yacht Club on the Amathus hotel gold coast just east of the city of Limassol. He had been afraid that events were developing to the point where he would have to leave quickly, and he figured that if he moved the ship, he could be well away—maybe even all of the way to Lebanese waters—before the Cypriots figured out how he had escaped. They undoubtedly would think first of the airports and only then of an escape by sea. He wasn't sure that they even knew he had a yacht in Cyprus, but if they did, they would be expecting to find it at its usual moorings at the Sheraton.

Abu Hani looked back at the retreating Larnaca seafront one more time before he went below. He didn't know if he ever would be returning to lovely Cyprus again. He heard a husky, lusty laugh from below. It was time for him to teach his favorite wayward crew member another lesson in humility.

Chapter Seventeen

Caitlyn was in an unbelievably hot room. But it wasn't a room at all. Its walls were lined with an enameled metal, a metal that radiated heat. Eric Isaksen was sitting on a large luminous red coil and was calmly talking about having been the main course in a dinner on a small deserted island. The baby was in her arms. It was crying, and sweat was running off its writing little body. It was dark in the room, although there was a large, cloudy picture window in one wall. Caitlyn started to move toward the wall with the baby—except now she found herself holding two babies, but she recoiled in fear, as the whole wall fell away and a huge, angry face jutted into the room.

"Where is he? Where is that little bastard? He'd better not be up there." And then the face pulled away and the wall closed again with a big bang.

The banging of the door to the shed backing into the Dhrousha hillside—a virtual oven under the afternoon sunshine—brought Caitlyn instantly awake. She brushed a few strands of moist hair away from her face and moved quietly and painfully, her joints stiff from too little movement, toward the shed door. Eric was asleep, but tossing, turning, and muttering, in the dirty straw at the far end of the earth-floored room. Caitlyn could hear an angry voice outside; a woman's voice. The woman, Widad. She was yelling at a man, probably whoever had been left to guard the hostages. Caitlyn could make out the names Ahmad and Abdul and something about a hotel, but the voice was too muffled and anger-slurred for Caitlyn to be able to follow the monologue.

The tirade stopped as abruptly as it had begun. Caitlyn turned back toward the interior of the shed, away from the shafts of light entering the loose stone, earth, and straw walls. Eric was beginning to stir. And not only Eric. Caitlyn could feel something else stirring within her. She stretched the fingers of both hands across her abdomen and began yet again to recite the comforting words of the Twenty-third Psalm to herself—"The Lord is my Shepherd; I shall not want . . ."

Widad al-Ghabra marched up the hill into the small village of Dhrousha. At the village square, she scanned the tops of the houses until she picked out the three-story Dhrousha Heights Hotel, incongruously dominating the southern skyline of the village, and strode off purposefully down a narrow lane that was sign-posted for the seaside town of Polis. As she passed the coffee shop at the center of the village, the heads of the old and idle—men all—turned in unison to watch her stride by. When she returned the stares, the heads were simultaneously tucked into collars as those of turtles were, and, after she had passed, necks reappeared and glances were exchanged. All exhibited the same unrelated emotions: curiosity, fear, respect, admiration, and lust.

Widad walked into the lobby of the Dhrousha Heights Hotel with authority and a determined air. The young girl at the desk started to address her and then thought better of the idea, shrinking into the room behind the desk and pretending that a reservation was coming in over the telex machine.

Widad knew what room Abdul had taken—one of the two-room suites with kitchenette on the second floor, with a balcony overlooking the full width of the Chrysochou Bay. Having found the stairway, she started to climb, only to bump into Ahmad at the stairs' curve. He was red-faced and was nearly crashing down the stairs in his haste to be gone. He was busy buttoning his trousers, and he was barefoot. His shirt and boots were under his arm. As was so often the case now, he looked mortified and deeply ashamed.

Widad slashed out at the young man, sending him lurching even farther down the curved stairs. She spat out indecipherable insults at him in Arabic. Pulling a knife, she lunged down the stairs. But he was gone—in one of three different directions she couldn't differentiate—by the time she reached the lobby level.

Widad retraced her steps to the floor above and took five paces down the hall. The door into Abdul's suite was open. Abdul was just inside the door, leaning against the frame, hands on hips—stark naked. His eyes had that heavily hooded look Widad so well knew as the signal that his desires had recently been satiated.

She started to speak but then saw the wisp of smoke rising beyond the figure of Abdul. She looked past Abdul into the bedroom, where a raven-haired beauty, also quite naked, was lounging on the bed and smoking a cigarette. As Abdul smiled and reached out for Widad, the raven-haired beauty gave a husky laugh. As if a spell had been broken, Widad whirled, stuffed her fist in her mouth to cover the urge to scream, and stumbled down the stairs.

A small Toyota sedan was parked in front of the hotel door. Widad could see through the window that the keys were in the ignition. It was an added satisfaction that it was "the bitch's" car. Widad was down the hill and driving hard for Paphos before she even began to collect her thoughts on where she was going from here—or even why she was fleeing from here. Luckily, she had carried her rucksack with her. She had her papers. She would go to Larnaca and see where the available airplanes were headed. She'd had enough of this. She had invested far too much in him.

Meanwhile, Ahmad had made the most of the time the absence of both Abdul and Widad offered him. When he returned to the shed, he found only one of the terrorists on guard duty. The others were dozing in another shed. Invoking the name of The Asp—whom the guard knew had just been with Ahmad—the young man managed to send the lone guard on a false mission to the other side of the village.

When the guard was out of sight at the top of the hill and beyond the edge of the village, Ahmad unlocked the door of the shed in which Caitlyn and Eric were being held hostage. He barely managed to sidestep contact with the large rock Caitlyn had managed to dig out of the earthen floor of shed in her determination to do something— anything—no matter how desperate to change the equation of Eric's and her imprisonment.

"Please, it is me. You know me. At last there is an opportunity to get away. But you must be quick—and quiet—about it. Not much of a chance, but something."

Caitlyn saw who it was and made an instantaneous judgment. "Come, Eric. We must follow this young man. Now."

Ahmad shepherded the two as quickly and gently as possible out into the sunshine and down the slope toward the west. They could not get far, but he had already found a secluded ancient rock-cut tomb among the large rock outcroppings toward Lara Bay on the island's southwest coast. If they could make it this far without being caught, they could hide until night had fallen. He had a little food and some water. They just might be able to escape. It was The Asp and Widad who he feared the most. But now that the other woman had appeared, it might be an hour or more before The Asp would notice they were gone and mount a search.

Ahmad thought for a brief moment about what he had just experienced. He had learned to numb his thoughts when The Asp was at him, but the addition of the beautiful woman had been a whole new experience—and not all distressing, although he knew he should be totally ashamed and disgusted. She had been so mesmerizing. Beyond his wildest imagination.

* * * *

It was a good day for hostages. Willie Hamilton had been able to outlast his captors. The Syrian ambassador, Munir Nahlawi, was the only one Willie had been able to see clearly before his hands were tied and the blindfold was put in place, but he could readily identify the voices of several of the others in the band. He had, however, not let on that he recognized any of them. And the Syrian ambassador had seemed all too eager to full himself on being able to keep his identity from Willie, who he had been introduced to directly on more than one occasion.

As he often said for his own amusement and to befuddle others, Willie wasn't born tomorrow. He had figured that as long as he didn't panic and didn't openly identify or accuse, he might be able to stay alive. And he had been right.

In the end, his captors seemed to have been more afraid of him than he was of them. As long as Nahlawi had remained at the small, open-air camp in the Cedars Valley area south of the village of Chakistra, there seemed to have been some sense of organization— and some sense of physical threat to Hamilton. But Nahlawi had been the first one to clear out.

Hamilton had been tied to a tree, but he was permitted to sit on the ground in a reasonably comfortable hollow. He was even allowed to relieve himself in the bushes before he was tied up and was given the whispered promise that he would be untied on demand when and if nature called again. Despite the guns present, none of these men seemed anxious to resort to violence—at least against another human.

The whispered promise had not fooled the newspaper reporter. He had clearly recognized the voice of the Danish CEO of the major off-shore soft drink bottling plant. But Willie had managed to bite off any sign of recognition of the man who had given the winning speech at the monthly Toastmasters' Club gathering just two weeks previously. The speech had been on protecting endangered species. Willie promised to share a hearty laugh about this at the next Toastmasters' Club gathering—should he survive to attend.

As the night had worn on, the heat from what was probably a large open-air fire began to fade out. Hamilton had been able to identify fewer and fewer separate, distinctive voices among those who were nervously discussing what they should do now.

At length Hamilton became weary of the endlessly repeated laments of self-pity and uncertainly and fell asleep. When he awoke, there was a new heat warming his face and he could almost discern forms through his blindfold. It obviously was day. It also obviously was very, very quiet.

After a short while, Hamilton called out, asking to be taken to the bushes. He wasn't uncomfortable yet, but he wanted to make sure he wasn't alone. When no one responded upon his third request for assistance, in frustration he gave a mighty heave on his bounds and nearly flopped on his face as the rope easily unwound and gave way. Either his captors were miserable knot tiers—which Hamilton considered highly likely—or some kind soul had unloosened his bounds before the last of them had faded out of the forest and into their Mercedes and BMWs in flight back to their important "normal" lives.

After taking store of his situation and assuring himself that he, indeed, was both alive and alone, Willie started off on foot in a southerly direction, lamenting the theft of his brandy flask during the body search the previous evening. He had mistakenly thought that he had been captured north of the village of Chakistra, and, in any event, he didn't want to stray into the buffer zone, so the southerly direction was taken as the most direct and safest route to civilization.

It was not long before he saw the Kykko monastery complex straddling a ridge in the direction in which he was walking. This identification of a known location was translated into a goal. Unfortunately, the complex looked like it was a lot closer than it really was, and it took Willie far into the afternoon to approach it through the pine and cedar forest. Not long before he reached the monastery—the wealthiest and one of the largest in Cyprus, the power base of the founder of the modern Cypriot Republic, Archbishop Makarios—Willie saw evidence of the massive search. Several helicopters were aloft over the forest area where he had been held captive, and the far-off ridges in that direction seemed to be alive with movement, as tiny figures systematically searched the forested slopes.

But the monastery complex was now much closer than the search area, so Hamilton kept moving in that direction. He didn't question that the searchers were out there to find him, and his spirits had been lifted by this show of concern. He took this as proof also that Mattas had escaped capture the previous evening and had raised the alarm. He had been worried about what had happened to Demetris. There were competitors, but they were friends and admired and respected each other's work.

Willie walked right up to Takis Koniotis and a group of policemen in the parking lot outside the Kykko tourist pavilion and stood beside the police chief for several seconds, listening to Koniotis efficiently direct the expanding search, before he was noticed. When Koniotis recovered enough at the shock of Hamilton's miraculous appearance to start asking questions, Hamilton revealed all—or almost all—about his recent ordeal.

He quickly told Koniotis that, although he *had* been captured by a band, it had not been the terrorist band that held Caitlyn Koniotis and Eric Isaksen. It appeared, rather, that he had been discovered by a group of illegal hunters who were poaching the Cedars Valley to bag the rare mouflon, which was on the endangered species list and thus could not be hunted legally—which, unfortunately only seemed to heighten the thrill for some hunters. Hamilton also identified Munir

Nahlawi as one of the hunters. Willie had no regard for that man and felt he was owed something by the Syrian for the indignity he had been put through. However, the savvy political reporter claimed he had not been able to identify any other members of the hunting party. It would have caused a major scandal if Hamilton had fingered all the prominent men—both Cypriots and foreigners—he had been able to identify by their voices, and he was fairly confident that they wouldn't attempt to play big game hunter again anytime soon. He also thought he himself could put their involvement in illicit activities to much better use in the future than Takis Koniotis could.

"But I think I can help you with some information on the terrorist band, Takis," Hamilton said, drawing the police chief a couple of steps away from the others.

"Oh?"

"Yes, I think there's an informant who had been feeding information from your side of the investigation to the terrorists that has permitted them to stay a couple of steps ahead of them."

"I think you're right, Willie. And I'd certainly like to get my hands on him."

"It's not a him. It's Suzanne Abu Hani. I found her playing hide the schlong with a rough character I think is the band leader in a south-coast hotel, and he's the one I followed to the villas above Paphos where I think they've been holding Caitlyn and Isaksen."

"Yes, that fits. Thanks for the tip, Willie. Where is this villa area in Paphos."

"I can lead your men there, but I'm sorry to say that Caitlyn and Isaksen are already long gone from there."

"OK. We'll get to that. Now I think we need to get a doctor to check you over."

"What about Demetris Mattas?" Hamilton asked. "He was with me when the hunters captured me. Is he—?"

"I think he's in worse shape than you are—an auto accident in getting away from your captors. But I think he'll be OK. Now for that doctor—and I'll get busy trying to track Suzanne down."

As they were finishing their little talk a man broke into their conversation and handed a mobile telephone to the police chief. "It's that British diplomat, Alec Stuart."

Alec Stuart had regained consciousness in his Averoff Street residence. He had lost a lot of blood and was seeing double, but he was confident he could make his own way to the hospital. His first act after he had become lucid was to start trying to track Takis Koniotis down by telephone.

Stuart had quickly reached Maria Solonos, but his male pride prevented him from being able to discuss with a woman what Suzanne had meant to him—and what she had done with and to him. Maria had guessed the score in an instant but had patched the British diplomat through to her chief, who, upon hearing the abridged story of Suzanne Abu Hani's treachery, placed a nationwide search and seize order on the woman. Such orders were beginning to pile up; find and watch orders were already out on both the Lebanese and Syrian ambassadors as well as Suzanne Abu Hani. As almost an afterthought, Koniotis asked Solonos to arrange to brief Safa Ziya and to ask her to issue comparable search orders in the Turkish zone.

The plot was beginning to unravel, Koniotis thought grimly to himself. This did not elate him, however. This was the most dangerous point in the investigation, for his wife and for the UN official. They had to move very carefully from here. One thing he was becoming sure of, and that was that the hunt should continue in the area north of Paphos.

* * * *

Ahmad and his wards had cleared out of the Dhrousha sheds none too soon. Widad's behavior and abrupt departure had angered The Asp and he had dressed and walked down to the sheds to admonish her, only to find, instead of Widad, the turmoil of his terrorist band out from under cover and frantically searching around the shed area for the missing hostages.

The Asp recognized the danger immediately. Surely the terrorists had now been seen by someone in the village and their presence would already be passing from villager to villager with the speed of lightning. Not only were the hostages missing, but so were both Ahmad and Widad—and Widad had driven away in Suzanne Abu Hani's car. Suzanne was now stranded and was one more person on the scene than he had wanted here, and, at a time that he needed to blend into the background, Suzanne Abu Hani was hardly an unnoticeable spot on the wall. He could not let her stay this close. He didn't even think he could let her live much longer, although he couldn't afford to let himself be connected with her death. She was too well placed in the hierarchy above him.

It was time to disband the brigade. He had already accomplished more with the band than he had intended, but everything was coming unglued. There were still a couple of things that needed to be cleaned up, however.

The Asp quickly told his best trackers, Mamluck al-Turk and Salah Hamad, to hunt down the hostages and kill them. He didn't much care what happened to the woman, but the assassination of the UN official, Eric Isaksen, had been the sole assignment he had originally taken on as his own avenue to fame within the Hizballah when he brought his band to Cyprus. The Hizballah had only invited Isaksen to Beirut under a flag of protection to buy time to consolidate their support in Lebanon. They wanted Isaksen to die before he reached Beirut. They had planned to have his plane go down en route from Cyprus to Lebanon, but The Asp had seen the opportunity to dispatch him in a way that would give The Asp the credit. All of the auxiliary operations he had successfully completed would mean nothing if he didn't fulfill his primary goal.

At the same time, The Asp was not a fool. Everything here was unraveling too quickly. He would send his best and most ruthless fighters—other than Widad, who herself had disappeared—to track down and kill Isaksen, but he would not endanger himself when the Cypriot police were probably hot on his trail.

The Asp directed Al-Turk and Hamad to search out by the rock formations in the near distance toward the sea in the west. This looked like the most logical path of escape. They were told that Ahmad and/or Widad were also to die if they were found with the UN official and the woman. He sent Salem Qazzar up through the village and toward the east on the off chance that the escapees had taken this route. Qazzar spoke Greek—he even had the typical handsome features of a Greek. He also was the best mountain man and was the most likely to be able to assimilate into the population and not arouse suspicion in the village.

The rest of those in the brigade were instructed to head for the fishing and tourist village of Lachi on Chrysochou Bay, where the brigade was already scheduled to link up with a vessel from Lebanon. They were to search for the escapees toward the north as they moved to Lachi. He instructed the three groups of searchers to meet up on the coast again after they had completed their missions or no later than the next evening. Meanwhile The Asp said he was going back to the hotel to pick up his gear and would be joining the band in Lachi later in the day.

Abdul *did* return to the hotel, but only to pick up Suzanne and to race, as fast as having Suzanne in tow would allow him, toward the southern—not the northern—coast in one of the vehicles he had taken from the villas near Ayios Neophytos monastery.

Suzanne was dragging her feet about leaving, and he had the greatest urge to do her right there and then. She was primping and dressing herself as if she was going to a tea party much later in the day rather than trying to escape a police dragnet. She even was carefully arranging a wide-brimmed hat on her head and pulling on gloves— both very incongruous in this rural village hotel. Abdul wanted to whack the woman, but he still needed her.

He would have to keep Suzanne with him until he could dispose of her quietly and without raising the suspicions of his superiors. She—and one other on Cyprus—knew entirely too much about him. He couldn't get at the other connection now, but he could make sure Suzanne didn't escape him.

In the event, Suzanne saved him from the clutches of the Cypriot police. After he had passed through the city of Paphos and was racing toward Limassol with the intent of continuing on to the airport in Larnaca, Suzanne made him turn off toward the Paphos airport. She told him that security at the Paphos airport was more lax than at Larnaca. She even had the cash to buy seats on a flight to London Heathrow, which was just about to take off, although she insisted that they purchase their tickets separately. London was the perfect destination. By the time the authorities would discover Suzanne Abu Hani and companion had flown to the UK, the two would be hopelessly lost in the protecting arms of one of the world's largest cities.

* * * *

No one had told Widad al-Ghabra about the dangers of using Larnaca airport. Therefore she did not manage to get anywhere near the flight to London—the same flight that later landed briefly in Paphos before continuing to London—before she was detected and arrested. Although she found this arrest very disheartening and frustrating, it undoubtedly saved her life. If she had made her flight, she could not have avoided meeting up with The Asp again between Paphos and London, and an annoyed asp is not a pretty sight in a confined airplane high over Europe.

When Koniotis was reached from the airport, he gave orders for the woman to be delivered straightaway to the police department in Paphos and to be confined there without having contact with anyone. Koniotis was on his way to Paphos and he wanted this one waiting for him—and he wanted her to be alive when he got there. Everyone who had come into contact with the suspect at the airport and knew who she was was also to travel together to Paphos. They were all to wait at the police department there and to have contact with no one else until Koniotis arrived to take charge. Koniotis didn't want anything left to chance. He wanted his wife back—alive—and so he was going to move very carefully from here.

"One more thing, chief," reported the police officer in charge at the airport before the line was cut. "The Al-Ghabra woman had keys to an automobile in her possession when she was apprehended. The key chain was a tag that identified the vehicle's registration number, and we found the automobile in the airport parking lot. It is a Toyota sedan that is registered to the Lebanese embassy, although it carries regular yellow-colored plates rather than the green diplomatic plates."

"The Abu Hanis again," Koniotis exclaimed with exasperation. "I can't wait to get my hands on Suzanne Abu Hani. She's showing up in all aspects of this investigation now."

But Koniotis would have to wait a good long time to see Suzanne again, although a meeting would not be prevented by what The Asp had planned for the siren. In fact, Suzanne was feeling much better than Abdul was when they reached London. She had taken a seat in the small, crowded nonsmoking portion of the cabin, while Abdul had been booked into the almost-deserted—but very commodious—smoking section at the back of the airplane.

Suzanne visited Abdul briefly while the flight was passing over the German Alps—a beautiful sight that could be clearly seen by the passengers from both sides of the airplane. Abdul had apparently decided to take a nap after visiting with Suzanne, and she thoughtfully covered him with a blanket when she left to go back to her seat, being careful to buckle his seat belt over the blanket so the stewardess wouldn't bother him before the landing. No one had noticed or remarked on her brief visit to the back of the cabin. The German Alps were a remarkably interesting sight from the air on this day and all of the passengers had had their faces glued to the plane's windows.

Suzanne was already through customs, hat and gloves in hand, and out on the street at Heathrow before anyone thought to even begin to check if the dead man in the smoking section—dead from chloroform followed by a long, nasty-looking hat pin into the heart—had been traveling alone.

Chapter Eighteen

The copyboy had made yet another swing around the room—or, rather, across the room to Demetris Mattas's desk and straight back to the editor's office. The circuits past Demetris's desk were becoming more frequent and more pointed. Most of the other writers and columnists in the large room had finished their work and retired for the evening to the local bars. The time pressure wasn't helping him, nor was his throbbing head and his aching body. But he knew Willie Hamilton would have his version of the events in Cedars Valley in the next day's edition of the *Cyprus Mail*, and he couldn't let Hamilton scoop him on this story.

Hamilton's version would, of course, be fuller and more exciting than his own. However, Hamilton would stick with reporting the events—and his part in them—whereas his own "Under the Grapevine" column could provide devastating parody on the illegal hunting activities of the Syrian ambassador, among others—and not just the illegal poaching of small birds out of season, but also the hunting of the rare and revered—and protected—mouflon. Jabs at the diplomatic community would, most certainly, make for good copy, but it was the "among others" that was causing Demetris to sharpen his wit and his pen. He suspected that many a Cypriot businessman and social leader would be squirming and looking over his shoulder for a good long time after his *Simerini* column hit the newsstands. It would all be parody, no one directly identified, but the characteristics given each one involved would be telling. Anyone who mattered would know exactly who he was skewering. And it was something that a Greek Cypriot could get away with that wouldn't be tolerated from the British newsman.

Mattas really should not have returned to work so quickly. In fact, he should not have left the Pedhoulas hospital for several more days. He had not been released. After he regained consciousness and determined that Hamilton was safe and the police had already received all of the information he could give them, his next thought went to his newspaper and to his column. Thorough professional that he was, he couldn't just concede the breaking of the story of the Cedars Valley VIP poaching club to Hamilton. Therefore, as soon as he was able to sit up in bed without being forced right back onto the pillows by the spinning in his head, he sneaked out of the clinic and engaged a taxi to take him straight down the mountain and to the *Simerini* offices in Nicosia.

It already was considerably past his regular column filing deadline when he arrived at the newspaper, but his editor was as excited as he was about the story he and Hamilton had unearthed and was keeping the presses silent to the very last minute to be able to front-page what Mattas was composing.

But Mattas's injuries from his automobile accident near the Kykko monastery were just too severe for him to be able to think straight. The editor had just about made the decision to force Mattas to give him an interview to cover the essential facts of Hamilton's kidnapping for the next day's edition, with Mattas's column to follow when he was in better shape and when they had more time, when the telephone on Mattas's desk started to ring. Mattas probably wouldn't have picked the telephone receiver up, but the ringing was felt in his head like a sledgehammer, he could see the editor and the copyboy beginning to circle toward him from different corners of the room, and he wanted to put off the inevitable for as long as possible.

The voice on the other end of the line was one of the newspaper's occasional "stringer" reporters from the Paphos area, a schoolteacher who sometimes was able to provide enough information from an unusually newsworthy event from that region to save a long trip by one of the full-time reporters in Nicosia. Mattas was about to put the teacher off on the excuse of an impossible filing deadline, when the teacher invoked the magical "Caitlyn Koniotis" name.

Mattas grabbed for a pencil and pad and wildly waved at the editor, who returned posthaste to his office to pick up his linking line to Mattas's telephone.

"I think I've seen her—and probably the missing UN official as well," announced the teacher breathlessly. "One of my students, a girl prone to fantasies, claimed she saw a group of foreigners hiding in huts down the hill from and to the west of the village. I didn't believe her at first, as she's always making things up. But this time she seemed so definite and was not content with just my usual words of agreement. In the end, she dragged me down to where we could see the huts without being seen ourselves, and that's when I saw them myself."

"Wait. Slow down. What village are you talking about and when did this happen?" Mattas interjected. His head was hurting worse than ever and he was growing faint.

"Dhrousha. We're in Dhrousha. In the highlands about a half hour north of Paphos and fifteen minutes south of Polis. It's been well over an hour since we were able to leave our vantage point and come back into the village and find a telephone. Shortly after the woman and old man left, all hell broke out and we couldn't move ourselves until the group of foreigners disbanded."

"Were the woman and man all right when you last saw them, and what direction did they go in? And what do you mean you couldn't move until the group of foreigners disbanded?"

"The couple moved off down the hill. They had a young Arabic-looking guy who was guiding them—he had a rifle and was herding them, so it looked like they were just being moved. We couldn't see much farther down the slope than the huts, though. We couldn't leave right away because shortly after that a large group of armed men poured out of the other two huts and began looking around. Then they were joined by another man who had walked down from the village and who seemed to be in charge. After a short, heated discussion, he went back up to the village and the rest of the men divided up and headed in different directions."

"Did any of them go down the hill in the same direction the couple took?"

"Yes, a couple, I guess."

"But the woman and older man were still alive when you last saw them?"

"Yes."

Mattas turned the teacher over to his editor to receive more information and swung back to his own computer terminal. He was still seeing double and his head ached even more now than before he'd received the call. If only Maria was here to soothe his aching head . . . although maybe she couldn't do anything about the type of ache he was suffering.

The thought of Maria made the face of Caitlyn Koniotis flash through his brain. And this thought was followed by the visage of her distraught husband, Takis Koniotis.

The copyboy was once again standing very close to Mattas and staring at him searchingly. It was long past the time he was supposed to be off duty, and he had a full night of studies facing him.

Mattas groaned, reached into his bottom drawer and pulled out yet another of his "contingencies columns," tossed it to the copyboy, and, picking up the telephone receiver once again, switched to an outside line. The editor could write up the teacher's story. Mattas knew that the honorable thing for him to do was to call Maria directly and do whatever he could to help the police get to Dhrousha and to Caitlyn Koniotis and Eric Isaksen in time—*if* there *was* still time.

"Maria, it's me. No, no, there's no time now to get into me about leaving the hospital. I think I know where they are . . . Caitlyn and Isaksen . . . yes, yes, still alive, but apparently still in the clutches of the terrorists. An informant just called . . . In Dhrousha . . . well, below Dhrousha now, heading down to the coast toward Lachi. Yes, yes, go ahead and get it rolling. We can talk later."

The copyboy's movement toward the editor's office was arrested by what he heard Mattas telling someone on the telephone. His eyes narrowed. Maybe he wouldn't get much studying done tonight after all. But maybe he would turn a tidy profit instead. Up to now he had only been able to give them tidbits of information he picked up in the newsroom. This, however, was a real bombshell and was directly of interest to them. After placing Mattas's contingency column on the editor's desk—the editor being fully engrossed in tapping out a flash news story on his computer to fill the space he'd been holding on tomorrow's front page, the copyboy quietly moved to another room and found a telephone. He searched in his wallet for the telephone number of the Russian embassy and began to dial.

* * * *

Demetris Mattas's call caught Maria Solonos at police headquarters in Nicosia about to leave for Paphos, where Takis Koniotis was headed to interrogate the woman terrorist who had been arrested at the airport. In fact, Maria would already have left, except that the American diplomat Paul Conte had dropped in to find out the latest news on the search of the Cedars Valley for Caitlyn Koniotis and Eric Isaksen. Conte had been very frustrated when he heard that the group Hamilton and Mattas had found were illegal hunters rather than the terrorist band holding Caitlyn and the UN official.

Maria received a telephone call and Conte was in the process of leaving the police department building when Solonos called him back and explained what Mattas telephoned to tell her.

"Then we must get to Dhrousha as soon as possible," Conte exclaimed.

"I'll start out after I've called Takis. Luckily he's already in the area, But I'd like to impose upon you to go somewhere else. It's important."

"Just name it," said Conte.

282

Therefore, just before calling the Paphos police headquarters to intercept and redirect Koniotis, Solonos sent Conte off to the Turkish zone to inform Safa Ziya what they had learned and to request that she get the buffer zone in the Morphou area sealed off, so that the Mouflon Brigade couldn't be able to escape across the Green Line again. Conte had said he was sure Ziya would get the Turkish army mobilized to seal the border, but he could see immediately that this suggestion disturbed Solonos.

"Please try to convince Safa to use other forces than the Turkish army, Paul," Maria pleaded. "You know how we feel about the occupation army—especially as brutal and trigger happy as they are. I'm sure that Takis would be very upset to learn that the mainland Turks were involved—even to help Caitlyn. Cooperating with the Turkish Cypriots—especially with Safa Ziya—is one thing, but cooperating with the Turkish army is out of the question."

"I understand," Conte quickly responded. "I'll see what Ziya can do." But he left determined to get the border sealed even if the Turkish army had to be used. He could understand the feelings of the Greek Cypriots in this regard, but this wasn't his fight, and it wasn't Caitlyn's or Eric Isaksen's fight either. They deserved the best chance they could be given.

* * * *

Takis Koniotis found the terrorist, Widad al-Ghabra, far more willing to talk about the Mouflon Brigade's activities and whereabouts than Faris Sukkar had been. It didn't take long to find out that she was the veritable "woman scorned" at the hands of the leader of the brigade. And what she had to say was both shocking and frightening.

She had proudly told him that the brigade was holed up in Dhrousha in preparation for being taken off Cyprus by boat near the fishing and tourist village of Lachi west of Polis and on Chrysochou Bay. Koniotis had nearly broken the interrogation right there and then to lead the police forces to Dhrousha before they could kidnap Caitlyn and Eric Isaksen to Beirut as they had previously done with Irina Lukenov. But as he was leaving the cell, Widad's taunting laughter brought him back to hear the worst possible news.

The Mouflon Brigade didn't intend to take Caitlyn and Isaksen to Beirut, she announced through hysterical laughter. They had intended to kill Isaksen here in Cyprus all along. Isaksen was not meant to reach Beirut alive, and her brigade leader meant to kill him here. The band's leader had just been embellishing on the assignment and teasing everyone to amuse himself. And they had no further need for Takis's wife either. Her kidnapping had, as he suspected, only been intended to confuse and slow the police investigation. They planned to kill Isaksen with the rest during their attack on the UN tour, but The Asp had wanted to toy with the situation. Now that Widad had left the band, she said, she was sure the hostages had already been killed. She let on that only her intervention had been keeping them alive.

In the face of this information, which the woman had delivered with glee—but had convincingly delivered—the call from Maria offered hope. She confirmed she'd gotten a report just now that the band had last been seen in Dhrousha, but she offered some hope that the hostages might still be alive, or at least were alive a couple of hours previously. In any event, the noose was closing on the band, and as long as Koniotis had a goal and was active, he could always hope that everything would turn out all right.

As the laughter diminished in the cell behind him, Koniotis quickly mobilized all of the police forces he could muster and raced for Dhrousha.

* * * *

Ahmad, Caitlyn, and Eric had been huddled together inside the old rock-cut tomb within the prominent rock formation to the west of Dhrousha for more than two hours. The sun was setting off Lara Beach below them, and it would soon be dark enough to strike out for freedom. Isaksen had been much weakened from the fast-paced escape following the days of inactivity. Caitlyn didn't feel much better, but the mere promise of freedom and refreshed her and lifted her spirits. The longer they went undetected, the greater was her exhilaration.

It was dark in the cave now and Caitlyn queried Ahmad in a whisper whether they could start their descent to the sea and to the nearest village—other than Dhrousha—that had a telephone. Ahmad answered that he was sure it was too soon to show themselves, but, in response to Caitlyn's insistent whispers, he rose and went to the mouth of the cave.

Ahmad disappeared for a second and shuffled about outside the mouth of the tomb. He turned, slowly walked back into the cave, a twisted, questioning expression on his face, and collapsed onto the earthen floor. He was clutching his stomach with both hands. A long handle was protruding between his fingers, and blood was spurting from a gaping wound.

Caitlyn started to scream, but Salah Hamad was on her in a flash. The terrorist struck her across the mouth with a back-handed slap that sent her reeling against the wall of the tomb and took the breath out of her.

The short scuffle with Caitlyn had brought Eric Isaksen's head snapping up. He had been sitting, head in hands, near the back of the tomb. In that same instant, however, Mamluck al-Turk reached Isaksen and pushed him back into the wall in a sitting position, a nasty-looking knife prodding at the skin of his throat, ready to be driven home in an instant.

Regaining her breath, Caitlyn was able to scream—or at least to start a healthy scream—before Hamad backhanded her again and brought his rifle up to a firing position, just inches from her body.

"No, not the rifle," the other terrorist cautioned in Arabic. "We don't want anyone to hear their deaths."

For a brief moment everyone was suspended in time. Ahmad coughing and groaning on the ground, the handle of the knife obscenely protruding from his belly; Caitlyn trapped against the wall, panting, her eyes darting about the cave; Eric Isaksen beginning to come out of his reverie, his eyes beginning to burn; Al-Turk poised in front of Isaksen, holding a knife to his throat but his attention on the woman; Hamad was holding Caitlyn at bay with the point of his rifle. But, unfortunately, time didn't remain in suspension for very long.

Salah Hamad was the first to break the freeze. The melting came in the form of a lascivious grin forming and spreading across his face as he watching the panting Caitlyn, her clothes almost in tatters from the days on the move from one hideout to another. He answered his comrade in Arabic: "They both have to die, but there is no reason we cannot have some fun first, is there? Me first and then you."

"Agreed. Let me off the old man first and then I'll come help you."

"No. Make him watch. That will be part of the fun. I can handle her myself."

With this, Hamad started fumbling at his trousers, which quickly fell down around his knees.

Caitlyn was panicked. She had understood enough of the Arabic and of the action to know what was going on—and that the terrorists intended to kill them all anyway. But what did Eric know of what they were saying?

She need not have wondered, however. Isaksen was fluent in Arabic and understood the situation even better than she did. With one push, he had Al-Turk on the ground, the knife clattering out of the cave entrance and into the night. Al-Turk half rose and moved toward the opening, but Isaksen tackled him and held on as best he could. The terrorist was too strong for Isaksen, however, and shuffled toward the figure of the dying Ahmad. He reached his hand out toward the handle of the knife that was ebbing away Ahmad's life. Ahmad, however, had both the strength and presence of mind to shuffle away, the knife handle momentarily out of Al-Turk's reach. If nothing else, he knew it was his only chance. If the knife came out now, he quickly die from the gushing of blood from his wound.

Meanwhile, Hamad's attention had been elsewhere, groping at Caitlyn as well as he could without losing the grip on his rifle. However, Eric's ploy was short-lived and a bit too noisy. Or perhaps Caitlyn had given the action across the cave away by looking in that direction when Hamad expected her to be watching him. In any case, Hamad eventually took notice that something was amiss elsewhere in the tomb and he backed off—which was not easy to do with his trousers around his knees—and swung his rifle around toward Isaksen.

Two shots rang out.

And then, after what had seemed like an eternity, the immediate threat had been lifted, and a hysterically sobbing Caitlyn was in the comforting arms of Ellen Larkin.

Chapter Nineteen

The once-proud city state of Polis is located in one of the most inaccessible areas of the Cypriot Republic. Known in ancient times as Marion and later, during the rule of the Egyptian Ptolemaices, as Arsinoe, after one of the thirty-some lovers and wives of the god Apollo, the micro kingdom was once the outlet to the world of the gold and copper mined from the nearby Troodos Mountains. But then, as one of the killer plagues of cities in the region—running a close third behind earthquake and sack—its harbor silted up, and the city sank into historical oblivion. Another harbor was established a few miles to the west along the Chrysochou Bay coast, but, until recent years, this harbor hadn't risen higher than the status of a small fishing village.

Time seemed to have passed the Chrysochou Bay coast by, aided significantly during the last twenty years by the Turkish invasion and the political division of the island. The region was isolated from the north by the Mediterranean and from the west by the wild and uninhabited Akamas Peninsula, now a national parkland. Therefore, when the Cypriot Republic consciously decided tourism would be its main industry and established the beach resorts of the southern and western coats, it neglected to include the isolated northwestern coast of Chrysochou Bay in its plans.

This proved to be both the Polis area's good fortune and its eventual shortfall. A particularly beautiful area, especially during the springtime display of the white-petaled almond and pink-petaled cherry trees, this quadrant offered unspoiled village-topped hills undulating down from the Troodos to the wooded Akamas Peninsula, with its legendary Springs of Aphrodite and Fontana Amorosa fountain of youth, and to pristine beaches and rocky coasts to both the north and the west. As tourists became more conversant with the glories of Cyprus and more adventuresome, they had, in recent years begun to "discover" Polis—and especially the quaint fishing village of Lachi, which became the home to small "getaway" hotels.

Unfortunately, although "getaway" was a good way to describe Lachi on this day, "quiet" didn't exactly fit the bill. In the last moments of twilight, the first wave of the Cypriot police forces that had been sent to the area by Takis Koniotis converged on the remains of the Mouflon Brigade just as they were reforming and coming out into the open in the main strip of Lachi to make their rendezvous off the beach with the boat from Beirut.

The fire fight was short-lived, helped by the disorganization of the band having no leadership in the absence of both The Asp, and Widad. As soon as the police forces realized that, open-air dining tourists or no tourists, the terrorist band was determined to cover its retreat across the hotel strip and through the restaurants to the beach with as much firepower as was needed, the police held fire and retreated to protective positions around Lachi. If nothing else, they reasoned, they would contain the terrorists within Lachi and not let them break out either to the west and into the wild terrain of the Akamas Peninsula or to the east across the barrier of the buffer zone.

But the remnants of the brigade had no intention of lingering any longer in Cyprus. When they reached the beach, they found, to their relief, that Ibrahim and the fishing vessel had arrived and were prepared to take them aboard even though they were arriving at Lachi one day earlier than agreed. Screened from the view of the police, who were trapped in the hotel complex across the road, the terrorists quickly climbed into the three small boats Ibrahim had sent up to the beach when he heard the sound of automatic weapons fire and vanished from sight.

It took nearly an hour in the gathering dark for the police to realize that the terrorists no longer were in Lachi and nearly an hour longer than that to calm down and patch up the tourists who had been caught in the brief, but withering cross-fire. The coastal patrol was notified that the terrorists had somehow escaped by sea, but it would take even more precious time for the patrol boats to steam around from Paphos to investigate.

Ibrahim was happy to have cleared off the terrorist band onto his awaiting fishing trawler without loss of life among those who had made it to the Lachi beach. But he was disturbed that neither The Asp nor his second in command, Widad al-Ghabra, were present. Even more disturbing was that Suzanne Abu Hani wasn't there either. He had explicitly been told by higher authority—much higher authority— that she would be linking up with the brigade for evacuation and that she was to be accorded every convenience. Ibrahim was scared and would not be steaming so hard away from the Cypriot coast and in a southeast arc toward the Lebanese coast if he had not feared he would be intercepted by the Cypriots. Even under this threat, he was not sure whether it would be worse to be captured by the Greeks or to return to Lebanon without the Abu Hani woman.

* * * *

Caitlyn Koniotis was struggling up the hillside toward the lights of Dhrousha for dear life—not for her life, but for that of the boy Ahmad. She had not stayed in the cave long enough to ask Ellen Larkin how she had found them or why she had been out looking for them alone, before she was sent off for help. Both of the terrorists had been killed instantly with just one shot each from the pistol in Larkin's hand. Caitlyn had not questioned why the fragile-looking young woman was such an expert shot. She could only think of Ahmad at that moment and how they must save the life of the boy who had tried so hard to save their lives.

Ahmad was bleeding badly and was close to losing consciousness.

"I'll go up to the village for medical help. This man needs it as soon as possible," Larkin said as she knelt beside the moaning Ahmad. "Can you cope, Caitlyn? Do you know what to do for the young man?"

"I have no first-aid skills, if that's what you're asking," Caitlyn said. "I'm afraid I'm not needed here as much as you are, if you do."

"I do, but you've been through an ordeal. I don't want you to—"

"Someone has to—and soon," Caitlyn said.

They both looked at Eric Isaksen, but he was sitting near the back of the cave, rubbing his leg and moaning louder than Ahmad was. In his struggle with the Mamluck al-Turk, he was bleeding from a

292

number of cuts and had seriously twisted his ankle in the fight. They both could see that he wouldn't be able to climb up to the village.

"Is it safe out there?" Caitlyn asked. She was holding her breath. She would go out there and try to get the village regardless—Ahmad's life depended on it, and he had tried to save them—but she was hoping there was some good news in all of this.

"I'm sure there are no other terrorists were lurking about. I've been watching and tracking these two for some time. I saw the rest of the band dispersing in other directions. I'd lost these two terrorists briefly too—but then I heard your scream."

"Wish me luck, then," Caitlyn said, and she slipped out of the cave tomb and into the dark.

As soon as she was out in the open, Caitlyn realized how dire her circumstances were. Here she was, still far away from the village above and hopelessly trapped in and confused by the warren of small, rock-walled plots between her and her goal, most of which were planted with lines of knobby-rooted grapevines. She couldn't find a road or a pathway through the plots, and she was growing tired and beginning to panic. She came up against a solid wall of loose rock and started to try to climb over it. But the rocks were too loosely laid. They came away in her hands and under her feet, and she slipped down to the ground in a frustrated sob—and closed her eyes in exhaustion.

She felt a light touch on her arm, and then there was the girl. Like an apparition. A girl with a strange smile and sparkling eyes. She gently took Caitlyn by the arm and guided her, slowly, but surely, to the hidden path and up to the lower edge of the village. Caitlyn turned in the dark to thank the girl. But she was gone—as eerily and completely as she had appeared.

Caitlyn was standing on a road above the sectioned fields below. She shook her head, not knowing how she had gotten here—whether the young girl who had guided her had been real or a ghost. But there was no time to ruminate on what had happened. She turned and moved as quickly as she could up into the village and toward the lights of the village square.

But she was not to reach the village square. As she passed across the mouth of a small side street, she was pulled roughly into the shadows and smothered in a breath-wrenching embrace.

"Caitlyn, Caitlyn. Is it really you?" exclaimed Takis Koniotis in wonder, the tears quickly welling up in his eyes. "It's me, Takis. Thank God I've found you and that you're safe."

Caitlyn collapsed further into her husband's encompassing embrace and began to sob uncontrollably—with joy, relief, and with the pent-up release of being able to give over control to someone else—to someone she trusted and who would take care of her.

She had to tell him about Ahmad. She had to get help down to the cave as soon as possible. But Ahmad's plight wasn't the first thing she was able to voice. She gathered her strength through her body-wracking sobs to tell Takis that Ahmad desperately needed medical attention, but, in the event, the first thing she said had nothing to do with Ahmad or with anything she was consciously thinking of.

"Oh, Takis, I'm pregnant."

"Yes, yes. Hush, my love," Takis managed through his own sobs. "I know."

* * * *

From the seaside terrace of his villa near Tripoli on the Lebanese coast, one of the small coterie of masterminds behind the activities of the Hizballah in Beirut and, not quite as commandingly, of the Mouflon Brigade in Cyprus looked down at his yacht, floating placidly in the clear waters of the Mediterranean below, its running lights aglow in the deepening darkness. He called out to the woman who had dozed off on the vessel's deck and who, when she awoke, waved her bikini top at him and disappeared below deck.

Ayman Abu Hani pushed the antenna of his mobile telephone into the handset and smiled at his friend and colleague—the hidden patriarch of the French shipping empire of the Piccard family—who was stretched out on a lounge nearby.

"That was Suzanne. She won't be arriving on the fishing vessel because she has just arrived in London. She said that Abdul got out of hand and had to be canceled."

"Pity," said Guy Piccard. "In many ways he was such a resourceful and creative man. But so unrefined."

"Hardly a pity, I fear," the wayward Lebanese ambassador to Cyprus responded. "He was out of control, unfortunately. The original, simple order was to unobtrusively conduct training. It was a mistake to let him know that we wanted Eric Isaksen killed before he arrived in Beirut and to do it in such a way that the Hizballah wouldn't be implicated. If he hadn't known that, he might not have formed his own, unapproved plans, and caused such a furor on Cyprus. But, with the stunts Abdul pulled, the Hizballah was implicated even before Isaksen was killed. At least Suzanne was able to assure me that Isaksen is dead by now."

"And the rest of the unit?" the distinguished-looking and reclusive shipping magnate queried.

"Ibrahim has messaged in that all who reached the coast were successfully picked up and are being brought here."

"Pity," sighed the Frenchman.

"Yes. They'll all have to be killed, of course. Including Ibrahim. Tehran is steaming mad about the whole affair. I've had to promise to totally clean up."

"And Suzanne?" Piccard asked delicately.

"Oh, no, not Suzanne," Abu Hani answered as the woman who had gone below in a bikini returned to the deck, dressed in a frothy cocktail dress, blew him a kiss, and climbed down to the dinghy for the short crossing to the pier below the terrace. "It's true that she almost committed a costly blunder in one respect, but it isn't really her fault. She could not have known. I didn't tell her about every aspect of our operations. No, I must remain faithful to my Suzanne. She still has several good years left in her. Perhaps when she no longer is able to drive men—and some women—crazy with lust . . ."

The sentence was not finished. The two men gave each other knowing smiles and clinked their glasses. Ah, this was the life. There was a sophisticated, golden lining to the business of international terrorism—as long as one didn't let ideology get in the way, of course.

* * * *

Ibrahim intercepted the call from the police forces in Lachi to the coastal patrol unit in Paphos. He was even then rounding on the tip of the Akamas Peninsula. It was getting darker and darker. As soon as he cleared the point, with its rocky outcroppings rising artistically out of the water just off the coast, he would direct the vessel's captain to steam straight out for international waters and sail a wide arc down and around toward the Lebanese coast. This would take much longer than a straight-line sail, but he didn't want to meet up with the Cypriot patrol boats. They couldn't hug the coastline as they normally would have done. To do so would put their trawler on a collision course with the vessels streaming north out of Paphos. He also was in no rush to get to Tripoli. Maybe he wouldn't go to Tripoli. Maybe he would take his chances and direct the trawler directly back to Beirut and try to disappear from his Hizballah colleagues there.

But, who could ever escape from the Hizballah in Lebanon?

He would think about his options, such as they were, later. For now, they had to clear the Cyprus coast and reach international waters.

But Ibrahim and his fishing vessel were not going to either Tripoli or Beirut. They weren't going to get any farther than the tip of the Akamas Peninsula. And when they reached there, they were going to go straight to the bottom of the Mediterranean.

As the fishing vessel rounded Cape Akamas, another, faster vessel appeared from the other side of the peninsula and bore straight down on them. The captain of the Beirut boat tried his best to turn the nose of his fishing trawler around, but he couldn't escape the faster ship.

Just as it seemed the trawler would be rammed, the other vessel neatly turned broadside. Ibrahim let out a sigh of relief—a short-lived sigh of relief. As the other vessel turned, a deadly barrage of automatic weapons fire honed in on the trawler. The gunfire caught the terrorists, most of whom were on deck, unaware and unprepared.

It also caught most of the terrorist band somewhere in their individual vital organs.

The Russians were merciless. Mikhail Lukenov was in the thick of the firing squad. His son, Uri, was there as well. They were relentlessly pumping vengeful lead into the fishing trawler long after all signs of resistance or movement had ceased.

It was almost an anticlimax when the fuel tank on the trawler exploded. The Russian vessel had to reverse its engines full to avoid being kissed by the flames of the fireball. The trawler sank like a rock, and, when the Russians had verified that there were no survivors from the targeted ship, they pointed the nose of their own vessel out to sea and opened up the engines. It wouldn't do for them to be found here by the Cypriot coastal patrol.

When the patrol vessels arrived on the scene, all they found was floating debris. They marked the site for a more extensive search in the morning light. They were sure this must be the ship they had been sent to intercept, and, as they knew their prey carried the band that been terrorizing Cyprus for more than a week, they were just as happy that they would not have to take the ship by force. But there was a mystery. As they approached the cape, there had been two blips on their radar screen. Now there still was one blip, which was moving swiftly away, even though a vessel had almost certainly sunk here—and recently; the debris was still aflame.

The one blip—a vessel that had ignored all of their radio signals requesting identification—was now well into international waters. They couldn't report a clean ending of the story to their government. Pity. Such always seemed to be the case with international terrorism. The new day was sure to introduce yet more such challenges and assaults

Chapter Twenty

A week after they were reunited in the village of Dhrousha, Caitlyn and Takis Koniotis were snuggled up together on a cushioned bamboo settee in the large covered area under the bedroom wing of their Acropolis home in Nicosia. The archaeologists working on the royal tomb Caitlyn had discovered in the hillside across the roadway were gone for the evening. The day had just reached that magical twilight time in the clear atmosphere of Cyprus when the waning light was tracing and accentuating the white stucco walls, red tile roofs, and lush greenery cultivated in otherwise dry and sandy gardens. The heat of the day had burned off, but the evening chill had not yet set in. There was no traffic. All of the Cypriots across the city were about to sit down to their evening meals, which would last several hours.

Takis was drinking a Keo beer. Caitlyn, who would much rather have had her customary twilight-time brandy sour, was dutifully swigging fresh orange juice. Takis was irreverently using a section of Roman column that had appeared from within the hillside only three days earlier as a footstool, and Caitlyn had her legs curled under her and was leaning heavily on her husband's shoulder. At a movement from within, her eyes lit up. She took the beer out of Takis's hand and moved the hand to her stomach. They both were lost in the thrill of prenatal parenthood for some minutes.

When the spell had worn off, Caitlyn's thoughts went back to the young man who had made this happy scene possible. This was really the first night since she had escaped that she felt like talking about her ordeal. Although Takis had told her something of what had happened since her rescue, he obviously held other information back until she was ready to absorb it. Well, she thought she was ready now.

"Takis," she said gently, "Ahmad will be out of the hospital soon. What will become of him? He can't stay here in Cyprus, can he? I suppose he just wouldn't be accepted." It was given as a statement, but she had meant it as a question, and Takis understood it as such.

"We were working on that earlier today. I think we may have found an answer."

"We?" queried Caitlyn.

"Yes, Safa Ziya and I. Ahmad has lived most of his life in northern Cyprus and probably thinks of that as his home—certainly much more than Turkey or Lebanon. And neither one of us thinks it would be safe for him to return to Lebanon anyway—even if he was willing to go there. Safa has offered him a job with her—replacing the detective Sami, no doubt—and said she would arrange for him to be able to live in northern Cyprus again. I conveyed the offer to him this afternoon, and he accepted it, with pleasure. It seemed like just having a job and someplace to live that is familiar to him will speed his recovery."

"I'm so glad," Caitlyn said with a sigh. "He really did save our lives. More than once. I will never be able to tell you just how much he suffered so that Eric and I wouldn't have to suffer any more than we did. Has anything been heard from his uncle? You know, I remember him now. He was that tour guide in Salamis I had found such an obsequious pest. It all seems so long ago now. I must have seen Ahmad then, too. He was there in Salamis, but I didn't really remember him."

"We haven't heard from the Lebanese merchant yet. In many ways his telephone call to Safa was one of our biggest breaks in the case. In any event, I don't wish him ill. He seems to be a survivor. I'm sure we'll see him again someday—someday when we least expect it."

"You say you saw Safa today? How was she? You must try to get us together soon. I know she did all she could to help rescue me, and I'd like to think her in person."

"Yes, she says she wants to see you too. But to tell you the truth . . ." and Takis couldn't help chuckling at the thought, ". . . she seems so head over heels with that agronomist, John Patterson, that I don't think she's thinking a great deal about anything else at the moment."

"Well, I think it's sweet," Caitlyn countered defensibly. "Safa's a fine woman, and she deserves all of the happiness she can find."

"No argument from me," Takis returned.

"Tell me more about the terrorists, Takis. I keep thinking about the second vessel the coastal patrol said was in the area off the Akamas Peninsula the other night and wouldn't answer their signal. How can we be sure there aren't terrorists out there who will be back or will be doing the same thing somewhere else?"

"I'm afraid there probably will always be terrorists," Takis said with a sigh. "That's what our world is coming to, I'm sorry to say. Of course we can't really ever be sure all of those from this band are dead or captured, but we think we got most of them—at least most of the lower- and mid-level terrorists. The fishing trawler went down in relatively shallow water, and the divers recovered quite a few bodies. The woman terrorist, Widad al-Ghabra, was very helpful in identifying them—up to a point. With the exception of the band's leader, Abdul Abed-Rabbo, and Suzanne Abu Hani, Al-Ghabra claimed to account for all of the terrorists between the bodies recovered from the sea and the two terrorists Ellen Larkin shot. But, for some reason, I think she double-checked over the bodies a bit too carefully. I keep feeling as if someone she expected to see there wasn't there.

"Other than Abed-Rabbo and Suzanne Abu Hani, of course. She was truly angry she hadn't found them among the dead. I didn't see any reason to tell her that Abed-Rabbo was killed on a flight to London—probably by Suzanne, who was booked on the same flight— but that Suzanne has escaped. An interesting point is that if Abed-Rabbo hadn't been killed, he probably would have gotten away scot-free. He wasn't in any of our systems; he must have arrived in Cyprus secretly by boat, or he was here before we put the ID system in."

Takis had already told Caitlyn about Suzanne's part in all of this, and she knew they had identified the dead brigade leader in London through fingerprints they found in the Dhrousha Heights hotel suite he and Suzanne had used.

"Just the lower-level functionaries have been identified and caught?" Caitlyn asked nervously.

"Yes, we haven't positively identified any of the more important leaders other than Suzanne, who probably was farther up the chain of control than anyone who was in the terrorist band here. I'm banking on her husband, the Lebanese ambassador—Ayman Abu

Hani—as being one of the bigger fish. He disappeared and hasn't resurfaced outside of Lebanon, and I can't help thinking he was very much aware of what Suzanne was doing to get her information."

"How *is* Alec Stuart taking the situation?" Caitlyn asked as delicately as possible.

"Just like the very rough diamond he is," answered Takis with a grim laugh. "He claims to be embarrassed and apologetic that Suzanne obviously got so much information out of him by making him believe she wanted him. But he certainly isn't acting apologetic. I'd think he'd slink out of the country in shame, but he's back at the Navarino Wine Lodge nightly, knocking the steins of Keo beer back and swapping dirty jokes with his drinking buddies."

"Don't be too rough on him, Takis. You know you like him for what he is. I'm sure the bravado is largely for show. I think he really cared for Suzanne and that her betrayal is almost more than he can bear without covering it with show. But," she continued, to change the subject, "what about Munir Nahlawi? Isn't he one of the kingpins of the Hizballah as well?"

"No," Takis smiled, "the Syrian ambassador is just a common wild game poacher and another one of Suzanne's easy conquests—and not even a good poacher or one of Suzanne's main lovers for that matter."

"But the vehicles that brought me over from the north. You said they were from the Syrian embassy."

"That's right, they were. But when we finally caught up with Nahlawi, he said he had lent them to the Lebanese embassy at Suzanne's request. Considering Suzanne's activities and methods, I believe him. She told them her embassy had a large group of visitors to take to the north and the Lebanese embassy didn't have enough vehicles to handle them all.

"Other than poaching the Cypriots' national animal, the mouflon, Nahlawi isn't in any trouble—since Willie Hamilton isn't going to press kidnapping charges. He doesn't seem nearly clever enough to be part of the Hizballah control group. In fact, I hear he's coming back to his post here—that the Syrians have the temerity to send him back. He couldn't be given more than a tongue lashing for poaching endangered species here. The Syrians seem to be laughing at Cyprus over the events. Although both Demetris Mattas and Willie have made references to the illegal hunting activities of certain diplomats and Cypriot and offshore business leaders in their newspapers, they apparently have been muzzled from making direct accusations. This is still a family island, you know. To the extent we have scandals among the wealthy and well-placed, you won't often see references to it in the public domain."

Caitlyn suspended the conversation to enjoy the reddish glow that radiated off the walls of the surrounding homes as the sun set behind the city. The sunsets were beautiful here. But, seen from their house, between the medium- and high-rise buildings of the surrounding commercial section, they weren't as spectacular as those seen from the open areas at the edge of the city. Caitlyn sighed and returned to the conversation.

"You mentioned Ellen Larkin and the two terrorists she shot. Weren't you at all surprised she was out there alone, looking for us? And with a gun, a gun she could fire so expertly?"

"No, I'm not surprised; don't underestimate Ellen Larkin," responded Takis in his best "you've said enough" voice, which he accentuated by lifting Caitlyn's orange juice glass to her lips and forcing her to drink. She pushed the glass away, laughed, and began to search for a good spot on her husband to tickle. She guessed she now knew that Larkin had replaced the Canadian high commission's spy master, John Dunsford, fully. She resorted to the tickling attack to take the edge off of both of them realizing she had learned something she really shouldn't know. Takis gave in to the intimate moment with relief that Caitlyn wasn't pursuing the point further.

This development, however, was cut off by the sound of the telephone from the house.

"Damn," Caitlyn declared as she rose and headed for the stairs to the front door.

She was gone for so long that Takis almost went in search of her. When she returned, slowly and dreamily moving down the front stairs, stopping twice to smell the sweet white jasmine vine that was entwined in the railing, she was wreathed in a look of contemplation.

"What is it? What's the matter, Caitlyn?"

"The matter? *Nothing's* the matter. This is wonderful, Takis. This is what I've dreamed for. I can't believe it happened." Her face was aglow with pleasure and wonder. But then a cloud passed over her eyes, and she sat down abruptly next to her husband.

"What's going on, Caitlyn?" Takis asked insistently.

"That was a lawyer. Someone by the name of Baroutis."

"Ah, yes, I remember. He called after you were kidnapped but before I knew about it. He seemed impatient to talk to you. Well, what did he want?"

"Takis. You'll never believe this, but . . . Eleni left me her house on the hill in Makedonitissa. You know, the one I admired so

306

much. The one just above the Makedonitissa monastery and overlooking the International Fair Grounds and the Markarios sports complex. Eleni Piccard left it to me."

Takis was stunned for a minute, and then when he recovered, he said, "That's . . . that's wonderful news . . . really. At least for you . . . for us. It's a little sad for Eleni, of course. It drives home the fact that she had no family left. That she had no children, not even a husband, to leave the house to. But, why the long face if this make you happy?"

At first Caitlyn didn't respond, and then she was evasive, but finally she leveled with her husband.

"I was happy, because I was lamenting to myself a bit about our inability to fully enjoy the sunrises and sunsets from this house— whereas they are quite remarkable when viewed from Eleni's house. That's only illustrative, of course. I love everything about Eleni's house. But then I remembered that this is your family home—built by your parents. I was only thinking of myself." Tears of remorse and, if truth be known, of frustration at being so near a dream but not being able to actually seize it started to well up in her eyes.

Takis pulled her back into his arms. "Hush that, Caitlyn, it's all right." And then, at length, he added, "Of course we'll move to the Makedonitissa house. I haven't really ever been comfortable in this house since my parents died. Perhaps it's because we were such a happy family here, and then they died so suddenly in that automobile accident. At the same time—together. And I wasn't even there to say good-bye. One day my father had left Cyprus, on top of the world, taking up the most important diplomatic position of his lifetime. And then, just a few weeks later, the telegram telling me they had both been killed in a road accident arrived.

307

"Listening to you talk so happily about Eleni's house is like having a weight lifted from my chest—one that I hadn't even realized was there. Of course we'll move to Makedonitissa. We can rent this house out; at least we can when you manage to get your archaeology colleagues to stop using it as the store house for ancient junk."

They were both laughing at this image when they heard a car stop on the other side of their garden wall, the tinny sound of a door clicking shut, and Eric Isaksen hobbling up to their gate—his ankle still wrapped but no longer so badly sprained that he couldn't move about. They greeted him like the lifelong friend that he now had become. It was amazing how several days in shared captivity at the hands of the Hizballah guerrillas could bring people to steadfast friendships.

Caitlyn quickly and happily told Isaksen about the beautiful hilltop home she had just inherited from her former mentor on the island, Eleni Piccard.

"Piccard. That rings a bell somehow," said Isaksen when Caitlyn's explanation was completed.

"Yes," Takis interjected. "Eleni Piccard was a shipping magnate here. A Cypriot, related by marriage to a French family shipping empire based in Marseilles. She also owned several resort hotels on the southern coast, was head of a handicraft export house here, and she was the power behind the archaeology foundation that brought Caitlyn to Cyprus in the first place. That's how Caitlyn met her and how they became friends. A sad story. her husband and son were killed in the northern harbor town of Kyrenia during the 1974 Turkish invasion; they never found the bodies, but there were so many such cases on Cyprus then. They weren't killed by the Turks, it turned

308

out, but by her husband's own nephew, who wanted control of the family holdings and who later was French ambassador here and was involved in some illegal drug and arms smuggling schemes of his own.

"Eleni was murdered up at her hotel in Kakopetria just a few months ago," Caitlyn interjected. "Very tragic."

"Hmm. Maybe I heard something about that. Still, it seems I've heard the Piccard name in some other connection—and not too long ago."

"Perhaps you've heard something in conjunction with your own kidnapping since you've been released," Takis answered. "We think the Piccard holdings have gotten involved in handling the travel accounts for some of the radical Middle East factions, including some of the branches of the PLO and Hizballah. Maria Solonos has already started researching the Piccard dealings for signs of links to international terrorism."

"Yes, that's probably it. That seems right; the name Piccard just seems to be registered deeper than that in my mind for some inexplicable reason. Of course, recent events have jumbled my mind. I think I'm getting to be too old for this peace-seeking work. I must admit that I'm almost relieved that the peace talks with the Hizballah that I was traveling to have fallen through."

Everyone was pensive for a few minutes. Caitlyn offered Eric a drink and went into the house to fetch a glass of white wine for him.

"Any purpose other than a social call for your visit to us, Eric?" asked Takis delicately.

"Yes, of course, Takis. I wanted to see how Caitlyn was doing, certainly, but I really came to see you. Let me launch right into it. I obviously am not going to Lebanon now to mediate with the

Hizballah. That means I can return to my real interest—the setting up of an Interpol-type office in the United Nations. You know I've been charged with establishing such a unit and have been given full responsibility for staffing it, don't you?"

Caitlyn returned with Isaksen's drink, handed it to him quietly, and went and stood behind her husband, one hand on his shoulder and the other mussing around in his hair.

Isaksen continued. "Takis, I want you to lead the UN's international investigations office. You were already at the top of my list, based on the work you have done here in Cyprus with your own similar unit over the past year. Now, after this Mouflon Brigade business, there's no one else I would even consider asking first to do the job. Please tell me you will accept the assignment."

Although when he looked up at his wife's face, Caitlyn was smiling at him, Takis had felt her hand involuntarily tense up and dig into his shoulder.

He thought for a moment, and answered, "I'm sorry, I've just been named police chief here in Cyprus. The president has asked me to take the job, and I accepted it; I can't go back on my word."

"I've already cleared it with your president. As a matter of fact, he recognized what an honor it would be for Cyprus for one of its citizens to be named to such a prestigious international post."

Takis looked up at his wife again. She was still smiling bravely, but the smile looked like it was frozen in place.

"No, I'm sorry, Eric. I appreciate your asking me, and I know it would be a great honor. But we're about to start a family and about to be moving into a new home in Makedonistia, here in Nicosia. I can't accept your offer."

The words were brave, but Caitlyn could feel her husband sag a bit into the chair cushions.

"Eric," she spoke quietly for the first time during this exchange, "If Takis took the job, could we live at least a couple of months during the year in Cyprus?"

"It's an international post and a newly forming office," Isaksen said with the smile of one sensing he was getting his nose under the tent. "He'd only have to spend part of the year in New York and Geneva. If he wanted to base the headquarters of the office right here, I'd see to it that he could do so. It would actually be a good location for such an office and the UN already has land under its jurisdiction here where the necessary facility could be built. I'd agree to almost anything to get the right person in the job. The main UN base here is on the next ridge over from Makedonitissa. We can build him a headquarters building there and he'd be just minutes from home."

"And staffing? Could I have a say in who the center would be staffed by?"

"Yes, of course. Not carte blanche, of course, but a strong voice." Isaksen was smiling. He had moved Takis to at least considering the idea. He sensed that Caitlyn held the balance in the negotiations now, and he looked up and into her eyes, appealing. He did what he could to convey to her how important this was to him— and, he though, to the world situation.

"In that case we accept," Caitlyn said, with finality.

Eric's eyes were twinkling as he lowered them to Takis's face. Takis was smiling wanly as well.

"Did you hear the last vestige of Cypriot manhood shattering just then, Eric, my friend? How could I ever face any of my Cypriot

311

friends or family if they could hear my wife accepting a job for me? But, of course, she's right. We'll accept if we can home base here in Nicosia and I can help determine staffing."

Later, as he was leaving, Erick inquired how Caitlyn's pregnancy was going and was delighted to hear that her tribulations at the hands of the terrorist band had not endangered her baby.

"And what name have you picked out?" he asked.

Takis responded shyly. "We discussed it and decided that we would name him Ahmad Eric—that is, if that is all right with his namesakes."

Isaksen beamed from ear to ear, as Takis continued. "Strange name for a Cypriot, of course, but we both felt our son should be named after the two men who took responsibility for protecting him and his mother during their most vulnerable moments. We hope that will meet with your approval."

"I'm honored, certainly," Isaksen bubbled over with joy. "I hope you will also permit me to relate to your child—to all of your children—as a grandfather. I don't think I would have survived the kidnapping either without the help and support of Caitlyn—taking nothing away from the heroism of Ahmad, of course. But I don't think I was truly living at all between the day my wife was killed and when Caitlyn and I were thrown together. She more than saved my life; she saved my soul. She brought me back to life."

All three were so moved that no one could speak for a few moments. Isaksen turned and limped toward the front gate, but, having been the first to regain his composure, he turned back to the couple he had grown to love as much as he could have loved the children he and his wife never had been able to bring into the world.

"But what will you name it if it's a girl?" he asked.

"A girl?" Takis asked in shocked disbelief. "Not a chance! The Greek way is to have a son first. Girls are for later—for when I can afford to start scraping together a dowry."

Eric spoke in mock resignation, "In that case, a salute to Ahmad Eric Koniotis." He drained his glass, handed it to Takis, who had moved to the gate, Takis waved him away, leaving Caitlyn momentarily alone and drifting into a trance.

She was standing on a mesa top—her quadrant of the mesa top, she now realized, looking down the Morphou plain toward the Mediterranean, the Troodos Mountains to her left, the Kyrenia Range to her right. This was her new home, and she felt an incredible sense of contentment standing here. When she turned, though, she saw not the house she expected but an open-sided Roman pavilion of graceful proportions. And then she realized she wasn't alone. She looked in the other direction and there, standing near her, at the edge of the mesa, straight-backed and gazing down the Morphou plain, was a woman swathed in a costume of flowing, diaphanous material that swirled in the updraft from the scrub plain below. The woman seemed to be floating above the surface of the ground they occupied, and, when Caitlyn looked more closely, she saw that the woman was holding something in her arms. The woman turned to Caitlyn and smiled a glowing smile. The bundles in her arms stirred, and Caitlyn knew without fully seeing that what the woman held so lovingly were two babies—and instantly Caitlyn felt she knew so much more than that and was infused with an unfettered surge of joy and purpose flowing through her.

In the darkness Caitlyn tossed off her own glass of orange juice—adorned in her secret, knowing smile—and, when Takis

313

returned to her side, snuggled more closely into her husband's strong, enfolding, safe arms.

"Eleni, we'll name one Eleni. And the other Charlotte, after my mother," Caitlyn whispered, as quietly as she could so that Takis wouldn't hear.

Gina Drew

Gina Drew is a retired American foreign service officer who specialized in investigating and countering international crime and espionage and who still travels the world in both the imagination and in fact.

Years spent working in Cyprus have left her with a deep love of this divided island and its people.

www.cyberworldpublishing.com